Created with Vellum

RADIANT'S HONOR

Founders Series Book Two

MARI DIETZ

I

VIC

Vic slid on her back across the gravel training ground. Loud laughter filled the air. As she pushed herself up, the pebbles bit into her palms. Dust entered her nose and mouth, making the training experience even worse. Before her exercise started, she'd promised herself that she wouldn't lose her temper. Her blood pounded through her ears. Punching him in the face seemed like a viable option.

"Flat on your back is fitting for you, isn't it, founder reject?" Landon tossed his staff in the air and caught it. Overly flashy but fitting to attract the attention of the other reapers training in the wide gravel area behind the Nyx Order. His lean build made him fast, and his years as a reaper made him a nightmare to fight. A few reapers tittered but didn't meet her eye when she turned to look at them.

Landon, the now second in command, paid special attention to the newest Nyx recruit. In the last week, Kai had struggled to keep the Order afloat. Vic could handle Landon, so she thought. His idea of training was more like bullying.

The personal barbs about her being a founder had grown more blatant as time passed. Her mind danced with images of his nose cartilage crunching under her fist and fresh blood pouring from his nose. Yes, punching him would feel great.

"If you're saying I get more action than you, that's probably true. I'm not sure what mog had to debase itself to sleep with you last." Her rebuke lifted her spirits, and she had to admit, the chorus of laughter from the audience gave her the warm fuzzies.

A shadow drew across his charcoal eyes, and he flicked his fingers toward himself. "Come and get another round, then. Not sure why our commander finds you so special, but if you have something besides magical bedroom skills, I can't wait to see it."

His mouth bent downward, over his weak chin, and he spat in the dirt at Vic's feet.

He assumed an awful lot. She clutched her staff and placed her foot behind the other. A breath of dusty air calmed her down. He wanted to get under her skin. Even if he won this sparring session, she wanted him to leave with bruises.

He smirked, and in a flash, he cut to the side. Even though his limbs were long, he had an amount of grace to his fighting. Vic diverted his first attack with a simple side-step. She knew he liked to feint. She flipped her staff to angle it at him and blocked his attempt to hit her stomach. He loved knocking the wind out of her. In his confidence, he'd grown predictable.

Their wooden staffs collided with a loud clunk, and her arms vibrated; she didn't have the muscle or weight to push him back, but she had enough to stand her ground. She planted her boots in the gravel, and the pebbles only gave slightly. Her calves burned from keeping herself steady.

While he tried to force her back, she gave in to his pressure. He faltered, leaving his left side vulnerable. With all her force, she swung her staff, connecting it with his ribcage. A pleasant crack sounded in the yard. She rolled to the side and bounced up before he could recover.

He didn't make a sound, but his arm hung lower, covering his injured side. A tic developed in his jaw, and Vic laughed. With a low growl, he darted straight at her. She dove out of the way. Moving too fast, he couldn't control his turn, and she whacked him in the back. He grunted in pain. Taunting him often led him to make a mistake, but it never fazed him for long. Landon had become the second in command because of his skills in combat. Even though he annoyed her, the other reapers respected him.

He swiftly recovered and didn't give her a chance to distract him again. He launched an all-out assault on her, and it was all she could do to keep up. Only the sound of their wooden staffs echoed in the training field. Vic's arms ached as she blocked him. Then one falter became all he needed. Landon's staff grazed under hers, and he yanked, driving the staff from her grasp. With one last swing, now that she was vulnerable, he sent her hurtling her to the ground.

Vic gasped as her breath left her lungs, and a large shadow stood over her. Landon held his staff over her, and she thought he might hit her again. He blinked and stepped back without offering to help her up.

Landon planted his staff in the ground and leaned on it. "It's a pity money can't help you improve. You can't buy skill."

Vic brushed the dirt off her clothes, and it came off in

brown clouds. She gritted her teeth. "If I had money, I wouldn't waste it on trying to prove something to a small, sad man who'd rather beat up someone than help them improve."

A whistle sounded in the training yard, signaling the end of her torture.

Landon cracked his neck. "You won't last long, founder bitch, even with Kai protecting your back. Enjoy sewer patrol. You go down there so often that you'll always smell like shit."

Vin groaned inwardly. Her team had ended up in the sewers every night last week thanks to Landon. The second in command made the shift schedule, and he'd decided that whoever lost to him in training got sewage patrol. The other teams rotated in fighting him, but Vic fought him at every session. According to him, she needed the most training.

An arm rested on Vic's shoulder, and Bomrosy nudged her gently. "Is Landon out here trying to prove he's the biggest jerk of them all?"

Before Landon could respond, Vic laughed. "He hasn't proved anything yet." She hurried away before Landon could take a jab at Bomrosy. He liked to remind her that she didn't have a relic and was thus a drain on reaper resources. Vic had grown tired of the second and longed for the day when she would no longer have to deal with him.

"Wait for me. I still need to run through the walls today."

Around the training yard, they had an obstacle course of walls that were flat, curved, smooth, rough, and anything else they could think of. The ability to scale a wall with their bare hands was sometimes a necessity in the streets. The wall Vic hated the most was the smooth one at the end. After trying multiple times, she gasped for air and wanted to kick the smooth stone. She wiped the sweat off her brow and grumbled to Bomrosy, "It's not like they make the houses of smooth stone in Verrin."

"Some are." Bomrosy glanced at Landon as he vaulted over the smooth wall with ease. "Do you tell Kai what he says to you?" She flipped her thick braid over her shoulder, her golden-brown eyes creased with worry.

Vic waved her hand dismissively. Had Bomrosy been worrying about this the whole time during the walls? "They're only words. I can handle it. He isn't the first to mention that I'm from a rich family and he won't be the last."

She wanted to help Kai with his burdens, not increase them over the petty second.

Bomrosy frowned. "It seems obsessive. He was always annoying, but he latched on to you."

She waited while Vic opened the stone shed where Nyx kept all the training staffs. The earthy smell of the dark room reminded her of a basement, and she welcomed the cool air on her sweat-covered skin.

"I'm lucky, I guess. He probably saw me holding hands with Kai and assumed I'd gotten in because of him. He might also assume I'm here because I'm a founder." Vic put up her training staff, and they walked across the training field and into the dining hall. "Honestly, I'd rather not waste any more of my thoughts trying to figure out what goes on inside that pea-brained mind."

"True, let's focus on tonight." The cook handed Bomrosy a plate with a portion of fish and a purple vegetable that looked like a carrot.

They could no longer take as much as they wanted, but they still got plenty to eat. Losing GicCorp's money and their spot as the top Order had hurt them. Kai had spent hours sorting through reaper complaints since he'd taken over the Order. The reapers knew Xiona had made mogs on purpose, but they didn't know GicCorp had involved her. The majority of the reapers believed GicCorp was punishing them by cutting their funding because of the battle with the Dei Order reapers. Landon tried to poke holes in the story. If he ever found out they'd purified Xiona, Kai's days as commander would be over. Kai counted on the reapers' trust, and they couldn't know he'd already broken it by lying to them and protecting the one who'd illegally purified their leader.

"What's tonight?" Vic sat down on a bench and shoveled in her meal. The purple carrots ended up tasting like the fish sitting next to it. If it filled her belly, it was all good with her.

No other reapers sat next to them in the dining hall, and the isolation got to her sometimes. She wanted to be part of their community but had entered the Order during a chaotic time. The other reapers' laughter echoed through the hall, and Vic stared too long at their playful nudges and smiles. Thankfully, Bomrosy had accepted her.

Bomrosy tapped her neck.

"Ugh." Vic swallowed down her glass of water. Her skin had healed, and they needed to rebrand her. No one in the Order knew Xiona had kicked her out. Xiona and her lackeys couldn't tell tales of her being kicked out since they'd all been killed in the battle with Dei and Xiona had been purified. Landon had asked about her injury, but she'd played it off as it being from the Dei battle. She still wore the bandages, even though they had long since healed her, and Landon had noticed. Creepy stalker.

"You'll get used to it." Bomrosy took their plates and

washed them at the sinks provided at the side of the dining hall while Vic waited for her.

After she'd finished, they headed to Bomrosy's shop.

"Does Kai even have time?" Vic played with the bandage around her neck. The new skin under it itched.

"Stop trying to get out of it." Bomrosy ducked into her shop.

The scents of metal and oil surrounded them, and unique tech inventions lay scattered around the room. Bomrosy swore the room was organized, but Vic couldn't see how. Although if Vic borrowed a tool without asking, Bomrosy would know exactly what she'd taken. Her proudest invention so far was the light created without magic or fire. Vic didn't know how it worked, but the radiant would love it. As she scanned the room, she jumped in surprise at the person sitting on the bench. They wore a scarf over their head, but Vic recognized the ex-commander, Xiona.

"What in the blight is she doing here?" Vic hissed.

Bomrosy turned away and guided Xiona back to her bedroom, which adjoined her shop. She shut the door behind her. "No one comes here, and I don't enjoy leaving her alone all day."

She organized bottles that contained dark liquid.

"It's not like she minds! If anyone finds her here, they'll revolt, then kill William, then Kai, then me." Sweat formed on Vic's brow. "What are you thinking? You know better than this."

Bomrosy went to her tools and placed them on small hooks on the wall. "I know. Xiona did so much for me, and I want to take care of her." Her back stiffened. "She didn't start out hurting people."

Vic tried to hold back a snort, but it slipped free. "Well, she *killed* a lot of people, not just *hurt* them. If you must take care of her, don't do it here. I can't believe you'd be so careless."

Didn't she understand what would happen to them if anyone found out?

Bomrosy hung up the rest of her tools with more force than necessary. "I was careful. I came in the back way, and no one saw us. She's alone most of the day and stays in my bedroom most of the time. She must have wandered out."

"Oh, no, she needs to be alone. What if she wanders around the Order? Can't you go to Kai's and watch her there?" Vic pressed her fingers to her temples. Was Bomrosy insane? Vic bit back the words she wanted to say to her friend. She wanted to yell, but that wouldn't help the situation. A small pounding formed in the back of her head. The last thing Kai needed was Bomrosy bringing the ex-commander into the Order.

Her lips formed a thin line. "You're right. I just ... I want her to know I'm here." Her fingers brushed a set of tools more worn than the rest.

"Take her back. Do it now. We won't tell Kai, and please, don't do this again." Vic paced the stone floor.

It seemed like Bomrosy would argue, but instead, she covered up more of Xiona's face and led her out the back. Few people came to see Bomrosy unless they'd broken their scythe, but the risk of keeping Xiona here wasn't worth it. She didn't care about the ex-commander's history of good deeds, according to Bomrosy, but Bomrosy was putting Kai at risk. Turning Xiona into a radiant hadn't been the plan, but there was no going back now.

Vic continued to pace, counting the minutes as she

waited for Bomrosy to return. Maybe they should have waited until dark to move Xiona.

The front door opened, and Vic jumped.

"You look guilty." Kai smiled and came into the shop. He checked the room, and seeing it empty, he pulled her into a firm hug.

"Guilty? Me? Ha-ha." Vic wondered if he could feel her heart pounding. She willed herself to calm down and enjoy this brief moment with Kai.

His russet curls were still damp, and the comforting smell of cedar surrounded her. He had either just woken up or, more likely, had tried to wake himself up with a shower after spending all morning dealing with founders and GicCorp. The dark circles under his brown eyes hadn't diminished.

He arched his brow and let her go too soon. "I was joking, but now I have a feeling you are guilty." He glanced past her. "Are you stealing tools from Bomrosy again?"

Before she could come up with an excuse, Bomrosy walked in the door and shut it carefully behind her. She paused, then grinned at Kai. "Hello, stranger. Can I put in an order for more fishy purple carrots?"

Kai sat down on the bench with his legs spread. "Don't mention it. If I hear one more person complain about how they should get more food because they took down more mogs, I will jump out the window." He rolled his shoulders. "I don't know how Xiona dealt with these people all day."

At the mention of her name, an awkward silence entered the room. Vic sacrificed herself and broke it. "So, who's ready to see me get branded?"

Bomrosy coughed and pretended to be fascinated with a glass object on her workbench.

Kai squeezed her hand, and his callouses brushed against her pale skin. "Sorry about this."

Vic shrugged. "I can't wear the bandage forever. Or I could? Make it a new fashion statement? The founders would be all over this. Bandage necklaces." She attempted a fashion pose and pursed her lips.

Bomrosy laughed, and the cheerful sound made Vic feel slightly better.

Kai raised his brows at her nervous rambling. "It's almost time to hunt, so we better get moving."

All three of them left Bomrosy's workshop, the hallways now empty of reapers who were probably resting before their shift. On the first floor, they went to the back room for branding ceremonies and glanced around before entering. The gloomy branding room remained empty. Vic thought it always smelled like smoky, burnt flesh. They flicked on the magic lights. The icy stone walls would be their only witness.

"I hear you're in the sewers again?" Kai asked as he gathered kindling for the flames.

"No comment." Vic stared ahead. Kai got to avoid the sewers since he took turns patrolling with each team. "Somehow, you're never with us when we end up there. A weird coincidence, no?"

Kai built the fire and swiftly heated the branding iron. "I don't know what you're talking about." The light from the fire hit his golden-sepia skin just right, making it glow warmly in the dim room.

"Sure." She grabbed the edge of the bandage and peeled it off, flinching as her already raw skin rippled in pain. This was a mistake. He took the iron out of the flames and held it close to her. The heat from the brand hurt, and Kai hadn't even placed it on her neck yet.

"Can I just keep the bandage on my neck?" Vic pleaded. She'd never imagined branding the tender flesh of her neck this many times.

She knelt in the empty room while Kai stood over her. Quite the difference from her first time getting the Nyx brand.

"I'm surprised the healed skin turned out so well. You did a glorious job skinning her, Kai." Bomrosy acted like Vic was one of her experiments.

"Yeah, he should put that on his list of qualifications: *good at skinning humans*," Vic growled.

Kai sighed. "Let's get this over with. This will be one less reason for Landon to bother you." So Kai was aware of some of Landon's harassment.

"Like it's any of that jerk's business." Vic pulled back her hair. "Make it quick."

Since they'd lost GicCorp's money, Nyx needed to pull in more mogs to do important things, like eat. However, in the last couple of days, they'd noticed a large drop in mogs in their territory. The reapers were getting restless. Fewer people changing into mogs was good, but Vic didn't think that was the issue.

Kai pushed the red-hot brand against Vic's neck, and she hissed. Tears ran down her cheeks. He quickly pulled the brand back, and Bomrosy placed a bandage over the wound. The mark cooled instantly. Hopefully, in a few days, she could take it off.

"Do we need to make a slight scar for her injury?" Bomrosy asked.

Vic glared. "Do you want to torture me? Why do we have to go that far for Landon?"

"He's strangely interested in you," Kai replied. Bomrosy had said something to that effect earlier. "He suspects something happened to Xiona." Kai plunged the brand in the bucket of water next to the flames to cool it and hung it up on the wall. "Bomrosy, you're keeping Xiona at my place? I'm thinking that isn't safe."

Bomrosy helped snuff out the fire. "Where do you want to keep her? In the cells?" She folded her arms. "What she did was wrong, but she had good intentions."

"Yeah, killing others. Very good." Vic understood having a blind spot for someone, but Bomrosy needed to wake up. If Kai knew Bomrosy had brought Xiona into the building, his head might explode. She hoped Bomrosy didn't do something like that again. Kai had enough to worry about. Vic lightly felt her neck, and it throbbed.

Kai waved his hand, tired of the argument. "Fine, just make sure she stays there." Bomrosy and Vic exchanged a glance. He walked to her and lightly touched her arm. "If it's too painful, you can stay in tonight." He ran a finger along the edge of her bandage.

Vic gripped his hand. "I'll survive."

They stood there, and Vic didn't feel the pain as much.

"Should I leave so you two can make out?" Bomrosy arched her brow.

Vic dropped his hand, and Bomrosy snickered. Kai glared at Bomrosy, and they all walked out of the room, only to find the reaper in question waiting: Landon.

He had his usual air of self-importance. With his dirty blond hair slicked back, he must have come from the showers. He squinted at the three of them, frowning as usual. "What are you doing in there?"

"Having a threesome," Vic deadpanned.

Landon's eyebrows shot up, and Bomrosy burst into laughter.

Kai stepped forward. "Did you need something, Landon? And do we need a repeat of our last meeting?"

Landon paused but took a small shuffle back. "No. We're ready to patrol. Do you want me to keep rotating among the other groups?"

Kai shook his head. "No, stick with your normal group. I'll keep the rotations this week."

Vic thought Kai should rest, but the change in leadership had made everyone restless, and he wanted to be there for the reapers to reassure them everything was fine.

Landon's eye flickered, but he said nothing. As they walked away, he eyed the door they'd come out of. Kai didn't want Landon complaining to all the reapers. He'd gotten reports that Landon was questioning his leadership because he favored Vic. She didn't want to make his leadership harder, so she tried to stay away from him, but she missed him and wished he would hunt with them tonight.

At her shop, Bomrosy waved goodbye and went inside. They paused at the entrance of the Order to meet with their team.

Around the corner, Ivy and Freddie waited with their backs to them, pointing at the board. Ivy turned around at that moment. Her light brown hair framed her face. Most might think Ivy's short stature would not make her a good reaper. They'd quickly rethink that if they ever saw her take out a mog. Her black reaper clothing fit her like a second skin, and her plump lips and long lashes added to the cuteness of her round face. Her wide whiskey eyes took in everything around her. Freckles graced her rosy skin. When she cocked her hip, Vic prepared for a lecture.

"Next time, let me fight Landon. Maybe we'll get out of the sewers." Ivy nudged Freddie.

Freddie scratched his shaved head, and his eyes softened when he looked down at Ivy as she bounced around. Where she was small and curvy, he was a solid giant. In one battle last week, he'd thrown Ivy at a mog, helping her take it out from above. The man was taller than Kai's six feet. Vic had run into him once and thought she'd broken her nose. His thick muscles flexed under his ebony skin. Freddie loved to cut the sleeves off his reaper shirts to show off his muscles to Ivy. Vic felt her spirits lift at their cuteness. On the outside, they were perfect opposites.

They worked well together, and Vic loved being on the same team. They weren't part of Landon's agenda. It reminded her that she wasn't as alone as she thought. They stayed positive, even though they'd gotten stuck with her. Maybe she wasn't part of the community because of her own lack of effort?

"I'll leave you here. Stay safe and dry," Kai said.

Vic nudged him. "Are you sure you don't want to join in on the fun?"

Kai backed away to another group of four reapers in the entrance. "Sorry, commander duties and all that. You know how it is."

Ivy stayed in her lecture stance. "You can't avoid the sewers forever, boss."

Kai laughed and saluted Ivy. He had to keep monitoring them all for morale. He trusted them the most, so he didn't hunt with them as often.

They joined the other teams on sewer duty. The entire purpose was to track humans who went down into the dark to change into a mog. If they were lucky, they caught them in time, but most of the time, at the end of the tracks, a mog waited for them.

The blight swirled in the night sky. Tonight, it faded from blood red to yellow as it drifted in the sky. Vic took a deep breath, enjoying the fresh air while she could. They reached the entrance of the sewer, and one by one they covered their noses and mouths with masks and placed their eyepieces over their eyes. The blight would glow brighter in the dim light of the sewers. The eyepiece also helped them see mogs before they jumped out of the sewage.

Ivy nudged Vic and jumped down after Freddie. The smell already seeped through her mask. Vic swallowed and followed them into the dark sewer.

❧ 2 ❧
VIC

Vic didn't want to become used to the sewer, but in the last couple of weeks, they'd grown familiar. Verrin's sewers remained the oldest structures in the city. She still worried about losing her way in the cavernous, maze-like tunnels. The more modern piping in the city above carried the waste down here and then to the swamp. On scorching days, the smell from the massive sewers rose up, and people would complain about how the city needed to restructure the sewers. Imbs would go down to clean the stone and push the waste through, but nothing permanent ever happened.

Greenish slime coated the stone, and some paths crumbled into the lazy river of waste headed to the treatment area. Apparently, everything remained on an incline to keep things moving. Water mixed in with the waste, but it didn't help the smell.

Even though the reapers sanitized and cleaned themselves after every trip, Vic swore she could smell the putrid stench coming from her skin for hours. As the reapers entered, the ticking sound of rat claws skittered away from them in the dark.

She paced herself behind her team. The shuffling steps of reapers and drips of—hopefully—water echoed in the tunnels. Team by team, they branched off from one another. Most sewer mogs were freshly turned, so reapers could handle one by themselves, but they never stayed more than shouting distance from their teammates.

Vic breathed through her mouth and waved at her team. She went first, so for this tunnel, she would run the farthest while Freddie and Ivy kept pace behind her a shout away. Once they finished their segments, they could get out of here. Since there were only three of them, it would take longer if they searched together. It saved energy by having only one of them run the full tunnel at once. They traded off after each tunnel.

She held her scythe to the side, still folded up. She scanned the water for any reddish glow of blight. Her heartbeat remained steady as she ran through the glow of the tunnel light. The rats the mogs had left alive stayed out of her path. The team's footsteps faded away, and she smiled behind her mask. These days, only running made sense to her. The tension in the Order had everyone feeling stifled and on edge.

There were many footprints left in the muck on the pathway. Either it had been a while since the steps had washed away, or a lot of traffic had happened recently. It would be impossible to track any individual human from the mass of footprints. She rubbed her neck, already tired from looking down. It was easier to track mogs or corrupted humans after a fresh rain. They might not find any people tonight using their usual methods.

As the thought crossed Vic's mind, a loud plop sounded in the distance. Something larger than a rat. Her gaze shot right, across the lovely river of sewage. In the shadows, a tall figure froze. Dressed and masked all in black, they didn't glow, so Vic hadn't noticed them in the dim light. They might be a reaper in the wrong territory or a freelancer. Either way, they shouldn't be here. They stared at each other, then the figure darted down the tunnel.

"That isn't suspicious at all." Vic gritted her teeth and chased them from the other side of the sewage river. "If I need to cross the feces river, I will kill someone," she huffed. If she got lucky, she'd find a bridge to cross, but there weren't many.

A crossroads appeared ahead, and she groaned as they ran left, veering farther away from her. They would soon be out of sight. Vic stopped and bit her tongue. She took one step into the river. With no rain, it wasn't deep, and her sealed boots would keep the waste out as long as it didn't go over the top. She navigated over the flowing sewage as fast as possible, but she didn't want it to splash up on her pants. She dry-heaved as something solid touched her ankle and continued down the river. With a quick thanks that it hadn't rained in a while, she crawled over the edge on the other side. She ran down the tunnel. Her boots dripped excess water from the surface. The figure disappeared down the tunnel, and Vic pumped her legs to catch up with them.

This side tunnel only had a small stream, making it easy to hop over. Reapers rarely went this deep into side tunnels. There weren't enough reapers to cover all this ground. Her mind raced with who this could be. Imbs were off duty. And why would another reaper run away if they weren't doing something bad?

Too well, she remembered those days of trying to get by without an Order's support.

She peered ahead to catch a glimpse in the darkness. Then, from the shadows, something plowed into her side. She swore as she sprawled on the ground and her folded scythe clattered away. Her exposed skin scraped against the muck and stone. She rolled to face her attacker, and a wooden staff clanked on the ground where her head had been. She flinched and struggled to regain her footing as the hooded figure approached. Her back hit the wall, and the silent figure swung again. She dove around their legs and jumped back to her feet. Before they could turn around, she slapped the side of their head, causing them to stumble.

Vick kicked out the back of their knees, and they hit the ground. She didn't have time to get her weapon. As she went to knee them in their side, they raised their elbow, blocking her. Her knee smarted from the contact.

The hooded figure swept their legs under her as they swung around to face her. She jumped over their legs. Their movements were clunky, even robotic. To her right, she saw something long and grabbed it. The slime made it slippery, but she had some reach now. She shoved forward to keep them down. They raised their arms, blocking the blows aimed from their head. She reached too far back, leaving an opening, and they punched up, hitting the side of her knee.

She scrambled to block the next hit. They pushed up to their feet, and with their longer staff, the hooded figure shoved her back. Vic stepped back to steady herself, but only found air as she fell back into the muck. Her back hit the stone wall, and she gasped for air. The figure froze, then ran off.

"Yeah, you better run!" Vic groaned as her back twinged.

She used her unfamiliar weapon to push out of the sludge. Careful not to further hurt her back, she bent side to side, testing the damage. It hurt, but she could function. She shivered as the air hit her wet clothing. The raw sewage smell snuck under her masked face, and she avoided looking down at her coated body. In her hand, she held a long object. It was a bone. She dropped it and went to wipe off her hand, but she didn't have any clean place left.

"I hope that wasn't human."

Mogs hungered for fresh meat, and they sometimes ate those in transition.

She took in the stone walls. Spiders skittered across the lamps, casting strange shadows.

"Where did I end up?"

In the fight, she'd gotten turned around. Vic checked the ground, but there were multiple footprints down this path. Everything looked the same.

"I came from that way, maybe?" She groaned and started walking. Her back throbbed with each step. It didn't take her long to come across another branch in the sewer, but it wasn't the major line. "Blight, I went the wrong way."

She needed to get back before her team started to worry about her. She already made their lives harder by being down in the sewers every night.

The tunnel marker had a different number, followed by two waves. She'd ended up in Boreus territory. She turned to go back, but a shallow voice stopped her.

"It's you."

Vic poked her head back out into Boreus's tunnel and blinked. "Tristan?"

HER FINGERNAILS BIT INTO HER PALMS AS SHE CLENCHED HER fists. Tristan leaned against the sewer walls. His arm covered his waist, and he sat in the sewer tunnel as if nothing was wrong. His normally sleek light brown was a disheveled mess. A ghost had more color than he did, but the stark ice-blue eyes still held their fierceness.

Vic stared at the GicCorp founder heir who had helped take her sister away. Her attacker had a smaller build than him. Tristan also had more injuries than she'd inflicted on the masked person. She couldn't tell if blood or muck stained his expensive black suit. Whatever it was, it was his problem now. She turned to leave.

"Wait."

Her back stiffened. "I have nothing to say to you."

A quiet laugh echoed in the silent sewers. "I find myself in a position where I may need help out of here."

"You got down here. Get yourself out," Vic spat. She faced him, and her arms shook as she held them at her sides. The future leader of GicCorp looked weak. "I won't cry if a mog eats you."

He blinked with unnerving calmness. "I didn't take you for a murderer."

Vic flicked her scythe open. It would be easy to slit his throat and leave him in the sewers. The mogs would cover up her crime. His eyes widened, taking in her blade. Her hand hurt from gripping her relic. Killing him wouldn't bring her sister back, but he had answers. He might call her bluff. Could she kill him? Probably not. As much as she wanted her sister back, she didn't know what had happened to her or if she was hurt.

He wanted help? Fine. She would find out how much help he wanted.

Vic kept her voice steady as she asked, "What happens to the vitals?"

A slow smile spread on Tristan's face. His stance maintained the same calmness as a member of GicCorp. A well-trained corporate gear. "They purify the magic so we can charge and not get corrupted."

Vic slammed the staff of her relic down on the stone. The clatter bounced off the walls, and Tristan leaned away. "I know the company line and what they tell us, and I'm not buying it. I'm tired of looking away when it involves my family. No one says *how*. How, Tristan? How do they purify the magic? Why are they connected to it? What happens to them?" Her heart raced. "Why do we accept this as normal?"

Down here provided them with a certain equality. She didn't want to waste this chance. She might not be able to kill him, but he knew something.

"You're acting like I'm the one who decided all this. It isn't easy to explain the relic they connect to, so that's the best way we can explain. This is how our world is, and maybe there's a better one out there, but we chose this way." As he held his side, he stayed calm.

He hid answers, always on the edge of truth. Did she not believe him because she missed her sister? Did she want something to be wrong? Maybe, but she would push until she got her sister back. "This isn't the time to toe the company line. It's only you and me, company boy, and you need me."

He tilted his head. "Otherwise you'll leave me here to die?"

Would she? She took in the crumpled founder. Even in this situation, she didn't hold the power. He knew she wouldn't kill him. "Is my sister alive?"

His smiles never reached his eyes. "We take excellent care of the vitals. Even though I can't personally go and see to them, every need is met."

Vic took a deep breath, and the rotten air consumed her. "Is my sister alive, Tristan?"

The pause lasted too long. His face became a mask he wore. The lighting in his eyes changed. It almost felt like she wasn't talking to Tristan anymore. Something shifted in the still air. Somehow, she knew she was finally talking to the right person. His voice came out slightly lower, asking, "Why won't you fall in line, Victoria?"

The corners of his mouth stretched too far up to be comfortable. The skin of his face molded to his teeth.

Ice crawled in Vic's veins, and she stepped back. Her throat closed when she tried to speak. What did he mean? What had happened to her sister? This person had changed from prey to predator. The sewer tunnels were too small. This man didn't need her help. Her heart throbbed, telling her to escape now.

The chilly smile stilled on his face, and his teeth glinted in the light. "It's hard to give up a family member to Haven." His face twitched, and his old gaze stared into Vic. "Remember, my sister is there too. Do you think I'd let any harm come to her?" Sincerity dripped from his voice like acid. It crept under her skin.

Vic shifted so her blade remained between them. "Who are you?" The words had left her mouth before she could stop them.

Why did his gaze seem to see inside her? "You don't know me very well, Glass heir."

"I don't think I want to." She backed toward the entrance.

He watched her move away. Shadows flickered. "One question."

"You didn't answer it." Her throat tightened. It felt like she was the one who needed help now.

Another slow blink. "That's all you want to know? Are you sure?" As he spoke through his smile, it didn't move.

Vic could ask him something that would help Verrin. She didn't care. This city wasn't her concern. "Is my sister alive?"

"I believe she is."

Those words pierced her mind. Fear curled up inside her. "What? How can you not know?"

This man wanted her help? She lifted her relic and swung the blade toward his neck. She paused, resting it next to his neck but not touching it.

Tristan leaned his head back and pushed his neck to her blade. His eyes never left hers. Her relic pressed lightly against his skin. "If I'm not back tonight, she won't be alive by morning."

"You're lying!" Vic's arms tensed, and she pushed the blade forward. A thin line of blood ran down his neck. "Why is her life tied to yours? If I hadn't found you here, she would have died anyway? Is that what you're saying?"

"Kill me or leave me to die, it won't change what I told you." Tristan closed his eyes. His body relaxed. "You know more than you should. Information is dangerous to have in Verrin, Glass heir."

"Didn't you just dig your own grave? I help you tonight and you kill me tomorrow?" What could she even do with this information? Try to storm Haven tonight?

His lips parted, and he chuckled. "If I thought you had any power, Glass heir, you'd be dead already."

A hollowness overcame Vic, and her arms dropped. Her senses floated around her. The expanse of the city entered her mind. She opened her mouth to rebuke him. Even if all the reapers believed her, why would they fight with her? Who did she have on her side? Kai? William? Bomrosy? Her father? She'd never made a list of allies, but now that their names had passed through her mind, the hopelessness of what they stood against filled her.

Tristan let out a bored sigh. His features shifted back to the familiar. Answer time was over. "What are you trying to do? Get your sister? She can't leave the relic. If GicCorp is gone, what problem are you solving?" He laughed. "It's kind of cute, really, the delusions you're entertaining. The blight will still be there, even if you get rid of GicCorp. People will still need to be connected to the relic. So I'll ask again, what are you trying to do? Isn't it childish?"

Childish? Cute? She was running around with no guidance, and Tristan knew it. It had started out with her not wanting her sister to leave forever, but the longer she dug into Verrin, the stranger it seemed. Something was off. When she'd discovered that Xiona had been creating mogs, it had proved that something else was going on behind the walls. Find one bad apple and you'll find an entire case rotted.

Vic tensed. "Go ahead and write me off." Her eyes burned. "I don't want you to see me as a threat."

"I look forward to it. I answered your question. Will you guide me to the surface? I wouldn't want to bleed out down here."

"It would be tragic." She folded her scythe, put it back in her harness, and leaned over to pull him up more roughly than necessary. All he did was chuckle.

Vic limped along with Tristan. Despite her effort not to have any more contact with him, his body leaned heavily against her. Her back hated the extra weight, and she shifted to relieve the pain. As they trekked back the way she'd come, she wanted to drop him and leave him to rot. He had answers. She doubted this version of Tristan would answer. What did that mean? She wished she could ask Em. Her sister often saw things others didn't.

Through her eyepiece, she saw a red glow form under the water. "Ugh, not now."

The black mass slunk out of the sewage and moaned low notes. This mog stood on multiple short legs, and its extensive body swiveled in an S pattern as it approached them.

Vic dropped Tristan and maybe even shoved him away hard. He fell with a pained grunt. She drew her scythe and flicked it open. The blade flashed, and her hands smeared muck on the smooth, warm handle.

"I'll have to shower for a week after this," Vic muttered.

The mog reared up and flailed its multiple legs at Vic, its movements not as smooth as those of other mogs. Vic found an opening, and her scythe heated as she hit its black flesh. It threw its weight against her blade, surprising her. Mogs usually avoided relics. Her blade cut into the mog, draining it, but one of its legs got closer and kicked her in the side of her face. She tried to go with the flow of its kick, but her scythe was lodged in the creature's flesh, not letting her move away. Tears blurred her vision. She didn't want to let go of her relic, but as more legs came to hit her in the head, she dropped to the ground. The mog moaned and plunged forward, its legs thrashing around her relic.

"Duck!" Tristan shouted from behind her.

Vic dove past the legs and hit the ground. An invisible

force flowed above her, brushing her hair to the side. The blast knocked into the mog and flung it against the wall. It gargled and its legs flailed as it tried to right itself, mimicking a bug on its back. She grabbed her scythe's handle and drained the mog until its misshapen bones clattered to the stone ground.

Her gicgauge was almost full from that one mog. She flicked her scythe closed and placed it back in her harness. She turned to Tristan, and he slumped to the side, his wand out.

"I think we need to go quickly," he said, his voice weaker.

Vic heaved him back over her shoulder, and she tried to walk faster. It had been a while since she'd seen that kind of imb magic—the Nordic magic of pure force. There was nothing to imbue, so how could he move the mog? They reached the main sewage line, and her team was where she'd branched away.

"There you are!" Ivy ran forward and paused when she saw Tristan. "Who's that?"

Freddie came forward and removed Tristan from her shoulders. She stretched out her back with a groan. "The GicCorp heir. I found him down a side path."

Ivy's brows shot up, and she took in Vic's appearance. "Did you bathe in the wastewater?"

Vic glanced down at her clothes. Her entire bottom half was covered in the muck, and the stench made her want to gag. "There was also a strange person who attacked me."

Freddie grunted and easily carried Tristan as they trotted toward the entrance.

"You had an eventful night, and we aren't even into the first hour." Ivy kept pace beside her and noticed how she tried not to limp.

"I have all the luck. I need to empty my gicgauge before I come back."

Freddie frowned, and Ivy shook her head. "No, we'll manage. Take care of him, and we'll handle it."

Vic's shoulders slumped. "I'm sorry."

She didn't want to leave them, but she dreaded the thought of running the rest of the tunnels covered in sewage. Her back ached, and her face burned from the mog's kick. She touched her cheeks, and they felt puffy.

Ivy held up her hand. "No need for that. You'd do the same for us." She looked thoughtful. "Don't let Landon see you come in early. I'd like to get out of sewer duty one day."

"Tell me about it." Guilt ate at her as her team helped her and Tristan. She always ended up needing so much help. When would she finally be the one to help them?

At the main entrance, Vic helped Freddie get the silent Tristan out of the tunnel. Freddie bent his head down the road, indicating that the nearest healers were down the block. Vic didn't complain as he carried Tristan for her. She thought it might look strange if she didn't go with Tristan. Even if he didn't see her as a threat, she didn't want Freddie and Ivy to get hurt later.

A healer greeted them at the door and rushed them inside. He cleared his throat at the smell of waste coming from them. Freddie left. Vic was now alone with Tristan.

He lay back on the wheeled gurney. "Thank you for your assistance."

The urge to punch someone came back in full force. "I may regret this."

He chuckled as the healers took him away. They glanced at her and stayed a good distance from her sewage-covered form. Without wasting another moment, Vic turned on her heel and walked out. Instead of going to the Order, she headed to her house. Her clothing clung to her, but she needed to talk to her father. With her sore body, she regretted not hiring a water taxi to her old home. Walking home in her condition was taking longer than normal. The streets were dark and strangely quiet, even though it was good that people weren't out with the mogs. The canal babbled softly in the night, and Vic stayed close to the alleys to avoid other Nyx reapers. She wasn't doing anything wrong, but Ivy was right. If Landon saw her leaving a shift early, he would make her life more miserable.

After almost an hour of walking, the Glass home stood silent and dark up ahead. She burst into her old home and tracked her mess through the clean halls, the clear glass walls muted in the night lighting. Light glowed in her father's office through the glass doors. She slammed open the doors, and her father's head shot up. He reached for his wand but stopped when he recognized her.

He strode to her. "What happened? Is everything okay?" He sniffed the air and coughed.

She paused at the concern in his voice. They'd never recovered their relationship, which had fractured in the last year, before Em had left. "I don't know. I met Tristan in the sewers tonight. What's going on? Do you know why he was down there? He said Emilia wouldn't live if I didn't get him back." The questions poured out.

"He told you that? Do you think he was lying?" His hand gripped his left arm, and he swallowed.

"I don't know." Vic slumped. "I don't know. I saved him." She met her father's eyes. "Did I make a mistake?" She didn't know if she could kill a human. In the Dei battle, she'd come close to killing Xiona, but William had saved her from that decision.

He sighed. "I don't know. He doesn't think you're a threat if he shared that much." His red hair was ruffled like he'd passed his hand through it multiple times. Her father looked like he'd slept in his suit for a few nights, maybe in his office chair. It seemed like no one was getting enough sleep these days. Bags had formed under his green eyes, which mirrored her own.

"Yeah, he pretty much said that. What's going on?"

He moved closer to Vic. "I wish I knew more. I've been researching the relic that the vitals connect to ever since Emilia was born. It has no history. I've failed her."

The sudden honesty surprised Vic. "I thought you were all about duty?"

"I had to play this part for many years. Do you think I could make any difference if I lost my place as a founder?" The rich office seemed to mock him. "It didn't matter. We might be too late." He fell back into his chair behind his desk.

Vic wanted to sit down but remembered she was filthy. She leaned on the wall with her elbow that was cleanish. "What do you know?"

"Did you notice anything different tonight while patrolling the sewers?" He tapped his wand and formed little figurines of glass with the sand he kept on his desk. The glass rose and fell as they talked. He claimed it helped him think.

Vic thought about the stranger in the shadows and their fight. "Someone attacked me, but am I supposed to know why?"

Her father shook his head. "That isn't good, but something else?"

She furrowed her brow. When she'd tried to track mogs tonight, there had been too many footprints in the muck to pick out a trail. "A lot of traffic. Too many people down in the sewers. How did you know?"

Her father laid his head back on his chair. "Before, they only took one or two. I'm not sure who they are. I think you'll find many people missing from Nyx territory now."

She pushed away from the wall. "How many?"

"I wish I knew. Hundreds, maybe thousands. Tell your commander to check the houses. The figures dressed in black seem to only be taking from you."

She tapped her fist against the glass wall. "That way, if they get caught …"

"They'll blame Nyx."

GicCorp needed to be stopped, but they'd found themselves outplayed. "We need to get into GicCorp."

"I'm looking in the sewers too. They're the only thing in this city that hasn't modernized. I'm trying to gain allies against GicCorp, but it's more trouble than I thought." He drew a figure in the sand with his fingers. "They seem happy with how things are and happy to believe the vitals are okay." He went to his drink cart and poured them each a drink. He handed her a clear glass with amber liquid. "They care more about who will be in charge of the rebellion."

Vic took the drink and swallowed it in one gulp, welcoming the burn. Of course the founders wanted power. They didn't care about the city. "You think they have something down there?"

"Maybe."

The masked figures could be protecting something. Why now? Her father reached, and she lifted her arm so he could take her hand. Vic studied his lined face. She'd never noticed him getting older, but he looked thinner.

She handed the glass back to him and gave him an encouraging pat. "He might think we aren't a threat, but I want him afraid for once."

A glimmer of fight flashed in her father's eyes. "We can do that."

❦ 3 ❦

VIC

Vic cleaned up before she ran back to the Order. In her bathroom at home, a spray bottle of sanitizer waited for her. Finally feeling clean, she went to talk to Kai. Outside his office door, she heard Landon inside.

"This is what they're doing." Something thudded in Kai's office. "What are you going to do about it?"

"I'm talking to Tristan today." Kai sounded tired.

"As your second in command, I should go with you. Something happened, and if we're being punished for Xiona's mistakes, we need to explain what happened." Landon's voice reached a new pitch unknown to the human world.

"I said I would take care of it today." A mean edge came from Kai, one Vic had never heard before. His temper got shorter by the day. With the amount of pressure he faced, she could understand why. Having Landon as a second must not make it easier.

Vic heard a shuffle. "Let me guess, you're taking your precious founder with you to the meeting."

"That isn't your concern."

"But it is!" Another thud sounded in the room, and Vic's hand hovered over the doorknob. "I'm your second in command, and you're keeping things from me."

"Then tell me what I'm keeping from you so I can get it over with!" A chair skidded across the floor. "If you spent less time torturing others, maybe I'd see you as someone I could rely on!"

"Fine, why don't you make the founder bitch your second?" Vic jumped back as the door flew open. Landon sneered at Vic. "Just in time."

Vic tried to move out of the way to avoid more damage, but he plowed into her and stalked away. Her back twinged painfully.

She peeked into Kai's office. Not much had changed since Xiona had left it. Kai tended to be more on the orderly side, but papers were strewn over his desk and dust motes floated in the air. He sat at his desk, his back outlined by the windows, his face resting in his palms. She went to stand behind him and lightly rubbed his shoulders. He didn't move to look at her.

"I'm sorry."

"What do you have to be sorry for?" Tiredness laced his voice.

Vic shrugged. "Nothing, but I suck at comforting people."

Kai raised his head and shook it. "I suppose you heard that?"

"Another Landon hissy fit? Yeah, I think the entire hall heard it." Did her relationship with Kai have that much of a negative effect? She barely saw him anymore. How could others believe he favored her when she went into the sewers every night without his intervention? Landon worked on a list of assumptions. She saw a large bone leaning on a chair. "What's that about?"

Kai followed her gaze. "According to Landon, Boreus is putting out meat scraps to attract mogs. He found these on the edge of Nyx territory. We can only assume they're baiting mogs to come into their lands from ours. That might be why our mog count is down."

"Meat? How can they afford it?" She rarely ate anything but fish, even as a founder. Her mind went back to her makeshift weapon in the sewers." I did find a bone tonight in the sewers."

"I'm guessing GicCorp supplied the bones for them. We can assume the theory about a mog's sense of smell is accurate." Kai leaned into her hands.

She felt a dozen knots in his neck.

"Are you really going to see Tristan today?" Vic wanted to go along. Her sister wouldn't be near Tristan, but she couldn't help it.

Kai half-heartedly picked up a yellow paper on his desk before setting it down again. "I have to go. Nothing will be done, but the reapers need to see me take action." He faced Vic. "Should I tell them we're suffering because GicCorp wants us to turn humans by force?"

"What are you afraid of?"

"They might be upset that I didn't tell them sooner, but I'm more afraid that they'll want to take part in GicCorp's plan." He pushed all the papers together on his desk and plopped them aside.

"I don't know most of the reapers, but you do. You're the

one who needs to trust that your comrades have a higher moral compass and would choose lives over money." In Verrin, people looked out for themselves. She'd hoped reapers would be better, but so far, she'd been wrong. "We need to remember that Xiona's group was small. Maybe it was small because only a few reapers would do something like that." Vic wanted Kai to have faith in his comrades.

"I thought I knew Xiona and those who helped her. Turns out they thought it was something they should do."

"Do you think Dei is helping?" Kai shrugged, and Vic continued, "Remember what Nel said? The numbers never went up despite how much blight was collected. Maybe we need to find out where all the extra blight is going and why people are still getting corrupted if there's enough purified magic for them to charge?"

"And how will we do that?"

She tapped her sides. "I can go in and see." And maybe look for other things while she was there.

Kai raised his brow. "And that has nothing to do with you worrying about your sister?"

"Maybe." She hadn't heard anything from her sister, which was normal, but with Tristan's involvement in harming their people, she didn't trust him that the vitals were safe.

"I get it. If my sister were a vital, I'd be worried too, but you're too obvious. We can't send you. They'll recognize you right away."

He was right, but she wanted to go herself. There was a short list of people they could trust. "What about William?"

Kai got up from his chair and sat on the desk to face her. "Send in the radiant?"

"We could find him a wand." The more Vic thought

about it, the more it made sense. As a radiant, he stayed away from magic and those who used it. His father was the leader, but William had yet to take over any responsibilities, so those in GicCorp wouldn't recognize him.

"We make the radiant use magic? That'll go over well. And find him a wand? You have one lying around?" Kai flung his hands out.

"As a matter of fact, we do." Vic bit her lip. Kai's family struggled since they only had his relic to support them. Founders had relics to spare.

"Oh." For the first time, she felt the distance between them. Part of her would always be separate because of being a founder. Vic had barely struggled growing up. She couldn't relate to most of the reapers who'd risen on their own, fighting against founders who had access to better training and resources.

"I'm not sure how this would work. Convince the radiant he needs to use magic?" He didn't meet her gaze and tapped his chair with his foot.

"He might." William stayed in Kai's house, and when she'd talked to him recently, he'd seemed off. His entire life had been turned upside down, so maybe he needed something to focus on other than his whole upbringing as a radiant being a lie.

"We can see, but he'll need to be willing. Why don't you go talk to him while I waste an hour with Tristan, trying to figure out how they justify letting Boreus into our territory? Actually, they'll probably say we're mistaken." Kai plopped back into his chair and put his face back in his hands.

"I'm not sure if you'll thank me for sharing more unpleasant news," she said.

He grimaced. "Pile it on."

"I found Tristan injured in the sewers last night."

"What was he doing in the sewers? I hope you left him to rot." He crossed his arms.

"He wouldn't tell me, and I wish I had." Vic didn't know why, but she didn't want to tell him she'd used up her question to ask about her sister. They were on team Nyx. "Afterwards, I went to my father, and he pointed out that there's been a lot of foot traffic down in the sewers. He mentioned that hundreds, maybe thousands, of people in Nyx territory are missing."

Kai slammed his hand on the table. "How did I miss this?" He shuffled through papers. "I'm sending reapers to check now. Of course they'd just do it in Nyx," he muttered to himself.

He'd reached the same conclusion that she and her father had. Vic paused before reaching out. Before all this had happened, she'd thought there was something between them. In their brief moments, they did casually reach out to each other, but she wished she could help him bear the weight of his position as commander. She slid her hand into his, pulled him next to her, then folded him into a hug. His arms tightened around her. The gap between them got wider by the day, and she didn't know how to stop it.

"I'm sorry I can't be around more," he murmured into her hair.

Vic pressed into his shoulder. He still smelled faintly like cedar, and she enjoyed being in his arms. "You have so much to deal with. I wish I could help, but it would only cause more problems with Landon."

He relaxed. "You're right. But I'd rather spend time with you than him."

She snorted. "I sure hope so. He totally isn't your type."

Finally, a laugh escaped Kai. "I don't know. He seems like a cuddler."

"You have poor taste in men." Vic leaned her head back and looked into Kai's face.

He brushed his hand against hers. "Good thing I have you, then?" They'd made no promises. They probably wouldn't until this GicCorp situation was over, whatever that meant. He needed to be a leader, and she could support him from afar.

Vic stood on her toes, and her lips brushed his. "I better get moving. I'll find William today and talk to him. If it goes well, we can see my father later and maybe get a wand." If this was all she could do, she would do it. Maybe it could give him strength.

Kai slowly released her and tucked a strand of hair behind her ear. "Be careful."

Vic left his office and quickly went to her room to take another shower. The nights in the sewers had left her always feeling dirty. Her cat, Scraps, slept through her routine, and she softly stroked his fur before leaving to see William.

As she stepped out of the building, the sun soaked into her black clothing. The mildew scent of Verrin surrounded her as she neared the canal. Normally, reapers slept during morning hours, but she couldn't sleep until she'd talked to William about going into GicCorp. He might not be what her father had in mind, but he might be all they had to offer.

She glanced over her shoulder to make sure no one followed her. Who knew how far Landon would go to bother her? They didn't need him finding Xiona at Kai's place. Maybe Kai should give him more to do. Then he might leave

Vic alone. To be safe, she took some random turns. There weren't many people around, though it might be too early. The familiar door appeared around the corner, and Vic knocked.

"Who is it?"

"Vic."

The door opened, and William gestured for her to come inside. The main room looked the same—small and cozy, with thick rugs made of warm colors. Samuel and Xiona sat to the side in wooden dining room chairs. Their calm faces and slight smiles made Vic shiver. Those who'd been purified always seemed peaceful but strange.

William didn't wear his usual white anymore, but various black clothing he'd borrowed from Kai. They hung around his broad shoulders. Kai had thicker muscles, whereas William had broader shoulders but a trim frame. His light brown hair was no longer slicked back, but rumpled as if he'd slept on it wet. His clear blue eyes flickered with distant shadows. The tan he'd gained from working outside as a radiant had faded now that he spent too much time indoors.

"Sit." He pulled out another chair, and it scraped on the wooden floor.

"Thanks." Vic eyed him. "How are you?"

"Fine. Is that all you came to ask?" He sat across from her.

"I should stop by more often." With the two smiling radiant watching on, Vic sat on the edge of her chair. She didn't like being here with them. She missed the old Samuel, and guilt ate at her about what had happened to Xiona. Vic would have rather died than become a radiant, and maybe Xiona would have wanted the same thing.

William laughed harshly. "We both know you're uncomfortable. What do you want?"

"I liked your brother." The past tense had slipped out before she could catch herself.

William's eyes flashed, and his jaw tightened. "He's still here."

"Yes. I mean ..." Vic didn't know how to recover, and she tapped her fingers against her thigh. "He's a bit different."

William stayed silent.

She took a deep breath. "I'm here to see if you'd be willing to use a wand."

His brows rose.

"Kai and I think you might be our best chance at seeing what's happening in GicCorp. I'm too recognizable, and so is he. Tristan might know you, but other than that, the radiant keep to themselves. We want to know where the extra blight is going—and maybe find a way into Haven." Vic voiced her own personal agenda.

William crossed his arms. "You want to know about your sister."

"That too." Vic pulled at a loose thread in her pants. "I'll be honest, I'm more worried about her. I'd like to think I'm a better person and say I'd put civilians before my sister, but I want to know she's safe." She broke the thread off her pants. "I'm trying not to be foolish and run in there and demand to see her. I can't do that, but you might find something. You honestly owe me nothing."

He turned his face away. "But don't I? It's only because of you I can stay here. Even though I feel more like a prisoner, Sam and I have nowhere else to go." He looked sad. "He'd find it funny, the thought of me using magic. I've already gone against the radiant by forcefully purifying two people. What's one more transgression?"

Vic couldn't read him. The prim and annoying William that she knew didn't sit before her anymore. "You don't seem okay with it, though. I don't want you to do it because you feel indebted to me."

"Then what other reason would I have?" He leaned forward. "I think it would be better if you called in your debt. I don't want to use magic. I want to honor my beliefs. I don't agree with what magic is doing to us." He walked over to his brother. "I want magic to end. Ask me to do this because we owe you our lives. Kai wouldn't have let us stay here if you hadn't fought for it. You saved my brother in the Dei battle. Tell me you want me to save your sister."

"Fine. Come over to the Glass house and see if you can bond with a wand. You owe me for saving your brother."

"I'll see you this afternoon." He brushed Samuel's hair. With his backed turned to her, he ended the conversation.

Vic left, saying nothing. Doubt filled her about using William. The radiant might not be as stable as she'd thought. Was he their only option for infiltrating GicCorp? Vic didn't have many people she could trust. She'd broken off contact with many of the founders she'd grown up with. The unstable radiant was all she had left.

Lost in her thoughts, she went back to Nyx. Kai's office was empty, so she went to get some sleep. Only a few hours passed before she woke up not feeling rested. Scraps purred at her side, his warmth comforting her back pain. She stroked his fur absentmindedly.

Thoughts of how to break into GicCorp took up her thoughts. How could she trust William? She didn't want to wake up Kai, but they needed to see her father today. He stayed in his own bedroom on the first floor. Vic had a feeling he didn't want to touch Xiona's things. No one was in the hallway when she reached his room. She knocked and heard a tired groan before opening the door. Kai was stretched out over his bed without a shirt on. The sun hit his built chest, and she blinked a few times before glancing away.

"Enjoying the view, Sparks?" He stretched and pulled the blankets up on his bed, then went to his closet.

Vic faced him as he put on a shirt. "Of your messy room?"

He winked. "You're more than welcome to stop by and look at my messy room anytime you want."

Things almost felt normal between them. "William's meeting me at my father's house. Did you still want to come?"

Kai groaned again. "I suppose I need to. Can we trust your father?"

Vic started. "That's a loaded question." He felt more like the father she used to know, but she didn't know his agenda. There was a bit of madness around him. Everyone she knew bordered on the edge of insanity these days. "I'm not sure what he's involved in with the founders. Do you want to talk to him about the missing people in Nyx territory? If nothing else, I know he wants to protect his family." Whatever else he was involved in couldn't hurt her or Em—she hoped.

Kai rubbed his forehead. "I sent out a small patrol this morning, and they found many abandoned homes with entire families missing. I'm thinking we need allies. Dei is out. Becks wanted nothing to do with us, and we may need some founders on our side. I don't know if they'll go against GicCorp. Do you know anyone?"

"I'm not sure. We can ask my father." She wasn't sure where she stood with him. He seemed like an ally. Vic couldn't help feeling hurt that he hadn't trusted her sooner. They could've worked together instead of her leaving the house. Childish. Tristan had been correct in that aspect. Her actions these last months had been useless.

"We'll sink without support. We've lost a few reapers already. There's enough food so far, and we pulled in a few mogs last night, but I hate to say it ... without people living in Nyx, we'll have fewer mogs and less corruption. The other reapers won't have a choice but to leave." Kai tied his boots and strapped on his harness.

"I'm surprised Tristan won't replace you as the commander."

"They don't get to decide. I have a feeling that could change, though."

They left his room and found Landon standing down the hall.

He eyed them and glared at Vic. "Where are you going?"

"Outside." Vic walked around him.

"Why are you going together?" Landon stepped in her path.

Kai pulled him out of the way. "Go start the training. I'll be back in an hour."

Landon clenched his fists and left.

"He's getting bold."

Did he stake out Kai's office to watch where he went? Vic shuddered.

"He's a good reaper but very territorial about his placement. He thinks you'll replace him."

"I think he has a crush on you," Vic teased.

"I wish that was it. Did you do anything to piss him off?"

"Me?" Vic blinked.

"Why do I bother asking?"

They left the Order and took a water taxi to her old home. The glass walls gleamed in the light, and William waited for them by the gate.

"He seems more rumpled than normal," Kai noted.

Vic was already on edge about trusting William. She didn't need him falling apart at the thought of using magic. As they approached, William didn't greet them and waited for Vic to open the gate.

The glass statues her sister had made remained in the yard like sentries waiting for their maker's return. Each one gave Vic a pang of regret over not having done more to stop her sister. Like William had told her, it had been her sister's choice. They'd grown up in Verrin, believing that vitals were heroes and her sister would leave to protect them. The more they uncovered about GicCorp, the less Vic believed anything the city told her. Did no one else care, or did GicCorp hold all the power?

Vic pushed open the front door, and the two men followed her into the foyer. She went straight to her father's office. He sat, drinking amber liquid from a glass tumbler. She frowned at him drinking this early, and he set it aside after noticing her disapproval.

He sat back when he saw everyone with her. "What brings my daughter, her fiancé, and her boyfriend here today?"

Kai and William shifted at their titles. Vic glared at her father's joke. He chuckled.

"We think William can get into GicCorp."

"The radiant?" Her father's tone came out flat.

Kai snorted behind Vic, and she glared at him to keep

silent. If she got early wrinkles from all the glaring, she would smack them. "Who else do you know? A random imb off the street? A founder they would recognize?"

Her father emptied his glass despite his daughter's disapproval. "I suppose you came for a relic, then? Nothing else?"

"What else is there?" Vic asked.

She curled her toes in her boots. What did he want from her? To stop by and act like normal? They'd connected last night, but now it felt off. The confusion of their on-again, off-again relationship hurt her head. "This is our best chance to see what's happening to the vitals and the extra blight. I thought you wanted that."

"I do." He looked past Vic. "What do you want, radiant? Can you use magic?"

"I owe Vic, and my brother would want me to help her. I don't know if a wand will even bond with me, but I'll try."

"Do you even know what you need to do to get hired by GicCorp?"

"I guess that's something you'll have to tell me."

Her father combed back his hair with his hands. He glanced at Vic. "This is a mission doomed to failure."

Kai stepped forward. "Magic users may not trust the radiant or even like them, but William went into battle with Vic, at a risk to himself. He may not look like much, but I honestly believe he will do everything in his power to help us."

William, who didn't care to sell himself, remained silent. Her father turned his back to them to shift a glass figurine on the shelf. He drew out his wand and slid open a panel. Vic didn't know what he did with his magic, but the wall opened, revealing the large door of a safe. He twisted the lock and used his wand again to open the door. A woodsy scent came from inside the room. Her father walked in and gestured for them to follow.

Vic had never seen the inside of where her father stored all the Glass relics. Kai and William followed behind her, and she gasped at the array of wands on the shelves. No other scythes sat in the room. The wands gleamed in rows with various colors of wood. They all had large colored stones attached to their ends.

"You might want to take off your ring." Her father pointed to William's hand. "I don't know if that will affect anything. Radiant don't need to bond with the rings, so hopefully it won't matter."

If William turned out to be a reaper, they'd be in trouble. In Verrin, you could either bond with a scythe or a wand. If your family only had one wand to pass down and you couldn't bond with it because you were a reaper, the source of income would be cut off since a born reaper couldn't use the inherited wand. To make matters worse, for the low-income individuals in Verrin, scythe were rarer, and the third-generation ones couldn't be counted on to drain a weak mog.

William stood there, taking in all the first-generation relics. "If I want to work at GicCorp, won't these imbue glass?"

Her father shook his head. "Your relic can imbue anything. It takes years and skill, so most stick with one product. The more practice you have with a relic, the less power you'll have to use to imbue resources. Then it won't drain as fast. If GicCorp hires you, they'll assume you have basic training in all areas." He swept his hand across a shelf. "You'll have one week to learn what it takes years for most. I'm hoping with your radiant training you'll already know control, although I can't relate to how it works to suck the magic out of someone's soul."

She elbowed her father, but William ignored the jibe. Her father was right. This project was doomed. She said nothing but turned to face Kai. His jaw tensed as he took in all the first-generation wands. He was the last in his family with a decent relic. Seeing all this wealth couldn't be easy for him. His sister, as an imb, would have no use for the scythe he'd pass down if something happened to him.

William shuffled forward, and something crossed his face when he removed his ring and put it in his pocket. His eyes traveled across all the wands and stopped on a simple-looking one with a large white stone and pure white body. He looked at her father for permission, and he nodded. William touched the wand. The stone flashed, then turned a soft white. The gicgauge on the side was empty, waiting for the user to perform magic. A gicgauge tracked magic used. It protected the stone from overuse and could be traded in for a small number of credits. Even if filled, it didn't give them much. That was why founder factories also paid them hourly. Otherwise, they couldn't survive.

"That was easier than expected," Vic stated.

Her father replied, "The magic draws us in. Except you. From the start, you went for the scythe. As an imb, he could have bonded with any of these wands and been okay, but some say it is better to have a friendly relic."

"Friendly? Like, it's alive?"

"Some say so."

Vic wanted to scoff but also understood. Her scythe almost felt alive when she used it.

William gingerly held the wand, unsure what to do with it. Her father guided them back out of the safe and shut the door with a whoosh. Then he shuffled through his desk and handed him a spare holster for his wand. William didn't put it on but continued to stare down at the white wand.

Her father turned to her. "Will he be okay?"

"Yes." No confidence reached her voice.

"I'd like to talk to you in private if that's possible."

Vic looked at William and Kai, who'd been silent since the safe. He nodded and guided William out of the office.

Her father went back to his desk, and Vic went in front of him. "What did you have to say?"

"If there is something wrong with the vitals in Haven, we'll need more founders on our side. Without their backing, we won't make it far."

They needed more. Kai had said as much too. Did her father not trust him with this information? She would feel more confident if she couldn't count everyone she trusted on one hand. "And what does that have to do with me? I'm not great with the founders."

"I think you'll have more luck in bringing in those closer to your age by privately letting them know what's happening in Nyx. The Nordics aren't letting that news out. Only a few will know about the forcibly turned people. You need to make connections with the founders to convince them the Nordics aren't the best leaders for the city. Like I told you last night, we're making plans, but with the founders, it's moving slower than I'd like."

"Wow, sounds super simple, Dad."

His lips quirked up when she said *dad*.

She shifted and didn't meet his gaze.

"It won't be. You'll need to come to parties." He barely hid his grin.

"Parties?"

"That's where all founder deals are made."

"Great."

His voice was tinted with mirth as he added, "You'll also need to wear a dress."

"Blight take me."

This would be worse than the sewers.

❦ 4 ❦

WILLIAM

In the faint lighting of Kai's home, William touched the wand. The box next to him contained different pieces of stone, sand, metal, and anything else Vic's father had thought he'd need to work on for his application to GicCorp. Sam and Xiona sat silently after dinner, leaving William alone with his thoughts again.

The wand warmed in his hands, waiting for him to use it. With one hand, he reached to straighten his cuffs but stopped when he realized he no longer wore the radiant uniform. He sat back and took a small piece of silver ore in his hand.

According to Conrad, those who worked for GicCorp needed to imbue many objects with precision. They did everything from repairing the lines that carried the collected blight to making repairs around the outside of the Haven enclosure. GicCorp ran the banking system for the credits. It would be useless for William to run around outside GicCorp, fixing charging stations. He needed to be closer to Haven, even though he wasn't sure how to get inside. They needed to find information before any move against GicCorp could be made. William hoped any information would help. Maybe it would reveal a weakness or a direction.

"They have too much faith in my abilities, Sam." He let the magic flow. At least her father was right about one thing: he understood control. The imbs worked the same as the radiant; they needed only a little magic to do a lot. If they ran out too fast, they couldn't work enough hours to get a full wage. The only thing going for him was that he had a first-generation relic that would take longer for the gicgauge to fill. He wouldn't run out as fast as others and might get hired based on that alone. It wouldn't do him any good, though, if he blew through his magic within two hours.

There was also the problem of Sam staying in the house. He had to lock him in when he went to meet Vic and Kai. His brother acted differently from other radiant. He still smiled and listened, but only sometimes. He wouldn't leave William's side, which was odd. Radiant never attached themselves to other humans. They worked together, but it made no difference who they worked with.

"I wish I didn't have to lock you inside." It felt worse to lock his brother in than having him sit still all day.

His brother didn't reply.

"Should I give you both a task?" Come to think of it, he'd never assigned them the normal radiant task to help the community. William squeezed the silver ore, and it bit into his palm. It felt off, ordering around those who hadn't wanted the radiant life.

They looked at him.

Xiona asked, "What's my task?"

Sam stared. "Do what you must."

William shivered. Sam's responses weren't normal either.

Radiant never talked much, and there wasn't much thought behind what they said.

"Why don't you both tidy the house?" Maybe a task would stop his brother from always following him. As they cleaned, William's stomach turned. "Never mind. Sit and read a book or something." He didn't want servants. He shook his head. No, they weren't servants. They weren't part of the community like they should be, and that was messing up his head. "Okay, go ahead and keep up the house."

He avoided glancing their way as they cleaned. *I hate this. I hate myself. What am I doing?* How could it be that only a few weeks ago he'd wanted a calm wife and his world had been black and white, everything clean and orderly? Magic was evil. The radiant life was honorable. Then his father had shown him the corruption. They were no different from the magic users. Did anyone in Verrin stick to their beliefs?

He focused on the small piece of metal. The magic flowed from the wand and into the metal, and he tried to pull the metal away from the embedded rock. The metal molded for a moment but then sunk back into its original shape. A metallic taste entered his mouth as he worked on the silver ore. He tried again, and the metal pulled like a taut rubber strand. It didn't want to separate, so he focused on keeping it connected. The wand warmed, and he plied the silver into a ring. The ring, cold to the touch, glowed in the light. Sweat beaded on William's brow, and he got up to drink something to get the metallic taste out of his mouth. Did all imbs deal with this side effect? He'd never heard of them tasting the metal as they worked. He frowned and ran his hands over his clothing to smooth the wrinkles. Maybe he did not have an affinity for metal.

While Sam and Xiona worked around him, William went

through all the objects, trying to form them. The unfamiliar stonework came easier for him, and instead of tasting it, he felt the texture come to life under his skin. The wand became an extension of his body, and certain types of stone felt like molding butter. The sensation on his skin became easier to deal with than the taste.

Long after the other two had gone to bed, he continued to work to get a handle on all the different materials he needed to imbue. He blinked when bright sunlight entered the room.

Before him, blobs of imbued materials sat on the table, his relic drained. The clang of pans and the smell of cooking fish startled him. Xiona and Sam were cooking breakfast.

He turned and saw Sam setting a place for him at the table. He sat down with them, and they ate mechanically. William gritted his teeth and pushed the plate away. He should have helped them make the food. Instead, he'd lost track of time.

"I'm going out."

Sam stood to follow him, and William didn't have the heart to lock him up again, so he let his brother come with him. He locked the door behind him, but not the outer lock that would keep Xiona trapped. She didn't wander off like Sam did. The blight glowed green in the sky today. His skin felt moist when the humid air surrounded them. "These black clothes are hot. Let's get something else to wear."

"Do what you must."

William bit his cheek. "I will."

He went to a charging station to deposit the credits he'd earned from working with the material. There would be none of the extra pay that a true employee would get. The number flashed before him, and his mouth dropped open at the credits. If a first-generation relic gave this much for molding materials, it was no wonder that those who had them had money. But then, living as a radiant on any amount seemed excessive. He didn't know what it cost to survive in Verrin since he now lived off Kai and Vic's charity. He frowned at his account number. There were more credits in there than he'd deposited. Had Vic put credits into his account without telling him? His theory on relics was dashed. For now, he needed the help. With determination, he promised himself he would find information on her sister. His debt grew larger by the day.

"I guess we can all get something new to wear." He rolled his shoulders at the strange feeling of wearing a harness for the wand. The heat bothered him, but he also wanted a jacket to cover the harness. He didn't want to advertise the relic to the world. He'd said nothing the other day, but he'd noticed the look in Kai's eyes when he'd seen all the relics stored in Conrad's safe.

William walked past the water taxis. It still felt wrong to take them. Even though it was hot, they made the long walk to the center of town. Sam remained his ever-present shadow. If people thought they made a strange pair, a man in black followed by a radiant, he didn't notice. William actively avoided meeting people's gaze. By the time they reached the center of the city, their clothes were soaked through with sweat.

The radiant tried to weave their own clothing, and the process didn't work out very well for most items. They tried to stick with factory-rejected linen, metal, or glass. The radiant grew their own food, but it took much longer.

Signs signaled various wares or tools made with magic. The House of Gold carried their own brand of delicate jewelry. The sun hit the rings and chains embedded with impressive scrollwork. The sign in the window claimed all the pieces were made with first-generation relics. Did that affect the quality? It would take longer to craft jewelry with a third-generation wand, so wouldn't it cost more? More symbols of status, he supposed. Could anyone tell the difference?

He caught sight of his image in the window and tried to smooth his rumpled hair. Now that he lived with magic, it should be easier for him to stay put together. William, now aware of his appearance, briskly walked to find a clothing store.

Clothing hung in a display window, and the cool air hit his face as he entered the store. A youthful woman with a toothy smile greeted them. Her gaze flickered when she saw Sam.

"How can I help you today?" She sidestepped to put more distance between her and his brother.

He crossed his arms. "Just getting some clothes." Did she think being a radiant was contagious? Trying to ignore her ignorance, he asked, "Do you happen to know what GicCorp employees wear?" He was probably getting ahead of himself, but he shouldn't waste credits from Vic or Kai on the wrong things. Judging by the prices in view, he did only have a limited amount to spend on them.

Her head tilted. "Most places are casual. You'd do fine with pants and a nice shirt."

William nodded and glanced through the clothes on the rack. He pulled out some light-colored shirts for Sam. His eye caught on a rack loaded with different blue shirts, and he gathered one of each for himself. He'd never thought about which color he liked. Maybe blue. They were all lightweight material that would feel better in the heat. He grabbed a cerulean jacket to hide his wand harness.

Then he added items for Xiona. He wasn't sure about her size, but they all couldn't wear black anymore. He thought maybe he could get Bomrosy to dye Xiona's hair. Maybe he should dye his hair too. They might want to be more cautious, in case someone saw Xiona on one of Bomrosy's trips. William almost wanted to ask his father if something had gone wrong when he'd purified Sam, but he hadn't seen his parents in weeks. He didn't want Sam to get taken away from him.

He took his items to the front, and the toothy sales person bagged them all and went on about some rewards program if he shopped there again. William nodded along and took his bags. Was this how those with relics lived? Nicer clothing? Finer shops? He felt out of place, even though he now had a wand. Most didn't enjoy having radiant in their shops. They went to market places and shopped quickly to avoid making people feel uncomfortable.

William and Sam left the cool air of the shop. The gicorb in his neck itched, so he headed to the nearest charging station to charge. He didn't need to worry about Sam or Xiona since the purified never turned into mogs. He placed his credits card in the slot and held the receiver up to his neck. Only a slight tingling from his gicorb let him know that he'd finished, and he replaced the receiver when it beeped.

"William?"

He turned to see his mother standing frozen in the path. Her body tensed when she saw the wand harness. Her gaze took in her sons in black clothing. She blinked rapidly and covered her mouth. A bag lay on its side next to her, and an apple rolled out onto the stone street.

William knelt and picked up the bag she'd dropped. He quickly brushed the apple off and returned it to the bag. His mother yanked the bag from him.

"Mother?" Why did she shop down here? His fingers twitched, and they stared at each other.

She grabbed his arm, covertly looked around, then led him to a nearby drink shop. They picked a table with three chairs, and his mom went to order. The imbs prepared the drinks, placing their wands on various machines for boiling some beans. Coffee was a luxury item, not as expensive as beef, but most couldn't afford it. They handed her a tray with three cups. Where had his mother gotten the credits for this? She returned and handed William and Sam their drinks, and she smelled her own coffee.

"I know it's wrong, but their coffee always tastes better. Don't you think?" Her smile quivered, and she took a small sip.

William stared down at the light-brown concoction. He never cared for coffee normally. The kind his mother sometimes bought merely had a taste and wasn't the genuine thing. When he tasted the bitter liquid, it flowed smoothly down his tongue and throat. He raised his eyebrows. "Way better."

Somehow, sharing the secret that his mom frequented a coffee shop made him feel better. Did his father not notice the missing income?

She put down her cup and traced the rim with her finger. "You see, some things are understandable. Radiant who have yet to be purified may take a water taxi or order food from a shop, and we get our clothing made by imbs since it has proven difficult to weave our own, even though we try to improve the process." Her face hardened. "But there are lines we never cross. What are you doing wearing a wand?"

Any hopeful feeling he'd had vanished. "I left, Mother. How can I provide for myself and Sam without magic?" A bitter coldness entered him.

"Samuel doesn't belong with you. He's a full radiant, and he needs to come back with me. Your rebellion has gone too far. Come back and ask your father for forgiveness, and I will never mention what I saw today." His normally submissive mother glared at him.

Even though he didn't like what she'd said, he preferred her to the woman who went along with what his father said without speaking much. William pushed his cup away. "Tell him. I won't be returning, and Sam stays with me."

Her eyes darkened. "No, he doesn't belong with you. Him being alone with you isn't normal. The radiant work together to provide a life without magic. That's part of the agreement with the city. Did you know that? Radiant stay in our area, where the imbs stay away. If we didn't live what we preach, we would be hypocrites."

William recalled the feeling of having Xiona and Sam help around the house. She was right, it wasn't normal. It wasn't like William had left everything to them, but it was a compact house and there was only so much to do. He studied his brother. Part of him wanted to let go of the burden, but he'd made a promise to him about the sky, and he couldn't leave his brother behind. *What color is the sky, Brother?* His brother needed to stay with him. He didn't trust his father with the radiant anymore.

"He stays with me. You can't call me a hypocrite as you sit

here drinking coffee made with magic." Maybe, just maybe, he could undo what he'd done to his brother.

His mother stood, and the chair clattered back from her rushed movement. "Samuel, come and get your duty for the radiant."

Sam's gaze lifted, but he stayed seated. His mother grabbed him and tried to drag him out with her. He stood, but he didn't budge.

"Samuel! Come and get your duty as a radiant."

Faces turned toward them, and William removed his mother's grip from Sam's arm. "He won't go."

"What do you mean he won't go?" she spat.

"He won't leave my side." He shouldn't have said anything, but he worried about Sam's abnormal behavior compared to other radiant.

Her brows shot up. "We must take him to your father immediately!"

William blocked her from his brother. "That isn't happening. We left the radiant community, and honestly, we were never given a choice to be part of it. Father has no power over those who don't choose the path."

"You're our sons!"

"That doesn't make us your property. Come on, Sam." William left his mother alone in the coffee shop. His hands trembled, but he didn't turn back to see if she followed. Not caring anymore, he hired a water taxi to take him back. They got out several stops before Kai's house and took a few turns to lose anyone who might be following. He didn't think his mother would follow them, but he didn't like the feeling he'd gotten from her. Did she think she and father owned them? Sam had had a point before he'd purified him. Everyone else got a choice except those born to the radiant path. No relics to pass down except the rings, and they needed the credits their family provided. Compared to reapers, the rings only collected a tiny amount of blight at a time. They weren't taught how to survive in Verrin.

William opened the door to Kai's house and placed the clothes in Sam's and Xiona's rooms. He slept on the sofa while Xiona and Sam got the beds. He took a shower and put on his new clothes. The blue made his eyes seem happier. As he toweled off his hair, he spotted red hair out of the corner of his eye. Vic sat on the sofa with Sam.

"The shower's open, Sam, if you want." Sam grabbed his new clothes and left to shower.

William sat down across from Vic. "What brings you here?"

The silver ring he'd made last night rested on her fingers. She slipped it on her finger, and it fit perfectly. "You're doing pretty well. It may not be as hopeless as I thought." Her smooth lips twisted in a wry grin.

"Glad you think so." Dark circles showed against her pale skin. Wasn't she sleeping enough? She brushed back her hair, revealing a minor cut on her face. "Rough night?"

"Hmm? Oh, just training."

William's jaw clenched. Who had cut her in training? "What kind of training leaves those cuts, and I'm assuming you're also bruised?" He went to get the med kit Kai left in the house.

He heard her sigh and a shuffle. When he returned, she was lying on the sofa. "The second doesn't like me, so he's training me personally. More like giving me a personal beating." She looked more comfortable in the house today.

His heart thudded, and he swallowed. He brushed her hair out of her face, then cleaned the scratches and applied ointment to them. It wouldn't heal her as fast as imbued ointment, but it would help. "Doesn't Kai know? Shouldn't he stop him?"

She crossed her arms. "I can handle myself."

He'd said the wrong thing again. He could never connect with her. There was always this feeling of distance that she'd never had with Sam until he'd become a radiant. "I know. I just think he should stop it."

Vic sat up and pulled her hair back into a bun. "He has enough on his plate."

"But you're important to him." Weren't they dating? Shouldn't Kai care more? Did William care too much? He put away the med kit.

"I need to support him. I can handle it."

"Fine. Don't get so cut up, then. Maybe dodge the attacks." He shut the cupboard harder than necessary.

"Got it." She started to leave, but William wanted her to stay.

"I'm about to make lunch. Did you want some?" His tone came out high pitched. What was wrong with him?

She paused, her face strangely blank. "Sure?"

Sam got out of the shower as William chopped up some carrots. "Sam, can you set the table? Xiona, can you grab the fish?"

Vic watched them cook from the doorway. "Can I help?"

"We got it." Maybe he should smile at her. Was that too forward? William settled for a half grin he hoped didn't look creepy. She'd come over before. What had changed? Maybe the fact she seemed so tired or alone. He'd missed it on her last visit.

"Why do you call Samuel Sam now?" She didn't miss much.

William finished cooking the fish and mixed it in with the vegetables. He handed it to Xiona, who dished out the meal for the four of them. Sam poured them water.

After a lengthy pause, he finally answered, "I'm not sure. I'd call him that sometimes before, but now he seems like a Sam." He gestured for Vic to sit, and he sat next to her.

She placed her hand on his arm. "He's still there." He looked down at her hand, and she took it away, blushing. "I'm sorry I was awkward around him. I didn't mean to leave you alone."

William nodded, and he suddenly wished her hand was back on his arm. "You have a lot to deal with. I-I want to see if I can bring him back." He stared down at his food. Why had he told her that? His hand came back empty again as he tried to straighten cuffs that weren't there.

"If anyone can do it, you can." Her face brightened. "I'll help you."

For the first time in weeks, William returned her smile. A full one. "What can an ex-radiant and a reaper do?"

She shrugged. "Who knows? But we can try."

William's heart pounded, and the meal had flavor today.

❧ 5 ❧

VIC

Vic passed the peppermint oil to Ivy, and she placed some under her nose before putting on her mask.

"Another lovely night spent in sewage," Ivy said and passed the oil to Freddie.

He grunted and put some under his nose.

The smell of mint had overwhelmed Vic at first, but it was preferable to human waste. "Wish we would have used this trick before."

"There isn't a lot of peppermint oil. You have to buy it fast. I'm willing to waste my credits on this to survive our new home." Ivy tucked her short hair under her hood.

Today, they were on sewer duty again, but tonight, they needed to find and gather any large bones. At the moment, they assumed Boreus reapers were leaving them to attract mogs into their territory. Apparently, other Nyx reapers had found more bones near Boreus territory. They'd brought the bait back to the Nyx Order entrance. That way, the bait would benefit them. Kai needed to go the political route. There were no rules against putting out bait for mogs, but no

Order had dared to try. Either Boreus wanted to boost their numbers or GicCorp was behind it.

Bomrosy was working on opening the sewer entrance in the back of her shop. She wanted to have more gates to prevent mogs from getting in, and she had some new tech she wanted to try out that would open the gates remotely. They had sealed it off a while ago because of the smell, but it would make accessing the sewers and baiting the mogs easier.

The other reapers Kai had sent out had reported more missing people in Nyx. The quiet streets seemed more eerie now due to the lack of light showing through the drapes of abandoned homes.

Their blight count lowered each day, and some had noticed the less-than-generous helpings of food. Nothing increased the tension more than hungry reapers, especially ones who'd spent the night on sewer duty. Ivy and Freddie never made Vic feel bad, but weariness would seep into their postures when they'd read the schedule.

They went down into the sewers to get the bait before the Boreus reapers came out at sunset. This time, every reaper took a different tunnel. They had orders to run and not stop for anything. Vic went down one of the main tunnels. She kept her eyepiece on so she wouldn't get any surprises, but she sprinted down the slippery path.

She focused on breathing in the sharp minty smell. It helped her feel cooler while she ran. Her boots thudded on the stone, and she soon reached the end of the tunnel. She'd hoped she wouldn't find any bones, but there they were, a bit out of Nyx territory. The long bones still had bits of meat hanging off them.

She quickly grabbed them, and the leftover meat

squished in her grip. Maybe they could attract more mogs. This wasn't an end-all solution, but GicCorp wasn't helping them. It seemed like they were headed for an end game, but only GicCorp knew the score. They barely had time to keep their heads above water or, in Vic's case, sewage. Tristan's words haunted her, and she couldn't avoid the feeling of powerlessness that permeated her thoughts. She needed to get her sister away from them.

Strange movement caught her eye, and she turned in time to dodge a figure that pounced at her.

"Not this time."

As they passed, she swung the two large bones and hit their back. They let out a small sound as they rolled into the sewage.

Vic pointed the bone at them. "It's your turn to take a bath."

She jumped down. Her boots splashed in the shallow river. The figure got up and ran away. She debated giving chase. Running through sewers holding mog bait was a bad idea. She didn't want to die that badly. She threw the bones onto the path and chased after the figure. This one seemed different. It was hard to tell, but they ran with shorter steps, and they seemed slimmer than the one who'd attacked her the other night. She hoped there wasn't more than one masked figure down here, but maybe it was Boreus.

She caught up to the figure. As she reached for them, the figure stopped, and she plowed into them. They fell over. She shot out her hands to catch herself and slid on the stone floor.

Her palms smarted as she stood. Black-clad figures crowded the tunnel ahead of her. The person she'd run into crossed their arms and faced her.

"Blight," Vic swore and turned to run.

She pumped her arms, the thudding of footsteps growing louder behind her. Fingers brushed against her shirt. She dodged down a tunnel and broke away from them. Her plan to get back to the main entrance wouldn't work. The smaller tunnel would only let a few of them run side by side. Vic tried to picture her location in the sewers. This tunnel should connect to the one Freddie scoped out. The path opened up in front of her, and the opening shone like a beacon. Then something hit her back, throwing her off balance. She slowed to catch herself, but someone kicked out her knees and pushed her face-first into the stone path.

They yanked her arms behind her and tied them behind her back. A fist smashed into her head, and her nose hit the stone floor. Blinking back tears, she twisted, but a heavy weight pressed her down. A shout sounded, followed by screams of pain. The weight left her body, and Vic scuttled forward, pushing with her feet. Her face and body scraped against the ground. A small pressure, then the ties snapped apart, and she scrambled to her feet, her head spinning. She turned to look at where her attackers had come from but saw only a wall of glass.

"Dad?" Were the sewers the new hangout for founders now? "Why are you down here?"

"No time." He ran toward the main tunnel.

Vic followed him and held back questions.

When they made it to the main line, her father said, "You need to return to your team. Don't come down here alone again."

"Wait, what?" Her dad ran off before she could make him answer. She gingerly touched her nose. "I don't know what's going on anymore."

Had her dad been following her? The sewers were getting too crowded. A disgusting new hangout place. Couldn't they all meet somewhere above ground? She tucked her hair back under her hood and jogged back to the front to meet up with Ivy and Freddie. Her dad hung out in sewers, William used magic, Kai ignored her, and Bomrosy wouldn't leave Xiona alone. Her small group was slowly going mad. Then there was the biggest question of all: GicCorp.

Up ahead, she saw her team, and Freddie's brows rose when she came from the wrong tunnel.

Ivy placed her hands on her hips. "You're covered in poop again."

"I hadn't noticed," Vic replied dryly.

"And your nose looks broken."

"Thanks, Ivy."

Her team member frowned. "What's going on?"

Vic brushed her palms off as best she could. "I wish I knew. I keep finding masked people in black down here. Tonight, a pack of them came after me."

"What in the blight?" Ivy tugged on Freddie's sleeve. "She can't go on her own."

Just what she needed: someone to babysit her. "I'll be fine."

"Tell Kai we can't be in the sewers. It's already hard with our team of three, and now you have people coming after you every night."

Vic knew Ivy didn't mean to sound condescending, but she flinched at the word three.

"Kai has enough to worry about. I'm sorry about all this." If they were coming after only her, she might need to be down in the sewers to find out what they were after. She couldn't possibly have been in the wrong place at the wrong time two nights in a row.

Ivy stood on her toes, which brought her up to Vic's chin. "Stop saying sorry, and let's solve this together. If you won't tell Kai, I will. Landon shouldn't keep us down here night after night anyway. He's abusing his power, and Kai needs to stop him."

"He's doing the best he can!" Was he, though? Vic tried to understand what he was going through. Landon would be hard for anyone to manage.

Ivy snorted. "Let's finish our rounds. I left the bait by the tunnel to the Nyx cells."

They finished the rest of the rounds in silence. Vic's nose burned, but she didn't complain. At home, she showered off the muck, and the healer set her nose. Her eyes were still watering from the pain as she flopped onto her bed. If her father hadn't been there, what would those people have done to her? She hated the feeling of being pinned down. Scraps curled on her lap, but Vic couldn't avoid the loneliness creeping inside her. If she supported Kai, who supported her? Vic missed her sister. She fell asleep. Her back and nose throbbed in pain.

"This is a horrible plan." Vic eyed the onyx gown in the mirror. It clung to her thin frame and glittered in the light of her room. The black material offset her pale skin flatteringly. In her mind, she showed way more cleavage than necessary to win over a founder. The long dress was a perfect tripping hazard, and she already itched to remove the scratchy material.

Her mother wrapped one arm around her and squeezed her arms to her body, holding her in front of the mirror. "It's so wonderful to have you back."

Vic's shoulders bunched up, and she looked awkward, like a kid playing dress up. Her mother, in an elegant flowing gown of light green, remained the image of put-together perfection. Blond curls were all in place, and even her smile stayed perfect. The grace of her mother couldn't be outdone, and the only ones who saw the sadness in her were her family.

"Mother, I'm here for the event. I'm not moving back." Vic stepped back from the mirror, only to trip on the hem. A frustrated sigh escaped her as she kicked out the bottom of the dress.

Her mother placed some vivid crimson heels down.

Vic groaned and stepped into them. The torture devices pinched her feet in all the right places.

"I see it's going as well as expected." Her father came into the room and placed a soft kiss on his wife's cheek. His dark gray suit matched her mother's dress. In the mirror, they all seemed perfect.

Light entered her mother's expression. She was more animated than usual. "About as well as expected. Emilia was the one who loved dresses." Her eyes faded again, and she lifted her hand to put away an imaginary loose hair.

Her father's expression tightened. "I need to talk to our daughter."

Vic watched her mother leave the room. "Are you going to tell me why you were in the sewers?"

"Yes, but not right now. We should meet in my office after the party. It isn't life altering." He went over to her jewelry box and lifted the lid.

"How much does Mother know about everything with Em?" She deserved to know since it involved her daughter.

"Everything." He shut the lid again and paced the large room.

Vic raised her brow. "Will she be okay?"

Her father glanced at Vic's reflection. "Your mother is stronger than you know. The disappointment hit us both. I became angry, and she became withdrawn. Acting like the perfect founder socialite gives her comfort."

Her father was being very open. It was strange to have him treat her like an equal. "I could've helped."

Vic had charged ahead and mostly made mistakes in the last year. She'd broken her connection with her family and assumed her sister would follow. Emilia was always going to do what was best for the family, and Vic should've seen that. The vital heroes didn't have much choice.

"I wanted to keep you and Emilia safe."

"Not a good enough excuse." Vic crossed her arms. "I already feel selfish enough because I didn't know you were researching the vitals. I'm a bigger fool now than ever." Vic kicked at the hem of the dress. "The founders see me as a selfish brat who left the house then pretended to be a radiant to torture her family. Who's going to listen to me?"

"That reputation will either help or hurt us." He handed her a list of names. "I think these people are ready to move their support or share information. I met with a few of them already. Most are after their own gains, but this may be all we have to work with. Our first move is to try to remove GicCorp the usual way. If not, then we may take more drastic actions. I don't know how far each founder is willing to go."

"Do we have any information to share?" Vic's world was flooded with reaper problems. William still trained with his wand, and they didn't know if that was the best path or how close he could get to Haven.

Her father replied, "We do now. Tristan all but threatened to kill your sister. We mourn the loss of our children, but we believe in our duty to the city. We believe they're safe."

"It's my word against Tristan's." He didn't run around acting like a fool—at least, not that anyone knew of.

"Yes, but we all know the vague lines we've been fed since childhood. That may work in our favor. Even though we were trained not to question, I think it's time to remind people of what they're giving up and that they should be asking for more from GicCorp." He rubbed his chin. "Maybe all we can do is have more of a power check with GicCorp and the founders. Or someone else can be in charge. In any case, don't they owe us an explanation? Even a picture of the relic? Anything." Her father's voice faded, and his expression grew blank.

This was his second time losing someone to Haven. Founders only needed to give up one child. Her father had become the Glass founder, and his sister had become a vital. Now he'd lost his daughter, too. "Did anyone try before?"

"There's no record. Tonight, once everyone is gathered in the ballroom, you'll need to create a scene. Appeal to their emotions regarding their lost children and siblings."

Vic grimaced in her heels. She already wanted to rip them off. "I can do that." She tugged at her father's jacket. "Will this put Glass house in danger?" After tonight, it would be clear they were against GicCorp.

He gripped her fingers in his calloused hand. "That's why we're being very public. There's no law saying we can't question GicCorp. In the accords, all founders are supposed to have equal power. GicCorp became the most important industry in Verrin. They hold the power to let us charge. GicCorp also manages the credit system."

A light knock sounded on her door. Vic answered it and found William standing in the hall. "What brings you here?"

William's eyes widened. His gaze flicked over her dress before settling on her face. "I, um, I'm here to get more materials to imbue from your father." Pink tinged his cheeks. He straightened his posture, and Vic grinned at how he tried to bring forth his radiant ways.

Vic twisted the ring he'd made, which she'd forgotten to take off. He caught the movement. "He's with me."

"I didn't mean to crash the event." He stepped into the room.

Vic ran her hands through her hair and smoothed the material around her hips. "The torture hasn't started yet." Vic winked. "Apparently, I get to cause a scene."

"I know you'll do an excellent job." He tugged on his blue shirt. "Is Kai helping you?" He glanced around the room like he thought the reaper would be in her bedroom.

Vic shook her head. "He couldn't make it tonight."

William tensed. "You won't have any backup?"

"I'll be there." Her father guided William to the door. "I have the materials in my office. We should get you out of here before they see you. Not that founders would notice you trying to get an entry job, but we should be careful."

William looked over his shoulder as if hesitant to leave. She bent over a small jewelry box. A new necklace lay across the top, and she touched the delicate silver chain that held a green flower pendant made of glass. "I'm fine, Will."

He nodded, and she called out behind him, "I like the blue. It matches your eyes."

His back straightened as he walked out of the room, making her grin.

Alone in the room, Vic practiced walking. She teetered on the heels, but it wouldn't take long to get used to them again. She couldn't help but examine herself in the mirror. It hadn't been that long since she'd left this life behind. The woman who returned her look didn't feel like the person who ran around in sewers at night. It only took a shiny gown to change someone's personality. Her skin glowed against the black material, but she couldn't hide her weariness. She hooked the necklace around her neck and admired her father's handiwork.

Now she could use her founder title to make a difference. Tristan's words in the sewers had affected her more than she liked. In this massive city, she felt like an ant trying to attack a lion. Maybe it was time that the founders remembered their power and did right by the people of Verrin. Maybe it was time to get rid of blight instead of keeping it at bay. William would love that idea. She twisted the ring around her finger but didn't want to take it off. Somehow, creating a planned scene made her more nervous than the stunts she'd pulled while at home.

Emilia would always roll her eyes as Vic dragged her into the aftermath of some disaster. It went best when she could convince her sister to go along with the plan. A few years ago, she'd gotten her to put a transparent glass coating on some doorways. Then they'd watched people run into them all night. Her father's lips had twitched as he'd lectured them on being proper.

Vic took one more glance at herself and kept her hair down, like a shield to protect her. She took a deep breath as music played below her feet. It was time to join the party.

＊ 6 ＊

VIC

"We tried to get permission to mine to the east, but the other founders won't budge." Emmet Steel reached for another fish cake and stuffed it in his mouth. "Those sewers have been blocked off for years! Why can't we mine?" In his rant, a bit of cake flew out of his mouth and landed on Vic's arm.

"Terrible. Very unjust." She flicked the fish cake off her arm without changing her expression.

His jowls jiggled. "My wife goes to the courts almost daily to plead our case. She barely has time to imbue at the factory. It's all left to me and my daughters. Not having a first-generation relic to help at the start slows down the production line."

"That must be hard on you." Vic discreetly looked for an escape. The room was full of founders in glittery clothing. They laughed and smiled since they could afford to. The magic lighting cast a flattering glow over everyone, with the perimeter kept dark so founders could whisper deals. More came to agreements at the events than in meetings. In the past, Vic had avoided all men of her age so she wouldn't get paired off. When she'd talk to a founder at school, the next day the parents would meet and discuss *options*. Vic had isolated herself from them early in life and more so in the last year. But all her founder classmates had grown older and changed.

He clutched his drink and took a long swallow. "Are you back to being the Glass heir now? Your poor family has no one else to inherit the factories. You must marry another imb, not that radiant. I have a nice son I'm willing to let go of."

Vic bit her lip. Was she supposed to play nice with this man? Everyone knew his wife had the actual power within the Steel founders. But her husband seemed more interested in human trade. "I'm part of the Nyx Order. I don't have any plans to get married."

"Pity. Your father will have to adopt. I have a nice son he can adopt." Another fish cake disappeared behind his jaws.

"Lovely." Vic looked at a tree in the corner. "Oh, I think I need to talk to them. I'll speak to you later." Before he could answer, she rushed to her new tree friend and stood behind the branches, hiding from view. When would it be time for her to make a scene? She'd lost sight of her father, and she didn't want anyone else trying to pawn off their sons on her. She felt like the last slab of beef at the elite market. After tonight, she doubted anyone would want their son to marry into the Glass house. A light tap made her turn. William, dressed like the hired wait staff, stood close to her. His hair, now a tawny brown, was combed back. He smelled like fresh linen as he brushed up against her side.

"Are you supposed to be here?" Vic whispered, her back to the wall. She glanced over his shoulder at the room.

William tugged on her elbows and turned his back to the party, helping her hide. "It looked like you needed a break."

"I preferred being rude to everyone." Even though she would never tell him, having him here comforted her.

"Why not treat them normally?"

Vic shrugged. "I don't know. This is my first time trying to overthrow a corporation."

"Same." He pulled her farther behind the branches. "Maybe you should let your father be the sweet talker and you be yourself."

William kept his stance alert, but he didn't let go of her arms. His grip was gentle yet firm. His body pressed in close, and though she knew he was only helping her hide from the room, her face heated.

As if he'd read her mind, he glanced down at her and dropped his hands. "Sorry. You looked a bit lost, and I wanted to see if I could help."

Had his eyes always been that blue? Vic tried to step back, but the wall stopped her. "Thanks, you already did." She pulled off the heels and rested her bare feet on the cold marble. She squared her shoulders and took in a deep breath. She gently squeezed his arm and stepped out from behind the plant. She lifted the hem of her dress so she wouldn't trip and marched through the crowd of founders. The older generation tried to corner her, but she stepped to the side. She needed to find those around her age. Spotting Tristan, she veered right and ran into someone else.

"Sorry."

The young woman, clothed in a pale yellow gown that flattered her bronze skin, turned to Vic. Her black curls cascaded down her back, and her icy blue eyes sparkled. "Vic? Blight and stone, where have you been?"

"Maddox?" Vic found herself engulfed in a tight hug from her old friend from school. They'd been inseparable throughout the years but hadn't interacted much since graduation.

"My father told me you were a radiant when I said I wanted to see you again." They lived on the far side of Verrin, so visiting each other outside of school had taken a while. The city sprawled over miles. The Glass house was lucky to be near the center, but most other founders needed to be close to their mines or quarries.

"Ah, yeah, I was faking." Vic fidgeted over lying to her old friend.

Her jaw dropped. "Whoa, that's over the line, even for you."

Her dress's shiny beading cut into her hands as she gripped the fabric. "Yeah, I was going through a bit." How honest did she need to be? If their goal was to get support, it might require some vulnerability. "My sister was leaving to be a vital, and I didn't take it well." She reached for a drink on a passing tray and took a long drink. "I'm still not."

Maddox nodded, and her brow softened. "Honestly, I get that." She hugged her ribs. "My parents decided that my sister would be the heir." Her voice trembled. She caught herself and stood straighter. "It's an honor that I will be among the next vitals."

Even though months had passed since she'd talked to or seen her friend, Vic ached for her. When they were younger, Maddox would run right alongside Vic, their hair in tangles as they'd come home to either house covered in mud. The elegant Maddox before her didn't match the one who'd stayed covered in dirt as she'd tried to imbue stone, making them countless forts for their childhood battles.

"It's okay to be upset about it." Vic reached out to comfort her friend.

Maddox jerked her arm away. "I'm not upset. It's an honor. We're saving the city's citizens from turning into mogs. As a founder, this is our duty." The sparkle in her expression faded with the rhetoric of the vitals.

"I'm not saying it isn't, but you won't get to see your family again, and you'll be behind a wall, doing something they've never explained." Vic tried to gently suss out where her friend stood. If Maddox could trust her, maybe she would share her genuine feelings about being a vital. Vic didn't know how she could help her since she'd already failed her sister, but she could try.

Her shoulders stiffened. "They explain it. Just because you don't like the explanation doesn't mean you have to take away someone else's honor." She smoothed the side of her dress and tossed her black curls over her shoulder. "As for never seeing my family again? You should know that's a benefit. They don't want me around, anyway." The last words came out tight, and Vic remembered they'd always stayed at her house when possible. On the rare occasions when Vic had stayed with the Stones, the father had drunk too much, which her younger self had thought was funny, and the mother had glared at them the whole time or lectured them on being ladies. Whatever that meant.

Vic wanted to poke holes in her resolve. The way Maddox fidgeted, she could tell she was unsettled. "Do you know how the relic works, then? Do you know how you'll connect to it?"

"It purifies the blight!" Maddox's voice grew shrill. People turned to them, and she quieted. "I know you're disappointed you were born a reaper but don't belittle my honor."

Vic clenched her jaw. "I'm not trying to belittle you! All I'm saying is that you have a right to be upset and a right to know what will happen to you. Why can't you know? You're the one who'll have to spend the rest of your life behind walls."

More faces turned, and Maddox waved for Vic to talk quieter. Out of the crowd, her father nodded to her. Vic took a deep breath and found the nearest table. She had a few people's attention, so might as well make the scene. She ripped out the tablecloth from under the drinks table. The red wine bottles crashed to the ground. The liquid bled across the floor. The broken glass skittered among the feet of Verrin's elite. Some screamed and stepped back from the noise. All eyes were on her.

"Ah, my fellow founders. Are you enjoying the party? I need your attention." A look she recognized grew on the surrounding faces. The look said: this is the Glass heir being a brat as usual. Vic was fueling the fire for their gossiping tongues.

The music quieted, and the room froze. Vic remained still in her bare feet as the wine trickled around her. She didn't dare move. Otherwise, she would probably step on glass.

"A few weeks ago, I lost my sister to Haven. She went because, well, that's what we do. We serve our city. You send your children off behind those walls and believe they're living a wonderful life."

Her eyes met those around her. Varying degrees of shocked faces came into view. Tristan stayed still in the back, assessing her calmly.

"Why aren't you allowed to know what they do? Why can't the magic be explained? Why don't they send pictures of your loved ones? Or are you okay with never seeing your children or family members again, with no actual explanation? What's the cost? So you can keep your position as a founder? Let's all hide behind our walls and keep giving our children away to be heroes. Heroes? What power do you all really have? Aren't there more of you than them?" Vic's voice rang through the silence. "You have no power."

A loud snap echoed in the room and banners fell from the ceiling. They were covered in faces. Vic recognized some of them from school, and then she spotted her sister's face. Normally, once a vital left, the family was strongly encouraged to put away any photos to help with the transition. They claimed it would help them deal with the loss. Now the faces looked down on them.

Emilia's gentle expression encouraged her. "I think it's time for proper answers. I want to know what the relic is. I want to know that my sister is alive. Don't you?" Vic faced Tristan. She stared down the GicCorp heir.

One by one, the founders turned to Tristan, following her gaze. He met all of their eyes and crossed his arms but said nothing, his face a mask that showed no emotion. The room waited in tense silence.

Tristan spoke, "I think the Glass heir had too much to drink?" A quiet wave of chuckles echoed in the room. "Another lovely stunt by the shamed heir of Glass."

Vic met his dead gaze. She'd known he would play on her reputation. "Maybe so. But it doesn't change what I said. Divert the question. It's still in their minds. What does the relic do, Tristan? Why can't we have pictures of them working? Everyone here went to school, so explain. I think we can grasp the concept."

"The party is over. You all need to leave." He shifted

slightly, but his mask stayed in place. He was no amateur and could play a long game. Vic could throw tantrums, but Tristan would wave them off.

"This isn't your house, Nordic," her father said. "You can leave first."

Something flashed in Tristan's eyes. He raised his glass, drank down the liquid, and left the room. The ballroom exploded with talk as he left. The music gradually came back, and people shifted and glanced at Vic standing in the wine.

A pair of arms surrounded her, and she recognized William. With his back to the room so no one could see his face, he quickly lifted her out of the wine and cradled her in his arms. The wine dripped from her foot and splattered on the drenched floor. "Tristan left, so I thought I'd take a chance to help you without him seeing me." He carried her toward the doors.

"I can walk now. I don't see any glass."

William looked down. "Just accept my help. You don't know how far the glass scattered, so I'll put you down once we're out of here."

He held her past the spilled wine. The staff cleaned it up.

"I should help them clean since I made the mess."

"If you track wine all over, that'll be more mess to clean." He turned to push open the door, and his shoulder rose to protect her head.

Her gaze traced his jawline. Nothing like viewing him from a fresh angle. He had a firm chin. "I see," she whispered.

He placed her in a chair. "Wait a moment." He left and brought back a wet cloth. When he bent over to wipe her feet, Vic jerked them back.

"I can clean myself."

His blue eyes met hers. "I know you can, but let me help." He pulled her foot to him, not caring that she got wine on his pants. He then carefully wiped off her feet, making sure no wine was left on her.

"Um, so, how's the magic going?" Vic looked anywhere but at her feet. It felt like a foot rub, and after days in reaper boots and tonight in heels, it kind of felt good.

"I can control the output, so that's in my favor." He put her foot down and picked up the other one. "The applications for GicCorp open next week. They may hire me based on my first-generation relic alone."

As unfair as that was, Vic agreed. "Are you doing okay?"

He put down her other foot and looked up. "Yes?"

She curled her toes against the icy floor. "I mean, with using magic. You're different from when I met you, and this is a lot to take in in a short time."

He straightened the cuffs of his waiter's uniform, and she grinned at the action. "I still don't think magic is the answer to Verrin's problems. The radiant are as corrupted as the reapers." He sat back on his heels. "I don't like who I became. I thought my father was who I should model my morals and beliefs after. The way he treated our mother. The way we weren't supposed to force the change. I can see now why Samuel was worried about me." He held out his hand to help her stand. "I think I'm becoming myself again."

"Maybe we should give Bomrosy your ring. She can help us figure out how it works."

His hand on which he used to wear the ring flexed. "I'd like that. The thing is, we have to fix the blight first. Even if we brought back Samuel, he still doesn't have a gicorb. I don't want to save him only to have him turn into a mog."

"Ah, I didn't think of that." Loud laughter sounded from behind the closed doors. The party went on as though she'd never interrupted it. "Do you think they even care?" The vitals became part of what Verrin stood for and believed. How could they change the entire system if they didn't understand it?

"I watched certain faces. Your father told me to. He provided a waiter uniform for me. Honestly, the woman you were talking to before you threw around glass bottles seemed most affected."

Vic snorted. "Wouldn't that have been a better scene? I'll toss one at Steel's head next time since he keeps wanting me to marry his lazy son."

"I may have overheard that." William laughed, his face lighting up, and Vic liked seeing him happy.

She nudged him with her elbow. "Then why didn't you rescue me? He was spraying me with fish cake."

William gripped her hand, and she faced him. "You don't need to be rescued, Victoria." His thumb traced her hand and rested on the ring she'd forgotten to remove.

They paused at the door. Something passed between them. He'd changed, and while she'd worried that he might fall apart as his world changed, he'd taken the chance to view the world in a fresh light. Vic swallowed as he tucked a stray strand of hair behind her ear. The soft touch warmed her, and she liked the changes she saw in him. William had proved she could rely on him. Now that he had a task, he could pull out of his guilt. If he could grow, maybe she could also try to see what a world would be like without the blight. Was it possible? What did they even know about it, except that it turned people who didn't charge into mogs? She made a silent promise to help him with Samuel.

"Thank you for the cleanup." Vic pulled her hand back.

"No problem." They peeked through the door. "It's winding down. I better head out to practice. Are you coming over tonight? This is your big day off from sewage work."

She occasionally complained to him about her sewer life.

"Yeah." These days, she found she preferred being with William than with the Order. Even though she wanted to make connections there, Landon infected everything. She was tired of him complaining about her being a founder.

He headed out the back door.

"You did well."

Vic jumped at her father's voice behind her. "Blight, let a person know you're in the room."

"Would you have noticed?" Her father straightened his tie.

Vic furrowed her brow. "What's that supposed to mean?" She fiddled with the beads on her dress. William was nice to be around. Calming. Was that a crime?

"Nothing." He gestured for her to step aside. "A few founders approached me. You must be extra careful. I don't think Nordic is worried yet, and that worries me." He looked at her like she was made of glass.

"I'll be fine, Dad." They both shifted. "Um, so, how's the magic going? Do you need me to throw around some food now or ..."

He shook his head. "Go. I'll let you know if there's anything new to report." He handed her the discarded heels. "Do you need any of the founders to help you with Nyx?"

"I'm not sure how the other reapers would take that. The second is already mad that I'm a founder." They probably needed something built in the sewers to corral the mogs they were baiting.

"Is Kai still letting you go down into the sewers? Did you find out who the masked people are?"

"You never told me why you were down there. It is after the party now."

"A wasted effort on my part. The sewers are massive, and I'd heard rumors of an old structure down there. I'm looking for anything related to Verrin's history, but I'm not having much luck."

"That's it?" She raised her brow. "With Tristan down there, I think there's more than that. I can keep an eye out, but I'm only in one section of the city."

He glanced away. "I'd rather you weren't down there, but that would be helpful."

She wanted to press her father, but he didn't seem as forthcoming as she'd hoped. "Well, I guess I'll be off then."

It felt like he wanted to hug her, but she went to her room to change.

She waited for the guests to leave, then snuck out the back. She avoided the partygoers and headed out under the blight-filled sky to Kai's house.

7

VIC

"If you break that, I will break your fingers." Bomrosy snatched the device out of Vic's hands.

"What is it?" Most of Bomrosy's devices didn't require magic. Vic didn't always understand the full effort of imbuing, but Bomrosy's tech—her term—was even more foreign to her.

"I'm working on a latch for the gates we're putting down in the sewers." Bomrosy held up a large metal clamp. "Put the bait in one of the divided cages, and as the mog eats, we close the latch, trapping them. Then you just stick in your relic and drain it."

"Wow, our lives are getting cushy." Vic reached over to steal a slice of orange off Bomrosy's plate.

"Are you here to eat my ration?" Bomrosy pressed a button, and the large hinges of the cage opened. She pressed a different button, and they closed on their own.

Vic put the orange back. "I haven't seen you since, you know, and I wanted to check up on you."

"You mean to make sure I'm not bringing Xiona here?"

"Should we be saying her name?" Vic glanced at the door.

"No one's here, Vic." Bomrosy faced her workbench, picked up a tool, and started working on a latch.

"More reapers will be here since the sewer entrance is through your shop." Watching out for Xiona was important to Bomrosy. With everything else going on, she wanted to make sure Xiona stayed away from the Order to avoid creating more problems with other reapers. Her shop wouldn't be empty during the hunting hours.

Bomrosy pushed aside the latch. "Yeah, the smells coming through have been great."

Normally, they entered through a manhole to stop the smell of the sewers from wafting through the Order, but they didn't want another Order to steal their stolen bait, so they were setting traps that would hopefully stay hidden for a while. When Boreus figured out their bait wasn't going to the mogs, they might stop placing it.

"Are you okay?" Vic asked. This seemed to be her standard question these days. Since the battle, everyone's lives had changed. "I only knew Xiona as the person who killed people, but you knew her before. I'm sorry if I didn't understand. It must have been hard to watch her change." She couldn't muster up enough empathy for a murderer, but she wanted to understand her friend.

Bomrosy sat back from the table. "The thing is, I don't think she changed. Her heart was always with the Order, and I'm sure when Nordic made the offer, she chose the reapers' lives over others." Vic opened her mouth, and Bomrosy raised her hand. "I'm not agreeing with the choice. Why do you think I sided with you and Kai? I'm only saying I understand her choice." She pushed back her braids. "I didn't know she would end up this way. Otherwise ..."

"You wouldn't have helped us?" Vic tried to see the situation from her side. She thought maybe it compared to how her father was acting differently. She hoped he hadn't killed anyone. The lines of right and wrong blurred more and more by the day.

"I would've still helped. I knew she might die in the fight, but you would have rather died than be purified." Bomrosy's expression was distant as she traced the latches, and her work paused.

"What if William and I find a way to reverse it? Maybe we could," she muttered, "reverse Xiona."

Bomrosy jumped off the bench and wrapped Vic in a tight hug. "Really?"

"I wanted to bring you his relic, but I didn't know how you'd feel. I know you see him briefly when you visit, but I'm not sure how you'd get along." The interactions that Vic had noticed had remained polite. She didn't expect Bomrosy to be friends with William. He'd broken the law, but they'd protected him anyway. After all, in a strange way, they were protecting Xiona too.

She stepped back. "I know changing her was the only choice. I may not like it, but I can't blame him."

"Too busy blaming yourself?"

Her lips pressed together. "Like Xiona, maybe he felt like he didn't have a choice. If we can reverse it, would there even be a trial for her crimes? Where do we stop?"

Vic slouched down. If Xiona went to trial, so would William. She rubbed her temples. Too convoluted. She didn't want to stick up for Xiona, but she didn't want to turn in William.

"Something like that." Bomrosy handed her a slice of orange.

The door slammed open, and they both jumped. Landon stood in the doorway, a sneer on his face. "Apparently, I'm now a messenger for founders."

Vic raised her brow. "Aw, got that promotion you always wanted?"

His eye twitched. "Another founder bitch is here to see you." He turned on his heel and shouted over his shoulder, "Don't be late for training."

She rolled her eyes. "I wouldn't dream of it."

"You should tell Kai."

"Tell him what? That I don't want to go down to the sewers? That there are masked people down there attacking me? That I can't handle it? The second makes the shift schedule. I don't need any more reasons to be the privileged person of the Order."

Kai hadn't said it outright, but he probably already knew. He wouldn't involve himself unless she asked. It didn't matter that Landon used to rotate between teams daily so others would get a chance at the sewer. But every day he'd pick her to spar with. Kai had enough problems. Vic could handle this.

"Wait, masked people attacked you?" The latched clunked onto the wooden table.

"Yeah, I have it under control." Vic waved her off. A minor detail that she'd almost gotten captured. Those thoughts could be shoved out of her mind too.

Bomrosy held up her hands. "Who's attacking you?"

"GicCorp lackeys, reapers, founders? Who knows? I keep running into founders down there, so maybe it's a masked ball I wasn't invited to." She needed to stay in the sewers to help her father look for evidence of Verrin's history. What did she know about the history of Verrin? That the first-generation relics had built up the city using magic to create a haven away from blight? There wasn't much information. The library had flooded before she was born, and they'd lost many historical journals and texts. No one had thought to recreate them. With all the magic they used to preserve and build, you'd think they'd have protected the books better. Unless they'd wanted to destroy them.

"You're not taking this seriously enough."

It isn't like she could do anything about Landon. "I'll stay with Freddie and Ivy, but I need to go see who's here. Take care, and I'll get William's ring to you."

Bomrosy's forehead creased as Vic left her workshop. Landon didn't say where the founder was waiting. She tried her room first.

Vic opened the door. Maddox stood next to the window, holding a purring Scraps.

"You always wanted a pet." Maddox grinned sheepishly.

Vic crossed her arms. "Yes. Is there a reason you're here, besides to pet my cat?"

Maddox gently placed Scraps back down in his sunny spot. "It was good seeing you at the event."

"Really? Did we have a different conversation I'm not aware of?" From the nervous twitching, Vic guessed that Maddox was ready to admit the truth.

"I don't want to be a vital," Maddox blurted.

"I figured as much." Vic sat on her bed and gestured for Maddox to sit in the chair. "Over the years, I learned when you're that defensive, you either did something wrong or would do something wrong."

Maddox sat and rolled her neck. She smoothed out her

black curls, and her lips turned up slightly. "I'm that predictable?"

Even though months had gone by since they'd seen each other before the party, Vic could feel them slip into a comfortable groove as though they'd never parted. "Your parents finally dropped the hammer?"

"So to speak." Maddox traced invisible wrinkles in her dress.

The Stones had played favorites with their daughters since they were young. They made them compete in everything. "When do you go?"

"The next ceremony. I'm of age, and there's no need to wait." Her fingers dug into her knees. "You're right, I don't know anything about being a vital. I'm supposed to feel proud, but I feel scared." Her lips trembled. "If I leave the house, they'll take my relic. But GicCorp says they'll take everything from my parents too. Your parents never officially kicked you out, so you got to keep yours. I'll either become a vital or a mog, or my family will chase me down." Maddox leaned in. "I want in."

"In?"

She jumped up. "In on the plan!"

The plan? Vic bit back a grimace. Did Maddox think they were organized like some rebel army? "Well, Mads, the only thing we're doing is trying to find out information about GicCorp. My father is organizing the founders." She wasn't sure how her father was organizing them or trying to. He claimed he had a decent number on his side.

"And?"

Vic flinched at her eagerness. "We're working on it." She didn't want to tell her they were sending William in as a spy.

Maddox was her friend, but her desperation might lead to loose lips.

Maddox slumped back in her chair. "After that scene you caused, there's no plan."

"We need founder support. The first step they want to try is voting out the Nordics." That might not happen in time to spare Maddox from becoming a vital.

"Well, my parents are out. They built this entire city with stone. GicCorp is generous to our family."

The Stone house had one of the largest production lines. They also went around fixing the roadways and sometimes the sewers. The sewers. "Wait. Did you see anything strange in the sewers?"

Maddox wrinkled her nose. "I don't go down there. Why?"

"My father is looking for the oldest parts of Verrin in the sewers for a hint of the history."

"A hint in the sewers?" Maddox said the words slowly, as if it would make them less vague.

"Yeah." Why had her father made her cause a scene? Vic grew embarrassed that she didn't have more to offer her friend.

"I came here because I thought you were organized and had a plan. From what I'm getting, your dad is wandering around the sewers, looking for something, and you're recruiting founders to do something." She rubbed her forehead. "This was a waste of time."

"We need the founders to overthrow GicCorp."

"And then do what?"

Vic understood her frustration. Her selfish goal of getting her sister back didn't work for everyone. She didn't care as much about her father's agenda. She stared at her friend slumped in the chair. "I'm sorry, Mads. We're just starting. I've been down in the sewers every night, getting attacked by strangers. Then we're trying to block the mogs inside Nyx territory so the Order can survive."

"I heard you weren't number one anymore."

"We're running low on tempers and food. We're stealing the bait that Boreus is using to lure mogs away, but we're trying to work it so the mogs stay in our territory. If we put up gates in the sewers, it may draw too much attention."

"Gates?"

Vic pointed at her bedspread and mapped out the sewer. "We can open up to the swamps to let them in. This is dangerous, so we want to close off the side tunnels so they'll only go to our entrance with the bait." She drew more invisible lines. "That way, we'll be safe."

Maddox scrunched her face at the invisible drawing. "Do you remember the doors in my house?"

The stone doors fit seamlessly into the walls of her home. Unless you knew where to look, you wouldn't know there were doors. "That could hide them during the day, but we're a bunch of reapers, and I don't think we can hire your family."

Maddox pointed to herself. "I can do it."

"But how would that help you?"

"I'll be on the ground floor, I guess. From the sounds of it, I'll need to wander the sewers like your father. I might have more luck than him since I can imbue the stone faster than a Glass."

Vic jumped and squeezed her in a hug. Maddox patted her back. "I'll do my best to keep you from the vital ceremony."

"Don't make any promises you can't keep." She gazed out

the window, her voice distant. "The trouble with being on the ground floor of a rebellion is that you might be the first in line to get sacrificed. If I can help your group against GicCorp, maybe it will help me. But can you tell me why Nyx Order is in trouble?" Maddox slumped slightly. Vic thought she wanted to know so she wouldn't feel out of the loop. If she was doing this much to help them, there was no reason not to share with her.

Vic explained what had happened and how Tristan wanted them to keep turning people into mogs. "Not everyone at our Order knows."

"Got it."

"Let's go tell Kai about the doors, and you can work with Bomrosy on the latches."

Vic guided her friend to the workroom. "Thank you, Mads."

"Yeah, yeah. I'll think of a large present you can give me later. You might have to throw it over the wall to Haven, but you'll still owe me."

"We will stop this."

"What if it can't be stopped?"

The question hung in the air as they walked. Vic feared that they would need to give up magic if they wanted to stop sending vitals. If using magic caused the blight, they might all need to give in to the radiant way of life. The founders wouldn't want to give up their comforts. This had been the way of life for centuries. They'd never had to fear turning into a mog due to their position. The founders didn't care about anyone else who lived in their world.

"We're going to try to vote out the Nordics, then figure out what the relic does in Haven. Right now, we're basing everything off a feeling. We might be wrong about Haven but not about the Nordics. We have to hope there's a better way."

"Ah, hope." Maddox grew silent as they reached Kai's office.

Vic knocked.

"Come in."

They entered the office, and Kai sat at his desk with a stack of ledgers.

Maddox tugged at her sleeve and whispered, "Okay, you can throw him over the wall as my present."

Kai looked up. He took in the two women and stood. "Who did you bring?"

"This is my friend, Maddox Stone."

His brow quirked at the last name. "A founder?"

Vic nodded. "She said she can help make the gates." Vic explained how the doors would be seamlessly built into the sewers and barely visible. "We'll need to remember to open them before we leave the sewers in the morning."

His face brightened at Maddox, and she blushed. "Really? That's great." He quickly shoved some papers aside. "If you're still free, I'd love for you to meet Bomrosy and get to work. I think it would be safest for you to do this during the day with a reaper, in case a mog appears."

"Would you be one of the reapers?" Maddox twirled her hair and batted her eyes at him.

Kai coughed, and Vic elbowed her.

"Did you get something in your eye?" Vic whispered at her flirty friend.

Kai pulled a file out of his drawer and piled in more papers. Ignoring her friend's antics, he said, "If I didn't have an endless pile of paperwork."

Maddox beamed at him, and Vic glared at her friend.

Maddox's eyes traveled between them. "Oh, are you two an item?"

Were they? "Um, well ..."

A knock on the door interrupted Vic.

Landon came in without waiting for Kai to answer, and Vic's heart dropped when she saw Tristan behind him.

"I guess he's here for your founder meeting." Landon glared at Vic, then left the room, slamming the door.

"You have founder meetings, commander?" Tristan asked. He noticed Maddox.

Maddox paled.

"There isn't a meeting. Maddox came to visit me," Vic replied.

"And she also came to visit Kai?"

"How is that any of your business?" Vic did her best not to let her hands shake. She was starting to become a threat. Would he kill her? He'd already said it once.

He calmly stepped to the side. "It isn't, but you offered the information. It's called polite conversation, Victoria." He held out his hand to Maddox, and he kissed her proffered hand. "I'm seeing your father this afternoon. Would you like me to see you home after I'm done here?"

From the tension in her posture, Maddox wanted to say no, but she wasn't new to the founder game of politeness. "That would be lovely." She plastered on a happy expression that didn't touch her blank eyes. She moved to leave the room.

"Wait a minute. This isn't important enough for you to leave." Tristan surveyed the room like he had plans to remodel it as his own.

Kai frowned. "Then why bother coming?"

"Sometimes, messages are better presented in person."

"I didn't know the GicCorp heir was a delivery boy," Vic muttered.

"You know very little about being a proper heir, so it's best if you stay quiet." A tinge of ice laced his words.

Vic tensed, and before she could reply, Kai spoke. "What do you want? Say it, then leave." He folded his arms over his chest and sat back in his chair.

Tristan sat and rested his hands on the arms of the chair. He leaned back as if he owned the piece of furniture. His ability to make any room seem as though it belonged to him was annoying. "I want to make sure you understand that the gates to the swamp entrance are not to be touched. It's for the safety of the city. We try to minimize how many mogs can get into the sewers from the outside." He tried to look concerned. The sincerity didn't reach his eyes. "I know you're struggling as an Order, but that's no reason to put people in danger. If you do this, I'll need to protect the city with force."

Kai's face didn't even twitch. "I think your sources have misinformed you. We'd never put the city at risk. *As you know.*"

"Delightful. I'm happy to hear it." He smoothly stood. "Maddox, dear, let's go see your father."

Vic stepped forward, but Maddox shook her head behind Tristan's back. When Tristan faced her, she put her hand on his arm. "Thank you."

Vic watched them leave, and when the doors closed behind them, her shoulders slumped. "I already put her at risk." The larger her circle, the more people Vic needed to protect.

"She knew the risks. I hope she's still willing to help."

"Yes, I'm sure she is, if that's all you care about. She has no reason to help us since we have nothing on our side."

"We're building a base."

"Not fast enough."

Kai pushed himself up. "How fast do we need to be? For every person we can trust, there are twenty we can't," His voice rose. "We haven't even put our plan into action, and Tristan knows about it. What does that tell you, Vic?" He slapped his hand on the desk. "GicCorp is always ahead of us. That was the entire purpose of his visit. He wants us to know that he'll always be ahead of any plan we make. While we're worried about feeding people, he can make actual plans to stop any founder rebellion that your father wants to have."

"Are you giving up already?" Vic's squared her shoulders. The fact that he'd said her name worried her. It felt like weeks had passed since he'd called her Sparks. An ache filled her.

"I didn't say that. Don't assume my meaning. But you feel it too. You said we weren't fast enough. How can we fight a giant?" He kicked his chair, and it slid back and hit the wall.

"You can fight it. Cut it off at the knees." Vic's body grew rigid.

Kai's expression darkened. "If you can't find the knees, it's pointless."

"Then for blight's sake, stab it in the toes until we piss it off enough for it to make a mistake!" Vic curled her fingers. He couldn't give up. He was strong, and he cared about his family and the reapers. If he fell, the entire Order would fall. She hadn't meant for her worry for her friend to drag him down. A bitter taste formed in her mouth. She'd been so careful to support him, and her few comments had derailed him. It was her fault.

They glared at each other from across the room.

Vic took a shaky breath. "We can continue with the plan, as long as we're careful. We'll keep the reapers afloat to fight the actual battles." She pushed her doubt aside. They needed to believe they could make something work.

"Don't you mean me?" He crossed his arms, making his muscles bulge.

"What?" Was he actually mad at her? This whole time, she'd tried to make his life easier. Her throat dried out as she thought of how to respond.

"I will keep them afloat!" Kai shouted. "I'm the one who has to battle them and Tristan. The reapers don't understand why we can't beg GicCorp for help again. They don't understand why our people are missing. Our district is dark at night. People are scared to leave their homes. While you're running around with your father, the radiant, and messing about with Landon, I'm here holding Nyx together! Don't pretend you care more about the reapers than your sister. The reapers are supposed to be your family, but you'd trade them in at the first opportunity."

The last words stabbed into Vic. Her voice lowered as she asked, "I can't care about both? This is coming from the person who always puts his family first? I've done my best to support you while you've left me in the dust. Messing around with Landon?" Vic let out a sound of disbelief. "Even though he tortures me and calls me names, I put up with it so I won't bother the commander with my petty problems. I've almost died twice in the sewers, and I go back for more. You may care about the reapers, but it's obvious you don't care about me as much as I thought."

Vic spun and left Kai behind in his office. She didn't slam the door but closed it quietly. She rubbed her eyes, annoyed with how they itched.

❄ 8 ❧

VIC

"All I'm saying is we keep what we earn."

When Vic stepped out onto the training ground, reapers surrounded Landon. His lean body was in a wide stance, and his weak chin was held high, almost like he thought he was the new commander.

"Some of us pull in enough mogs and credits not to be rationed. Why do we have to feed everyone? Since we lost all the money from GicCorp, there's been no return on the credits we give the Order."

Vic swallowed at the nodding heads around him. Landon grew bolder by the day.

"Until the day GicCorp forgives Nyx, we can survive comfortably."

Vic snorted, and they all turned to face her. "Who gets to decide which reapers get the more populated mog routes?"

Landon smirked. "Those who've been here the longest."

"Shouldn't it be a rotation?"

"You've been getting plenty of mogs, sewer girl. Don't

worry about it." He turned back to his crowd. "Does she think she's important enough to have a voice?"

They all laughed with him.

"I think she's right," a deep, gravelly voice said. Everyone had to lift their heads to look at Freddie. "We rotate." He flexed his muscles. His eyes glowered down at the group of reapers, and his head turned side to side, but they didn't meet his gaze.

Everyone decided they needed to train. Landon glared at Freddie for all of two seconds before he too looked away.

Vic closed the distance between them, and she scuffed her boots in the dirt. She tipped her head back to look at her teammate. "Thanks."

Freddie paused and spoke again. "I know you can fight your own battles, so I stayed quiet. But you can rely on us too."

He turned to spar with another reaper. Even though Landon was the second, everyone knew Freddie could beat him. He didn't enjoy talking to people, so he'd declined the position. Vic loved that Freddie could shut Landon down. He would have stepped in earlier if she hadn't stubbornly insisted that she was okay and could handle him.

Vic picked out a training staff. Hollowness had been eating at her since she'd come down from Kai's office. They only cared that GicCorp had all the power. She could see it in the ragtag group of people. She'd always wanted to trust others in the Order and her team, but she wanted to do everything on her own. If they could help each other, they might make it out of this alive.

For some reason that might start with the letter F, Landon left her alone during training, but her team still got assigned to the sewers.

Ivy tucked her hair under her hood. "Honestly, we get more mogs down there, so he is helping us get credits." She passed Vic the peppermint oil. "We'll stick together tonight. No need for the masked weirdos to attack you."

"That would be good." Last time, they'd pinned her down. Vic shuddered.

"Do you know when we'll be using the entrance from our Order?" Ivy pulled back the metal cover, and their team entered the sewers first.

No matter how many nights Vic had spent down here, the smell still overwhelmed her. The peppermint didn't combat the sewage smell as much tonight. The heat of the day had only made the stench worse down here. She tightened her face mask. "Once the gates are in, we can focus on that tunnel, I believe."

"That'll make our lives easier."

Unless Tristan has us arrested, Vic thought. They separated from the other reapers and hunted out their tunnel. They all ran together so Vic wouldn't be alone for her black-clad fan club to grab her. Freddie led the way, his broad back blocking most of the view.

"Did you talk to Kai about Landon yet?"

Vic shook her head. There was no need to talk to Kai anymore. Her chest hurt as she ran. Deep down, she knew he'd only said those things because of the pressure he was under, but he'd still said them. The whole time she'd been supporting him, he'd felt isolated. She hadn't shared her burdens with him, but maybe in doing so she'd unintentionally isolated him. "We aren't on good terms."

"Oh?" Ivy waited, but Vic didn't say anything more.

They reached the end of the tunnel and drifted over into

Boreus territory to see if they'd placed any bait. They found one long bone with a bit of gristle hanging off it.

Vic picked it up. "I know we have limited cattle, but they seem to have an endless supply of bones."

"Only the founders would know the exact number."

In Verrin, only cattle that stopped producing milk made it to the butcher. Did it matter if GicCorp killed more cows for Boreus? They'd have to be paying the Dairy founders a ton of credits.

Then they had a group taking people too. Kai had stayed with a group in town to stop people from disappearing. They hadn't found a trace of other reapers, but still people went missing. Nyx territory was slowly becoming a ghost town. What the old Dei commander had said haunted Vic. There didn't seem to be a jump in blight collection, even though people had gone missing. What were they doing with them?

"Blight, is that the person who attacked you?" Ivy whispered.

Vic followed Ivy's finger as she pointed at a figure in the shadows. They all ducked into the tunnel. The figure ambled along, their back to the group. Vic didn't think they'd spotted them.

"I have no clue." None of the masked figures stood out from each other.

"Should we follow them?" Ivy reached back to grab her scythe from her harness, and her stance widened.

Freddie frowned at Ivy.

She returned his look. "Oh, come on, we should find out who's been attacking Vic."

"I can follow them. You two can stay here," Vic replied.

They glared at her, and she raised her hands. "Fine, we

can all go together. I don't want you to get hurt." Vic had a feeling the masked figures were after only her.

Ivy pointed her folded scythe at Vic. "And we don't want you to get hurt. Trust us."

"Point taken." They watched as the figure turned down another tunnel, going deeper into Boreus territory.

"Do you think Boreus reapers attacked you?" Ivy asked.

It was possible, but why only her? They carefully followed the figure. The sound of flowing sewage covered up their footsteps. They stayed as far behind as possible. There wasn't much for them to hide behind, especially Freddie. The figure continued to move forward with purpose, and Vic hoped they were so focused on their destination that they didn't turn around.

They navigated the sewers, and Vic thought they were heading toward the center of Verrin. It was hard to tell down here. They could get out by using any manhole, so Vic wasn't worried about getting too lost. However, she still carried mog bait with her. She wished she'd put it down when they'd been by Nyx.

Then their luck ran out. The figure halted and turned. No side tunnel was next to them. They all stood looking at each other.

"They aren't running," Ivy stated.

The figure looked beyond the group, and Vic turned to look. More masked figures were in the tunnels behind them. "They don't need to. We're the ones who were being followed." Vic swore. They'd been so focused on looking forward that no one had bothered to look back.

"Three to one," Freddie said, meaning they'd take on the lone masked figure in front of them instead of trying to get through the mob. He pulled out his scythe and flicked it open. "Get to a manhole."

Vic nodded. Without giving the group behind them any time to charge them first, they rushed the lone figure. Ivy peered up and to the sides, searching for an escape.

The figures thundered after them. Freddie pushed past the one figure, but Vic guessed they didn't want a fight. She didn't dare look back to see how close the large group was.

"We need a main line!" Ivy shouted.

Freddie ran in front of them to ward off any frontal attacks. They left Ivy in the middle. He took a sharp turn, and they followed. Vic hoped he had a better sense of direction than she did. The sounds of running and breathing filled her head as she kept pace with Ivy and Freddie. She didn't need to look back at the group; she heard them getting louder.

They still weren't in a main line.

"Split up?" Vic called out.

"Don't even think about it," Ivy answered.

The masked figures were after her. She didn't understand why, but if she left Ivy and Freddie, they would be okay. She didn't think about it. When the sewer tunnel forked ahead of them, she silently veered left while Ivy and Freddie went right.

Vic swallowed as the masked figures pounded behind her. In front of her, the tunnel dropped off. She skidded to a stop. Dirt and pebbles fell over the edge, and after a moment, she heard them plop into liquid. The rush of water sounded louder here. It might be a main sewage line. The light didn't reach the bottom.

She pulled out her scythe and turned to face the group of

masked figures, the large bone in her other hand. She couldn't count how many there were.

The sewage behind her roared in her ears. She whimpered slightly. "My life repeats itself."

They didn't answer. Vic closed her mouth and pretended that she was about to jump into water and not sewage. The thought made her gag. As her legs bent, a masked figure reached out to grab her, but they were too slow. Her stomach leaped as she fell down the tunnel. She wanted to scream, but her mouth stayed shut as her body slammed into the water. Cocooned by water, she floundered, then her head broke the surface. She pushed down her mask and gasped for air.

The smell overwhelmed her, and it got harder to breathe.

It's only water. It's only water, Vic repeated to herself as she swam in the liquid. The current dragged her along, and she couldn't make out much in the light. Her vision wasn't adjusting fast enough. Her scythe stayed warm in her hand. There could be mogs in this river. Her teeth chattered as she tried to clamp them shut.

Eventually, the current slowed, and she found herself in a larger pool. A bank appeared in the darkness, and she frantically swam to it. Her feet touched stone, and she ran out of the sewage. Finally on dry ground, she fell to her knees and pulled off her black hood and jacket, dropping them to the ground. Then she tore off her soaked mask from around her neck.

She gasped in the putrid air and gagged.

"I will not think about what's covering my body," she muttered to herself. Her clothing clung to her, and she rose while holding her arms away from her body. Somehow, she still hung on to the bone and the scythe. With a clunk, Vic dropped the bone to the stone floor and squelched forward. Liquid leaked out of the tops of her boots, leaving a trail of liquid behind her.

Vic shivered when a cool breeze hit her. "This is gross. Gross, gross, gross."

Her little chant echoed in the stone room. The smooth walls arched overhead into an enormous dome. Unlike the gray and green walls of the normal sewers, these gleamed an inky black. Vic stood dripping in the middle of the room with multiple gloomy tunnels ahead of her. The sewage water lapped on the shore behind her.

"I guess I pick a path?"

Was there another sewer under the original? Would that make this the original one? These walls looked nicer than the ones she patrolled every night. She reached out and touched the cold stone. She could hardly see a seam where the stones connected. Either it was extremely well built, or there were people managing it. She didn't know what the other factories managed. She should ask Maddox if her family had gotten hired to smooth out a line of the sewer, but why bring down different rock than the main lines?

"Ugh, does it matter?" Was this what her father was looking for?

Vic picked a path. They all looked the same, so she took her chances with the first door on the right. Unlike the normal sewer paths, this had a curved ceiling like the walkway. No trickle of sewage appeared. The lights were dimmer down here, and she couldn't see very far ahead. The breeze she'd felt earlier disappeared, and the only sound came from her breaths, steps, and pounding heart.

When she thought the tunnel wouldn't end, it widened into another large dome. This time, instead of a sewage lake, junk was piled all over it. She frowned. Twisted lumps of metal, shattered pieces of wood, and strange stones lay in the room. She bent over and grabbed a stone. The cut reminded her of the stones attached to wands. It didn't glow; it was a dull and empty color, like someone had used the magic and it needed to recharge.

She put one in her pocket and navigated around the piles of trash. The sound of water echoed in the domed room. She did not want to get back into a feces river. On the other side of the room, she spotted a passageway. Once she reached it, darkness fell around her. She froze, and her hand shot out to touch the tunnel wall. The darkness consumed the space. She held up her hand but couldn't see anything. She let out a shuddering gasp. *How am I going to get out of here*?

ॐ 9 ॐ

WILLIAM

William hoped that Vic would stop by before his job testing. She'd been coming by after every shift before passing out on the sofa or going back to the Order to sleep. He pulled on his sleeves and combed his darker brown hair back. His shoulders shifted under the weight of the harness. He still couldn't get used to the feel.

The table, already set, contained the morning's meal. Only Sam ate, and William frowned. Had Bomrosy come and taken Xiona again? She didn't listen to him or Vic. Vic had mentioned that Bomrosy sometimes kept her in her room connected to the workshop, but she worried about the reapers finding out about Xiona.

Maybe they needed to change the locks on Kai's home. He would ask Vic the next time he saw her. It would be harsh to lock Bomrosy out, but it was a matter of their safety. He swallowed down the breakfast, tasting nothing.

"I'm going to the job testing. Stay here, Sam."

"Do what you must."

William left the house but locked Sam in behind him. The blight swirled a cheery yellow in the daylight. He took it as a good sign. He'd practiced his control over draining the stone every night, but he still ran out too fast. His only progress was that it took longer to drain his relic.

He hired a water taxi, and it took him past the center of town. The job testing took place at GicCorp. Few people knew him in the city, but Tristan might recognize him, which would end their plan before it even started.

Luck stayed on his side. A sea of hopefuls all moved in the same direction as him, and he blended in with the crowd.

"My father finally passed down the relic last week. I'm hoping to work with stone. They pay the highest for side jobs," a young woman stated.

"Really? Where did you hear that? The mines always need workers, and they sometimes let you make your own metal items."

The young woman scoffed. "Yeah, if you survive a cave-in."

The couple passed William. As he eavesdropped on the other hopefuls, no one mentioned applying to GicCorp. Tables appeared, and they all separated into lines according to which factory they wanted to join. The shortest line was GicCorp's. He assumed it was so hard to get in or nobody wanted to work for them.

A scrawny man with a hooked nose pinned a number onto William's blue shirt. "Go behind the black door, and we'll give you your task."

"Thanks."

The man waved him away.

William went to the door and opened it. A musty smell

permeated the inside. Multiple doors were built into the wall. None of them stuck out from the other. A tall woman stood in front of the doors and didn't make eye contact with any of the people wearing numbers. Her clothing fit her tightly, and she tapped her foot and sighed every few seconds. Everyone remained apart and didn't talk. He kept to the side. The person closest to him stepped away, even though they had plenty of space.

What was with the atmosphere? He shifted and held his hands to his sides so he wouldn't mess with his sleeves. A few more entered, then at the top of the hour, the woman spoke.

"Thank you for your interest in joining the GicCorp family." Her voice was monotone, and she still didn't look at them. "As you know, we value many traits, so the test will contain various materials. You have until midnight."

Midnight? Nice of them to keep them here after dark.

She continued in her bored tone. "You are to build a small one-room structure in the middle of the swamp. Use what materials you want. You're encouraged to use them all. Make sure it's a functioning living area. Pick a room."

Everyone separated to the different doors, and William turned to the one nearest him. He opened it, and the musty smell grew. In the middle of the floor was a large pool of swamp water. To the side was a pile of materials, and a clock glared down the time at him. Sand, rough stone, metal ore, and various woods waited for him, but no instructions on how to build a structure. Did people assume they could hold anything together with magic?

William grabbed some larger stones. A firm foundation was key before he could build the room. He took off his shoes and clothing to avoid getting them full of mud.

Nothing like doing a job interview while in his underwear. Mud squelched around his feet and calves as he got into the swamp. As a neat person, he didn't enjoy this task of mucking around in the dirty imitation swamp.

After an hour, sweat dripped down his face and into the swamp mud. The makeshift swamp only rose to his knees, but slogging in and out of the murky water had tired him quickly. Warmth spread through him as he imbued the stone. He didn't want to waste too much magic at the start. The longer he worked, the more he could tell the difference between the stone. The marble made him push harder, as though he'd gotten stuck in thick porridge. The granite molded well underneath his wand. As he drove the iron in the stone, a metallic taste filled his mouth.

William wasn't familiar with making a foundation, but he created nine main pillars and thought they seemed solid enough. They just needed to hold until midnight.

He imbued more stone to lay flat across the pillars. The biggest problem he had was tracking mud all over his project. Couldn't they have given them a towel to clean with? How would he wipe down his body before getting dressed again? Those clothes would be filthy. He glanced at the time. Four hours had passed, and he only had a platform.

"I still have twelve hours." He sighed. If he didn't get hired after all this effort, Vic would be disappointed. She needed his help, and he wanted to show her how thankful he was for all her support.

The stone in his wand only had half the power left. He took wood for the flooring. He decided to only shape it, then he used tools to install the floor. He knew how to build a house without magic. It would take too long for him to do the entire structure, but he could conserve magic this way.

The hours passed, and William used up the last of the magic. He dragged more stone over, his fingers slipping more than once. With a loud crash, he dropped one over a grate. He grimaced and pushed the heavy stone away. The latch broke away under the stone. He eyed the door, and no one came in. He would tell them after they'd hired him that he'd broken the grate. They must use it to drain the swamp after the tests.

With only an hour left, his one-room structure didn't look that great. It was supposed to be functional. William glanced at the sand. Was he supposed to make lights?

His heart sank. He'd made a radiant home.

No running water or magic-running lamps. His wand gem produced the dull gleam of being used up.

"Blight."

How could he have overlooked this? William sank to the floor. He didn't belong in this world of magic, and he'd let Vic down.

The door opened, and he jumped.

"Naked building. That's new." The instructor tucked a loose strand of hair behind her ear and held a clipboard in her hand. Her cheeks turned pink.

"Ah, sorry. I didn't want to be covered in mud at the end." He ran to the side and pulled his shirt over his head.

Her eyes traveled slowly up and down his body. "By all means, don't get dressed on my behalf."

William paused in reaching for his pants. "Um, I didn't want you to feel uncomfortable."

She leaned on the wall and licked her lips. "I'm here to check your progress. For you, there's only an hour left."

William shifted. She didn't look away. "The room is over

there." He pointed. Under her focused gaze, he still felt like he wasn't wearing a shirt.

The lady laughed and came closer. "You're funny."

He pulled at his sleeve, and when he reached for his pants, her hand stopped him.

William fidgeted. Her grasp made him uncomfortable. "I should get dressed. This is a bit—"

"I'm fine." She bit her full lips.

William cleared his throat. "What do you think of my room, then?"

She hadn't even looked at it once.

She let go of his hand and sighed. Then the bored expression came over her face again. "Not functional. Decent build, but you didn't use every material." She faced him. "You'll need extra points to make it past the interview." The corner of her mouth turned up, and her eyes traced his lips.

Was she flirting with him? Women didn't flirt with him. They found him off-putting. He stepped back. Did he need to seduce this woman to get a job? She stepped closer, and his gaze flitted from the radiant structure to her. He held his pants tightly. He didn't want to do anything with this woman. Vic's sad expression, in her desperation to find her sister, came to mind.

He swallowed thickly. "What extra help do I need?"

The woman was mere inches from him, and her finger traced his chest. The shirt had molded to his body from all the sweat. "You seem like a smart man. What do you think you can do to improve your grade?"

"I-I don't think this is the right way to get a job." Did his voice have to come out a whole octave higher?

She wrote furiously on a piece of paper. "Fine." She tore

it off and handed it to him. "You're out of magic, and the structure isn't functional. Fail."

William's hand shot out to stop her from handing him the paper. "Wait, I still have time!"

"How will you make lights without magic?"

A sick feeling filled him as he assessed his radiant room. He clenched his hands and stepped toward her. Her eyes widened and held up her clipboard as if to protect herself from him hitting her. Instead, he gripped her upper arms and pulled her to him. He slanted his mouth over the woman's. Her lips were dry, and he moved his mouth mechanically. She let out a soft moan, so maybe she thought he was enjoying this or doing a good job. As she wrapped her hands around his neck dropping the clipboard, he pulled her closer. In his head, he imagined that her hands belonged to someone else. The woman tugged at his hair, making it messier. He gritted his teeth and pushed his hands between them to unbutton her shirt.

A clank echoed in the room. The woman shoved William away, and their gaze zeroed in on the person standing in the room with them.

Vic's mouth dropped open. She was wet, and a horrible odor entered the room as she eyed them. "What in the blight is going on here?"

❧

"She made me kiss her!" William wanted to sink into the ground. He didn't know why Vic had popped out of the ground like a mog, but he wanted to dive into the grate she'd come out of.

The woman huffed and folded her arms.

Vic's eyes narrowed. "Who are you?"

"I'm Ginny, and I'm conducting a test for Gic Corporation." She quickly bent over to pick up the discarded clipboard.

Vic put her hands on her hips. "Kissing is part of the test?"

Ginny hugged her clipboard as if using it as a shield. "He wanted help since his grade was bad."

Vic glanced at the house and at William. "What was the task?"

"We had to build a functional room."

Vic stepped forward, and the stench coming off her grew stronger. William didn't think this was the time for him to cover his nose.

"Ginny, I think he passed, don't you?" Even though it wasn't directed at him, William got chills from her dark tone. Covered in who knew what, Vic still commanded the room.

Ginny opened her mouth, then shut it. She nodded and handed William a piece of paper that contained a day and report time.

"Now Ginny, I think you need to leave before I tell the head of GicCorp that his employee is sexually harassing others."

Ginny ran out of the room and slammed the door behind her. Vic's glare shifted to him, and William shoved his pants on despite the dried mud on his legs.

"How far were you going to go with her for this job?" Vic rubbed her forehead. "Blight, you already had your pants off. If I'd been a few minutes later, I'd really have seen a show."

"My pants were already off," William blurted.

Her brows shot up. "You were already half naked?"

"I put my shirt on when she came in," he mumbled. He faced any direction but where Vic stood.

"You built this naked?"

"I had my underwear on." His face burned. He'd wanted to stay clean. He should have ruined his clothing.

They paused, then burst into laughter. William's eyes filled with tears as he gasped for air between fits of laughter. Vic doubled over and used her scythe to hold herself up.

"Will ... Blight ... Why would you?" Vic gasped.

He took a deep breath to calm down. "She would have failed me, and I didn't want to disappoint you. I know you're doing so much, and this is the only way I can help."

"I wouldn't want you to sleep with someone to help me, Will." She shook her head, but her eyes were still bright.

"I know, but ..." He plucked at his clothing. "Can we not tell anyone about this?" He shivered as he remembered the woman's dry mouth on his.

"If you take up naked building, I might say something then."

William walked over to the broken grate. "Why did you pop out of the ground in my testing room? And do I want to know what that smell is?" He didn't want to hurt her feelings, but he stayed apart from her as they left the room. The woman was nowhere to be seen as they left.

"That was the first grate that finally opened. I'd been wandering in the dark for I don't know how long before I finally saw the light."

"The masked people?"

Vic nodded. "They trapped us. I need to get back and see if Freddie and Ivy made it out okay." She rolled her eyes as he stepped farther away. "I get it, I smell. Do you want to walk a block ahead of me?"

He moved next to her. They walked at a fast clip toward Nyx. He almost suggested they get a water taxi, but he changed his mind since Vic's clothing would mess up the poor driver's boat. His legs burned as he walked with her. He'd spent most of the day hauling around stone, and he wanted to shower and pass out.

William focused on putting one foot in front of the other. Close to the Order, a rather large, muscular man with a short, curvy woman waited. The woman ran to them and screeched to a halt before giving Vic a hug.

"Blight, you took another sewer bath?" the small woman stated. She craned her neck to look at William. "And you picked up a man?"

"I guess so. I got lost, and you don't want to know how badly I need a week of showers."

"Girl, I see it. We ran around in the sewers all day looking for you. We were about to start another round."

The tower of muscles nodded and stepped next to the woman. William swallowed at his attention.

"This is Freddie and Ivy. They're on my team. This is my friend William."

Ivy quirked her head. "He looks familiar."

William shifted and adjusted his harness over his sweaty shirt, but her attention had already shifted off him.

"Team?" Ivy reached out to smack Vic but stopped before she got dirty. "You keep acting on your own. We would've gotten out together. You don't get to sacrifice yourself!"

Vic flinched away. "They were after me."

"So? You. Don't. Leave. Us." The short woman yelling up at Vic would have been comical, but William had a feeling she could win in a fight against all of them.

The small woman glared at Vic. William had never seen Vic so cowed before.

"I'm sorry."

"Trust your team." A moment of silence passed, and she sighed. "Go shower. I'm too tired to keep lecturing you. William, look after her."

He felt like he should salute, but he nodded instead. They walked away. "Kai's house?"

"Yeah, I don't want to see Landon while covered in sewage." They walked at a slower pace than before. "I'm sorry I didn't come to wish you luck this morning. I was a bit busy." She'd spent all day wandering in the dark, smelling like dry poop, and she was apologizing to him?

William warmed at the thought. After everything she'd gone through, she'd remembered that she'd intended to stop by. "Don't worry. I completely understand. You have good teammates there."

"I really do. I think I'd rather do everything myself and take the blow than let someone else get hurt."

They reached Kai's house. "Is it because your sister wouldn't let you?"

Vic removed her boots in the doorway. "Hmm, maybe. Do you care if I wash up first?"

William gestured to the bathroom. "Go for it. Put your clothing outside the door, and I'll get you something to wear."

Vic gingerly touched the door and entered the bathroom. After a moment, he heard the shower running. He went to the room Sam slept in and grabbed an extra set of his sleepwear. William ignored Kai's extra clothes, and he didn't grab Xiona's clothing, even though it would fit Vic better. He checked Xiona's room, and it was still empty. Sam was asleep in his bed.

He waited a long time before Vic reached out to grab the clean clothing. The smell of his body wash wafted out of the room. She emerged dressed in his blue shirt and pants. William swallowed. He liked how she looked in his clothes. She ran her fingers through her damp hair.

"I also cleaned the shower and floor—just in case."

His throat felt thick, so he bobbed his head in reply. He went to shower, and the room filled with steam and the smell of cleaner. William ran the hot water and washed the dried mud off his legs. His thoughts drifted back to Vic wearing his clothes, and his skin heated. He turned the water slightly cold. Now it felt like a radiant bath.

He shut his eyes under the spray of water. Now that he had the job, he would somehow need to hold on to it until he found out information on the vitals. The plan lacked any more details since no one knew how to get inside Haven. Even if he did, would he connect to the relic? He rinsed his hair and let the cool water pound on his back. What did it matter? It wasn't like he cared about magic, but if he did connect with the relic, he wouldn't be able to see her again.

William shut off the water, dried himself off, and dressed in an outfit that matched Vic's.

When he came out, the floor smelled of cleaner, and the scent of melted cheese filled the room. Vic set two large sandwiches on the table. "I'm sorry I used the last of your cheese."

"No, that's fine. Help yourself."

She used a knife to cut her sandwich in half. "So, you like blue?" Her fingers brushed his as she handed him the knife.

William's neck heated. "Yeah, I guess so."

The air grew strangely thick between them. They both looked away, and he bit into his food. "This is fantastic." Cheese, veggies, and eggs danced on his tongue.

"Melting it makes all the difference. My sister and I ..." She stopped. "I know I talk about her a lot."

William lightly touched her hand. "Go ahead. I enjoy hearing about her."

Her lip trembled. "When I talk about her, it makes it feel like she never left."

"I get that. I talk to Sam like normal most days." He glanced at Sam's door. "He isn't like most radiant. He mostly says, 'Do what you must,' and it almost feels like he's judging me like he used to."

Vic furrowed her brow. "I don't mean to sound insensitive, but maybe those with the forced change don't take it as well?"

"Xiona seems normal." William debated whether he should tell Vic she wasn't here. Bomrosy did always bring her back. He would talk to her first, then tell Vic. She'd barely finished her sandwich before drooping at the table.

"Get some sleep."

Vic fought to open her eyes. "Sit with me on the sofa for a bit?"

Why did his heart pound every time those green eyes met his? "Sure." William tried to act normal. She came over often, so why did it feel different tonight?

They sat on the sofa, and as they leaned back, their bodies shifted closer. They shared stories of their siblings, and Vic eventually closed her eyes, a peaceful look on her face. William moved, and her head rolled onto his shoulder. He smoothed back her brilliant red hair, and he let himself, just this once, fall asleep with her in his arms.

The smell of clean linen surrounded her. Part of her wanted to stay in William's arms. As soon as that thought crossed her mind, she scooted away so as not to wake him. She looked down at his sleeping form and admired his peaceful face. The ruffled hair made him seem vulnerable, and she stopped herself from putting it back to its normal order. He'd changed so much, from a person she couldn't stand to be around to someone she found steady and comforting, almost like a journey in a calm part of the canal. Maybe this was him before he'd taken on the responsibility of a relic for his father. Samuel had mentioned how much he'd changed, and she hoped that he would be proud of who his brother was becoming.

The door opened, and Samuel was in the doorway. He nodded at her and went to make breakfast. Vic didn't want to eat any more of their food, so she grabbed her clean clothes and boots out of the laundry and changed. She felt relaxed as the smell of William surrounded her while she dressed.

She left the brother behind and ran to the Order. Vic and

Kai hadn't had time to talk since their fight, and it left her feeling uneasy. His not understanding her frustrated her. Trying to think ahead of GicCorp was hard enough, and they needed to stand together. She understood the frustration of the early stages of planning, but they couldn't fall apart yet. The flame had only sputtered; it was time to coax it gently into an inferno.

Vic reached the Order and jogged up the steps to her room. She opened the door and balked when she ran into Kai. Her bed was rumpled but no different from normal. Her bed never got properly made, but from the looks of Kai's slept-in clothes and how her blanket was folded, he must have slept in her room.

"Where have you been?" he asked. She couldn't read his face. She saw the same black circles under his red eyes.

"I was checking on William and Samuel," Vic hedged carefully.

His eyes clouded at the mention of the former radiant. The weight of their last exchange crowded in the space between them.

"Did he get the job?"

"Yes."

The silence ate the room.

Kai gestured at the door. "I've been looking for you. Maddox is here to start on the doors. I figured she'd be more comfortable with you."

"Oh, okay." He walked out. "Kai?"

"Yes?"

She got the feeling he didn't want to talk. Maybe he'd come last night to air out their fight, but when she mentioned William these days, he closed off. "Are we okay?"

He looked at her without seeing her. There was no

intensity in his face, and he treated her like they shared nothing between them. "Don't make Maddox wait too long."

Vic's heart sank. She took a deep breath and followed him down to his office. They needed to talk, but she didn't want to distract him from the job. Maddox sat waiting in the office, and her brows rose as they entered the room. Vic trailed after him like she'd broken a rule and was about to be disciplined. The ease of their relationship had taken a vacation, and she didn't know if it would return.

"Now that you're back, get her some of your clothes before you go down." He sat at his desk and shoved some pens into a container.

"Fine."

Vic left with Maddox without saying another word. In her room, Maddox opened her mouth to say something as Vic handed her some clothes, but she shut her mouth and got changed into reaper black instead. She eyed the masks Vic placed on the nightstand. "Do these help?"

"You'll still smell the lovely sewers, but they kind of help."

Maddox grimaced and put on more than one. Vic stifled her laughter. They avoided the other reapers and headed down to Bomrosy's workshop.

Bomrosy was busy putting hinges and latches into a bag, and she left a few out on the table. She swung her head around as they entered, her braids swinging over her shoulder.

"Just in time." She handed the pack to Vic. "I'm guessing you're the packhorse?"

She took the heavy pack and put it on. "Yeah."

Bomrosy held up the latches and hinges to Maddox.

"They'll need to face this way, and this side goes on the tunnel side. They can then be released remotely."

"Remotely?"

Bomrosy practically shook with excitement. Her eyes lit up as she showed off her latest brainchild. "Yes! It sends a communication to the latches and hinges so we can close, open, unlock, and lock them. You see, this sends out the signal." She pressed buttons and chattered on. "This way, we don't need to rely on magic energy or running down to shut the doors in the sewers. The tracking from using that energy could get us in trouble. But it all comes down to the signal and which frequency it's on. Since no one else uses this tech, there's no worry that anyone will intercept it."

Vic's eyes glazed over as Bomrosy spoke.

Bomrosy poked Vic. "I lost you, didn't I?"

Vic started. "Oh no, very interesting transmitty thingy." She'd gotten used to Bomrosy's excitement over the last few weeks, but her mind wandered back to Kai and their interaction. She wanted to fix their relationship, but she didn't know how. Shouldn't he apologize for his assumptions? She mentally shoved out all those thoughts. She needed to stay focused to help Maddox. Even though it wasn't too late in the day, it still wasn't safe in the sewers.

Maddox laughed. "I think the radiant would appreciate it more than us magic users. It's neat, though."

Bomrosy groaned in a long-suffering way and put the last three items in Vic's pack.

"Oh, I have something for you." The stone she'd found still sat in her pocket. She hoped it getting washed hadn't damaged it. She handed it to Bomrosy.

Her friend's eyebrows shot up to her hairline. "Where

did you find this?" She sat down and pulled out various tools and a microscope.

"I hate to say it, but I got lost in the sewers and found it in a room. Is it important?"

Bomrosy held it up to the light, and her eyes glimmered. "I don't know, but it might be. If it is, I hope you can find that room again."

"It's at the end of a swim down shit river ... so I'm not sure I want to." Vic didn't know if she could find that room again. If she went down the feces river again, maybe, but for a few rocks, she didn't want another bath. Maybe she could let Bomrosy have at it. Toss over a boat and wish her luck.

Maddox pulled down her masks, her face already beaded with sweat. "You've developed weird hobbies."

Vic heard a noise in Bomrosy's room, and her gaze shifted to her friend. Maddox hadn't heard anything and was putting her masks back over her face. Vic leaned forward and widened her eyes at Bomrosy, then flicked her head toward Bomrosy's room. Had she brought Xiona back?

Bomrosy looked away from Vic and found her tools very interesting to stare at.

Vic closed her eyes. They couldn't talk about it with Maddox right there. "Let's go build some doors."

Maddox nodded, and they went to the back of Bomrosy's shop. Vic slid the giant stone door aside and shut it behind them. Then they walked down an extensive set of stairs to another stone door. The smell grew thicker as they continued down. Her skin itched at the thought of being down here so much. After the dunk in the river, her skin still didn't feel clean. If these doors worked out and she didn't need to run around in the sewage anymore, Vic swore she would kiss Bomrosy.

Vic slid open the last door, and the smell hit them in the face. Maddox stepped back.

Vic chuckled. "Welcome to my world."

⊛

"I MIGHT AS WELL BUILD A HOME DOWN HERE." VIC PLODDED through the sewer with Maddox at her side. She held back another yawn as they walked through the main tunnel toward the swamp. They'd decided on the line farthest from Boreus territory. With Tristan's threat toward them if they modified the sewers, the doors Maddox built would help not make the new gates obvious, although they couldn't be sure how Tristan gained information.

"Gross. Why would you do that?" Maddox's voice was muffled through multiple masks.

"Might get more sleep if I stay down here." The sight of people's waste was more welcoming than Landon's indignant face. With all her problems swirling in her mind, the second felt like an excellent target for her anger.

Maddox cleared her throat. "So, when I came today, you weren't sleeping in your room, but Kai was. And he didn't know where you were, so he stayed there without you? Like, does he cuddle your pillows or something?"

Vic's stomach did a strange flip. She'd assumed as much when she'd run into Kai this morning. He must have sent Maddox to wait in his office while he'd stayed. She'd missed out on her chance to talk to him. "I stayed at his house ..."

"With someone else?" Maddox teased. "Could it be the man who lifted you out of your wine puddle?" Her eyes danced with mirth as Vic's face grew red behind her mask.

Her teeth clamped down, and Maddox crowed with

laughter. "It is! With that glare you gave me over flirting with Kai! You have another man!" She shoved Vic playfully.

"No, he's a friend." Vic continued to the next passageway and handed Maddox the next latch and hinges.

Maddox continued to laugh, and her wand glowed as it formed a door big enough to span the tunnel. "Does Kai know about this friend?" She held out the hinges, and the stone molded around them. Next, she placed the latch after swinging the stone door closed so it fit the side tunnel. The door stayed the same texture while in the wall, but it was smooth when it was shut. Someone would have to be looking carefully for the hinges and latches if they wanted to see them in the gloomy lighting of the sewers.

Vic didn't understand how the hinges worked. She kept Maddox safe from mogs while they placed them in the right direction. Tech stayed foreign to her, but if more people cared about Bomrosy's devices, then the problem of blight could fade into history. Maybe she should talk her father into investing in Bomrosy's inventions. They could squeeze that in between trying to stay alive and rebelling against GicCorp.

Maddox finished the door and stood back to admire her handiwork. Her eyebrows rose when she faced Vic. "You aren't going to answer my question?"

Vic kicked a loose rock into the sewage river. "Kai knows he stays at his house."

"Does he know that you stay there?"

"I don't!" The words shot out, but she thought about most of last week, when she'd stayed on the sofa more often than in her own room. "Well, not too much."

Maddox stopped walking. "You like him."

"I don't!"

"You like him. Why is that a bad thing?"

Vic continued to walk, leaving Maddox to catch up with her. "I'm with Kai. I like Kai. Can't a woman have a male friend without it being about romance?" Like the ex-radiant? Never. Not all relationships with the opposite sex needed to be romantic. So what if she stayed over there more often than at the Order? Being with William was less stressful. It didn't matter that she felt more relaxed with him. With Kai, they had a thing. Right?

"Are you with Kai, though?"

Was she? She seemed to be the one chasing him while he put her at a distance to protect her from the other reapers. "We haven't talked about it. He's trying to keep Nyx afloat." What kind of person would she be if she demanded all his attention in the middle of this so they could build a relationship? A small thought popped into her mind. *You built a relationship with William.* Vic squinted and shooed the thought away. William didn't have the same responsibilities. He was only risking his life going undercover. Vic groaned.

Maddox nodded. "Yeah, overthrowing a government will strain a relationship."

"I'm there to help him if he needs me."

"Sounds more like a friend to me," Maddox muttered.

Vic tucked a strand of hair under her hood. "Okay, let's talk about your love life for a while, then."

Maddox finished the next door and tested the hinges. "My love life doesn't involve multiple men. It dried up after they declared me the vital of the family." She swung the door, and it didn't even creak. "Other vitals now find me attractive. I guess we can make our own families behind the walls. But have you ever seen any kids come out of there?"

"Maybe you can't have kids?" Vic shook her head. "Why am I defending it? We both know something's going on."

Maddox shrugged. "You're trying to make me feel better."

"I'm not doing a great job."

"No, you're not." They glanced at each other and snickered. "I guess if I get taken, I'm hoping you'll still be out here, fighting to get me out." She twisted her wand between her fingers. "I remember the first thing I formed with stone. Do you?"

"Oh yeah, a small heart. You used the walls of the school. Our teacher was so mad." Teaching a bunch of adolescents coming into their power would tax anyone.

"Well, you didn't have to tell on me!"

"We both got in trouble, anyway, because you told him I gave you the idea." Destruction of school property. She'd never known her parents' faces could turn that shade of purple.

"I made it for you," Maddox huffed.

"I thought you made it for Gavin." Vic leaned her elbow on the wall while she waited for Maddox. "Even back then, I was jealous I couldn't make things."

Maddox locked arms with her. "Yeah, but now you're a badass reaper fighting the good fight."

"I think I'd rather build houses."

"No, you wouldn't."

Feeling more uplifted, Vic followed her friend. They fell into a comfortable pattern. They came to the last pathway before the grate that led to the swamp.

"Good, it's getting dark out, and we don't need to be down here together." Vic noticed a new latch already on the grate. She didn't know that had happened yet. Kai hadn't kept her in the loop. She peeked out the grate and glanced at the path below the grate entrance. Bones were piled on the walkway in the swamp. The sun dipped down, and the lights glowed in the darkness.

A strange feeling came over her. "We need to move out now."

"I'm almost done. What's wrong?"

"I have a bad feeling." There was no reason for a pile of bones to be out in the swamp next to the grate—unless someone wanted to attract a bunch of mogs.

"Okay, then let me finish." Maddox acted calm, but her hands shook as she held the hinges.

Vic paced back and forth while Maddox finished the last door. They latched that one shut. Bomrosy would release them all in the morning, after they'd brought in mogs for the night. A chorus of low moans rose from the swamp.

"Blight, what's that sound?"

"Mogs." Vic glanced out the grate. Piles of mogs came up to the bones and munched on them. The sound of the mogs' teeth grating on the bones was accompanied by the sick slurping sounds as their long tongues sucked up the crushed dinner. The rotting smell from the mogs mixed in with the sewage, making the masks useless and turning her stomach.

Maddox shivered. "I'm with you. Let's get out of here."

As they turned to leave, Vic heard the echo of latches clicking, and the doors swung open. They froze. Vic turned back to the swamp grate, and mog eyes glowed at her as they stuck their limbs inside the sewer. The gate opened on its own.

"Run." Vic grabbed Maddox's hand and yanked her along the path, the moans of mogs at their heels.

WILLIAM

William's eyes watered as he held back a yawn. When he'd woken up this morning, Vic had already left. She didn't seem to get very much sleep these days. Normally, reapers slept past noon. The time on the clock flashed in front of him, and he jumped off the sofa to get dressed. He wished he could shower, but he shouldn't be late on the first day at his new job.

Sam already had breakfast out, and William gulped it down. "I have to go to work, so I'm sorry, but I need to keep you shut in here all day. Would you like some books to read?"

He had never seen a radiant read. They didn't have many books in Verrin. Only founders could waste their money on something that wasn't food. But the radiant might want to read. He might snag some books from Vic's family or grab some newspapers.

"Do what you must."

William put on the harness for his wand and stared at his brother. Sam moved back and forth from the table, clearing it. "I miss you, Samuel." *What color is the sky, Brother?* For a moment, he thought Sam paused, but he continued to clean the dishes with the methodical movements of a radiant, no wasted time or effort.

William went out of the house and locked the door behind him. He ran to the nearest water taxi and took it all the way back to GicCorp. The paper said he needed to go to entrance C. He walked down the line until he spotted a bright red C above an iron gate. Employees went in and out of various entrances to GicCorp. Other factories didn't give off a friendly image, but with its high walls, this one felt more like a prison. The feeling might be coming from his purpose of spying. There were few windows or escape routes if he got caught snooping. Would they fire him or turn him in to the city officers?

He took a deep breath and walked through the entrance. He was supposed to report to a person named Julian. In the middle of the stone courtyard, a woman with deep smile lines on her tanned face and a booming voice directed other imbs. Her slicked-back hair came to a tight bun at the nape of her neck. The muscles in her arms pushed against the jumpsuit. Her friendly manner encouraged him, but she could pin him to the ground without breaking a sweat.

He inched toward her, and her topaz eyes zeroed in on him. "Ah, the recent hire?" She stepped down from the stone platform. A wide hand engulfed his, and the callouses scratched his skin. "I don't know who you pissed off, but welcome to the glamorous side of GicCorp in the sewers."

"Julian?"

"You found me. Go get a jumpsuit and mask. You're with me today, fresh bait." She slammed her palm against his back, and he kept his face neutral as his shoulder smarted.

William nodded, then moaned inwardly. Vic had told him tales of spending every night in the sewers, and now he got to join her. She'd joked about living down there. Maybe she was right. They should build a home and get used to the smell.

He went to a side entrance that other men and women in bright red jumpsuits came out of. The color wasn't flattering on anyone, but if they needed to find a body, they could spot it for miles. As he stepped aside so he wouldn't impede the other workers, he came to a sizeable room that matched the musty smell of Verrin, but with the body odor of humans mixed in. The clang of metal lockers surrounded him, and he spotted names at the top of most of the beat-up metal.

William found one with his name. When he opened it, a bright red jumpsuit blinded him. He swallowed and took a quick sniff. The scent of fresh material greeted him. At least the only sweat on this would be his. The smell of the room and thoughts of the sewers already made him nauseous. Samuel used to tease him about how he'd kept his white uniform as a radiant so clean. Wouldn't he laugh now at his brother going into a sewer wearing this caution sign of a uniform? To complete the joke, he slid on the pair of matching boots. William felt like a giant bloodstain. On the top shelf was a lock with a code written on it. He quickly folded his clothes and locked them inside, committing the code to memory. With that completed, he held the mask as he went outside to join the other red blotches.

Julian nodded at him and eyed the jumpsuit. "Looks good on you, bait. We're luckier than reapers. Our suits are imbued to keep the stench out, so you mainly get to smell yourself. But it doesn't change the fact we're around feces all day."

"What are we doing exactly? They didn't say when I was hired." Even if he didn't have to smell the sewers, he didn't want to get defecation on himself.

Julian laughed. "Wow, they sent in the freshest bait. We repair the lines directly into Haven."

William's heart thudded. His luck had turned around. This was exactly where he needed to be. After almost not getting hired, this seemed to have worked out too perfectly. He glanced around to see if Tristan watched him, as if this might be a setup.

"Got somewhere to be, bait?"

"No. I'm ready to learn." This might give them a chance to make their own way into Haven if they couldn't find one.

Julian let out another booming laugh. "Love the attitude. Let's go down into the dark. If a mog pops out, it's best to run. You good at running, bait?"

William swallowed. "You're not calling me bait because I'm the one who'll get eaten, are you?"

All of Julian's teeth showed. "That's up to you ... bait."

William got in line with the rest of his group, and they headed toward a door at the end of the complex. Julian took out a key and unlocked it. They went down some stairs, and every so often, they would need to stop to unlock more doors. Just getting to work took a long time. This line to the sewers was well guarded.

"Why so many locks?" William asked a worker next to him.

The jumpsuit billowed around the man's narrow frame. "We're between the city and Haven. You can't get here from any other entrance. They don't want mogs to get in here, so everything is patched often. Our leader may tease you about mogs, but there aren't any here. We check all the grates and lines daily. The only thing bad about this job is the smell if you need to take off your mask for a drink or to eat. The smell tends to cling even after you put it back on. It can get pretty hot."

If Vic needed an entrance to her sister, this was it. William couldn't believe it. He silently thanked Ginny for hating him enough to put him on sewer duty.

WILLIAM CURSED GINNY FOR PUTTING HIM ON SEWER DUTY. Heat radiated from the tunnels, and he stewed in his own sweat. The soupy mixture of his sweat made the suit stick to his skin. If anyone wanted to lose weight, this was the way to go. Was there even any water left in his body? He wanted to wipe his eyes as sweat dripped from his eyebrows, but he didn't want to disturb his mask. The seams to the Haven side were smooth, and there were no entrances except for small pipelines that no human could fit through.

He wanted to scream in frustration. Halfway through the day, they ducked into a side room, which Julian had to unlock. Everyone removed their masks and took out cloths to wipe the sweat from their faces. Then they got out packs with their lunches. That was one thing he'd forgotten to bring. At the moment, he didn't care and leaned back against the cold stone, enjoying the air on his damp face.

Julian squatted next to him. "Take some of mine, bait."

His mouth salivated at the sight of her drink. "No need. I just forgot."

She nodded and handed him a drink and half a sandwich. "You need to stay hydrated, so take it."

He gulped down the lukewarm water and bit into the sandwich. His group chatted quietly as they ate.

Since he was new, he could use his ignorance to ask questions. Julian seemed open enough to tolerate it. "Is there no need for repairs on the Haven side?"

Julian coughed. "You don't want to do that. You'll end up as a vital. They take care of it from there."

"The vitals do?"

"They bring them food through a system at the gate from the back of GicCorp, but other than that, they need to handle their own repairs and purify the magic."

"Have you seen them?" William asked.

"Down in the sewers? Don't kid around, bait. You should know as well as anyone they aren't seen after they go inside. You couldn't have grown up in a cave, shut away in the dark." She tried to hide a shiver. "Almost makes me glad I wasn't born a founder brat."

"Me too." As a radiant, he'd grown up in the dark, but no one knew much of anything about the vitals. The ones who did would never talk to William.

She quirked her brow. "A nice relic, though, for someone who isn't."

William glanced at his wand. He'd rehearsed the story with Vic's father. "It's the last one in my family. My father retired from working in glass, and he passed it on to me. I'm the only one supporting my family now."

Julian nodded. "Your family must always be wary of laws."

"Yeah, even though you might never break a law, you worry you'll accidentally break one you never knew about."

First-generation relics were rarely found outside of founder homes. Once you broke a law and lost your relic, others could bid on it. Only founders could afford the price. The thing about Verrin was that those with other generational relics were often forgiven since there was no value in their relics. The laws made by the rich benefited the rich. William pulled at the sleeves of his jumpsuit. There was no way for others to rise in this system. Could they fix it if they got rid of the Nordics? Or would another founder take their place and stomp on those without power? He'd taken this job to help Vic, but maybe they could do more for the city.

"Nothing like a recipe for paranoia to follow you throughout life. I hope you make enough one day to buy more relics for your family. That kind of pressure isn't easy."

William liked Julian's easygoing manner. From the morning shift, he could see that the entire group respected her. She didn't sit back and let others do all the work, and that could be part of what drew everyone to her. Julian got in the thick of it more often than everyone else.

For the rest of the afternoon, he was on the lookout for hidden passages. Maybe there would be hidden doors down here. He needed to be on his own to take a closer look. He couldn't very well search for cracks in the wall with his coworkers around him. Maybe he could come back after hours. But first, he'd need Julian's keys.

They finished their meals and went back to the tunnels. Julian directed them to break apart into the smaller tunnels. William worried that his magic was depleting too fast. Together, they cleaned and repaired the lines that transported blight into Haven. Apparently, the blight lines corroded quickly. With only an hour left in his shift, he ran out of magic. A few raised their eyebrows at the first-generation relic holder, but Julian slapped him on the back.

"Don't worry, bait. First-timers are always too enthusiastic and use too much. Stay with us until the end of the shift."

Just like that, everyone accepted it. Julian would let him get paid for the last hour, when most places would have sent him home. As he walked with the smaller group, he pressed his hand to the side of the wall to see if he could feel anything. Nothing but smooth stone met his fingers. They might need to find another way in. Vic and her father were counting on him to find something out about Haven, so he hoped this wasn't a dead end.

At the end of the shift, they all trudged past the many locked doors to the locker room. Julian hung up her keys inside her locker. It would be easy to get to if he knew her combination. Everyone put their jumpsuits in a large hamper to be cleaned, and William eyed Julian's lock. His hands trembled as he shifted his gaze around the room. He gripped his lock in his hand. It looked like Julian's. No one was looking his way. He quickly changed their locks. His heart pounded as he stopped himself from looking around. Nothing like acting all spy-like. No one said anything as they left the room. William went to the washroom that was full of toilet stalls. He went into a stall and got up on the toilet. This didn't seem like the best place to hide, but there was nowhere else. The noise outside quieted down, and then all the lights went out, plunging him into darkness.

He drew in a shaky breath and exited the stall. William spread out his fingers and found the wall. His hand touching the cold metal of the locker, he shuffled forward to where he thought the door might be. Then the lights flicked on, and Julian was at the door with her arms crossed.

"Get stuck in the dark, bait?"

William froze. "Ah, sorry I took so long." This was it. His

brief career as a spy had come to a halt. He found it hard to keep his breathing under Julian's gaze. His mind raced for a plausible excuse, but his brain only rewarded him with blankness.

Julian's lips thinned, and she assessed him. "You didn't shout when the lights went out."

"Oh." William begged his mind for something. "I figured I could get out," he hedged.

Her eyebrows rose. They stood there in silence, and William couldn't quiet the screaming in his mind. She made a clicking sound with her tongue. "I get it. You must not have a place to stay?"

Huh? The mindless roar in his brain quieted for a second.

"I know we just met, and it can be embarrassing. The outer doors get locked up in about an hour. I'll take the clothing out to the laundry so no one will come in here." She went to the laundry cart and flipped in a stray pant leg that hung over the edge. "You're fine to stay here this week, but after payday, make sure you find somewhere else."

William could only nod. Her kindness made him feel guilty. Julian's face softened, and she took the laundry with her. She didn't lock the room from the outside.

He sat on the bench. She'd helped him out with the timing. The clock ticked by slowly, and he waited for over an hour before going to her locker and putting in his combination. It clicked open. Just in case, he left his lock on her locker until he got back.

William's hand paused over the door leading out. He hadn't even started yet and he was sweating already. His stomach felt filled with stones. With a shaky hand, he opened the door and glanced around the empty yard. No one in sight. His heart pounded in his ears. He went to the first door and flipped through the keys. There were too many. With each failed key, he glanced behind him. His fingers shook so much that the keys jangled loudly in the empty, darkening night. He gripped them to stop their clattering, which would surely announce his presence to every living being in Verrin.

With a click, the first lock popped open. He quickly entered the next room and shut the door behind him. Most of the keys looked the same, but he tried to remember their position. Now onto the next door.

William didn't know how much time had passed by the time he finally found himself in the sewers. He wasn't sure of the order of the keys anymore.

He hoped Vic didn't worry about him not being home tonight. He shook his head. "Why would she worry?" He'd gotten too attached to her, and she and Kai had something going on. It wasn't right for him to pine after a person in a relationship, especially with Kai letting him stay in his house. It's not like Vic liked him. He walked in the tunnel. When he'd first met Vic, he'd basically been his father's mirror. He flinched as he remembered how he'd acted toward her. At his core, he still thought Verrin shouldn't depend on magic, but here he was, using magic to help. Even though he hoped it was for the greater good, he recognized the hypocrisy in his actions, and that couldn't be attractive.

With every step, William didn't know what to look for. If he got caught down here, there would be no talking himself out of it. Out of kindness, Julian had assumed he was down on his luck. Then he realized Julian would get into trouble since he'd stolen her keys. The guilt ate at him for having abused her kindness.

Dripping water made him jumpy, and he took care to tiptoe in the empty tunnels. Unsure of the passing of time, he took a break in a side tunnel. He should have borrowed more of Kai's clothes to blend in with the black walls. Vic liked the blue. His face warmed at the thought.

Then he heard voices coming down the tunnel. William's mind buzzed. He hadn't thought he would find anything or anyone down here. Now here he sat with no protection and his wand drained. Even if it hadn't been, he didn't know how to use it as a weapon.

For now, he would watch. Maybe next time, he could bring backup with him. He carefully peeked out of the side tunnel. Dark-cloaked figures wearing masks entered the tunnel. They opened the wall, and a wide tunnel appeared. The masked figures entered, carrying large bundles on their backs. He'd correctly assumed that the doors would be well hidden in the wall.

Was that food they carried? No, it almost looked like people. Vic had mentioned that the people in the Nyx district who'd disappeared were being turned into mogs. There were too many of them. William punched the stone wall. Pain bloomed in his hand, but he ignored it. This city would kill people before it went without magic. His anger grew into despair as he watched people go to their deaths. Was there something he could do besides watch? That was all he did while everyone else took action. Vic would stop them. Kai would charge in and take them all on. William watched.

The last of them entered the hidden room, and William sat. Shame came over him for having done nothing. He eyed the landmarks in the tunnel, and his shoulder slumped as he headed back to the entrance.

He didn't pay attention as he went back through all the locked doors and then to the locker room. He put the keys back in Julian's locker and then placed the correct lock on it. He didn't want to stay here all night. He dreaded telling Vic how he'd watched helpless people being carried to their deaths, but she needed to know.

The blight swirled in the night sky, and William went to the main doors to see if there was a way out.

A side door seemed hopeful, and he gripped the handle and unlocked it, his mind on the people doomed to be turned. Then a black cloth bag went over his head. Arms gripped him as he struggled, but then a strange smell hit him and he knew no more.

Vic frantically tried to shut one door, but it wouldn't budge. She hoped they could run down a side tunnel and block it off. "Blight!"

Fear filled Maddox's eyes. Vic ran, pulling her friend behind her. There were too many mogs for her to take on. Even with Maddox, she wouldn't want to try to drain one.

Vic tore off her mask and dropped it so she could breathe better. Why were there so many? After weeks of finding only a few at a time, they'd come en masse. Either she or Maddox had to smell amazing, or the bones had worked better than they'd thought. Vic didn't take the time to turn around, but the sound of the mogs grew louder.

"We should try to make it to Nyx," Vic gasped as she ran.

Maddox didn't reply but pumped her legs so she now ran next to Vic. Nothing like fear to give you a boost.

Her lungs burned as they approached the Nyx entrance. The door was wide open. Vic gulped, and they ran up the stairs. All the gates were open, and she tried to push them shut.

"No use, founder. We can't shut them!" Vic had never thought she'd be thankful to see Landon in all her life. He pulled them up the rest of the stairs. "What happened?"

"Mogs. So many."

His brows shot up. "Come on."

They ran through Bomrosy's workshop, and a group of reapers greeted them outside the door. Landon slammed the door shut behind him.

"Report."

Vic caught her breath. "They're right behind us. Over a dozen large mogs came out of the swamp. The grate opened on its own and wouldn't shut."

To back up her words, a loud crash sounded in Bomrosy's workshop.

Landon pointed at Maddox. "Take her to Kai's office. That's where Bomrosy is." He turned his back on them and shouted, "Cover the halls! Once your gicgauge is full, run to empty it if you can. Don't leave anyone behind. Try to dodge the mog until the other returns to drain it."

Vic grabbed Maddox's hand, and they charged up the stairs as Bomrosy's workshop door burst open. Landon lanced the first mog. They ran to Kai's office and banged on the door. A wide-eyed Bomrosy opened it.

"Stay here. I need to go back." Vic pulled Maddox into the room.

"Vic!" Bomrosy grabbed her hand, stopping her.

"What?" Vic tugged her hand free and tapped her fingers at her side.

"Xiona is in my room!" Tears filled Bomrosy's eyes.

"I don't know what I can do, but I'll try." She gave Maddox a pointed look not to let Bomrosy know about the state of the workroom. There was a chance the mogs would ignore the shut bedroom. The reapers might tempt them more.

Vic shut the door to Kai's office, barricading them in the room. She practically tumbled down the stairs to get back to the main hall. Shouts and moans echoed in the halls as the mass of mogs poured out of the workshop like a broken water line.

Large mog bones lay in the hallways, and fallen reapers tried to pull themselves out of the way. A large mog crushed a reaper under its bulky form, cutting off the poor soul's screams. With dismay, Vic knew these were old mogs, and it would take more than one reaper to drain them. Working in their favor, the mogs were so huge that they couldn't freely move in the Order's halls. Dozens of reapers fought in the hall, but they weren't enough to stop the flow of mogs. Three massive mutated mogs rose in the main entrance and swung at the reapers trying to drain them.

She found a group to join, and they pulled down a large mog. Their blades cut into it. Her scythe burned hot in her hands, and the blade sliced through the flesh, catching on the mog's bones so it couldn't shake her off. The mog pulled at the group of reapers, and some of their bodies dangled in the air as they desperately gripped their scythes. The blight drained out of the mog, and the bones fell to the ground, along with some of her comrades. Her gicgauge was almost full from one mog. They all met each other's eyes. They couldn't drain another.

"Go drain your gicgauge and come back quickly," Vic told the one nearest the Order exit.

The reaper nodded and ran off. The rest of them stayed, and now it became a distraction game with the mogs.

A fat mog waddled up to them. Its wide mouth grinned,

and it opened its maw to reveal long, sharp teeth good for shredding human flesh. Its size made it slow, but as they cut into its flesh, their gicgauges filled. The mog still had plenty of energy. It used its massive form to push them back. Its teeth chomped as it ignored their useless blades. All four of them stabbed and pushed at the large mog. Vic frantically looked around the room for help. As soon as a reaper got back, their gicgauge filled too fast. They couldn't hold the mog back.

More mogs came into the entrance of the Order. Even though they'd drained a few, six massive rotted mogs came from the workshop. They used their mass to push back the reapers who could no longer drain them. There weren't enough reapers left in Nyx to handle this attack.

"Back to the walls!" Kai shouted. "Take a position around the walls!"

The walls were closer to the charging stations around the Order. They needed space to move.

"We need to block the entrance."

Vic swore. Maddox didn't have much magic left, but maybe she could do something. The fat mog backed them into the wall, its putrid breath bathing their faces. Soon, it would crush her group. A reaper propped his scythe handle against the wall to hold it back. Vic heard a cracking sound as the wooden handle gave. They exchanged glances, and Vic yelled over the screams, hoping someone would hear her, "Help! We're pinned. Help!"

The other reapers caught on as they slid down the wall under the fat mog's weight.

Then the pile of flesh from the mog melted, coating her group in smoking flesh. The bones clattered to the ground, and Vic stumbled from the lack of mog to push against. Two reapers saluted and ran off to find more mogs or to drain their gicgauges. Vic bolted to Kai's office. On her way, she met Freddie and Ivy. She glanced at them. They had empty gicgauges.

"Come with me!"

Without question, they followed her to Kai's office. Vic opened the door, and Maddox sat to the side, comforting Bomrosy. Their faces were full of fear until they saw Vic.

"Do you have enough magic to block the door?" Vic yelled.

Maddox started and glanced at her wand. "I don't know. Maybe a cave-in?"

Bomrosy shot up. "But my room! Xiona!"

Ivy frowned. "Who?"

Vic pursed her lips. "We're going to the doorway. Can you do it?"

There wasn't time to worry about the ex-commander while Nyx reapers were dying in battle.

Maddox drew in a shuddering breath. "I can try."

She left her chair, and her wand arm trembled.

"Cover us while we get to the entrance," Vic directed her team.

Ivy and Freddie nodded.

"Try not to use up your gicgauge. Mine is already full. Maddox, stay next to me. Freddie, lead." They only had two reapers to get through, and they couldn't drain more than one old mog. They didn't have a say in how fast the gicgauges would fill, but the words gave her some comfort.

They left Bomrosy in the office while they ran downstairs. The reapers retreated to the walls. Only a few remained to push the mogs out into the courtyard. The reapers acted like bait with calls and slashes. Shouts came from outside to attract the mogs' attention. One false move as bait and they could end up as dinner.

They got to the workshop entrance, and Landon blocked their way. "Get outside. Didn't you hear Kai's orders?" He slashed at a mog and hooked it with another reaper. They tried to direct the mogs outside where the other reapers waited. Blood and sweat coated his skin.

"We're blocking the door." Vic shoved past him. They didn't have time for his ego.

Landon snarled, "If you die, fine."

As the reapers cleared the mogs, they ducked into Bomrosy's workroom. All her tools were scattered about the room. They could hear the moans of approaching mogs.

Maddox's wand gem glowed dimly as she glanced at the tunnel's archway. "I can collapse the tunnel." Maddox pulled on Vic's arm.

Freddie and Ivy shoved forward to drain the next mog coming out of the tunnel.

"You have only a minute, Mads!"

Maddox adjusted her wand, and the rock in the tunnel ceiling melted. The sides of the tunnel folded in with the ceiling, making the entrance smaller and smaller. The mog's bones curled in with the shaping stone, and the next one reached through the wide crack. Then the stone stopped moving, leaving a small window. The mog's arms stayed stuck inside, twitching as it reached for the food in the workshop.

They all took a breath of dusty air.

"I'm all out." Maddox leaned on the wall but avoided the mog's arm that looked like a grotesque wall hanging.

"That will stop more from coming in. Thanks, Mads."

"I'll take her back," Ivy said. "You and Freddie go empty

your gicgauges and help clear the rest." Ivy led Maddox out of the room.

Freddie watched her go, frowning. He didn't like to leave her alone, even though he knew she could handle herself. They both ran out of the room.

"We shut the passage!" Vic yelled to Landon on her way out. They did their best to help push the mogs out, but they couldn't drain any more. Vic sliced into a mog with another group, getting it away from a reaper lying prone on the ground.

Too much blood covered them, and Vic swallowed. A pack of reapers fought at the gates, and they let them pass. They ran to the charging station and finally emptied their gicgauges.

Vic ran back to the mogs and drained them again and again. Some reapers fell with a shout, and Freddie would plunge in to pull them out. The last mog fell in a pile of bones.

The reapers remained still as if they didn't believe what had happened. There was no time to rest. They gathered the injured and the dead. Most had had their limbs torn off by hungry mogs and bled to death. Many could've been saved had they gotten to them sooner.

Her mind flashed back to the battle with Dei and how the blood on the courtyard had made her ears ring.

"Are you injured?" Kai asked.

Vic shook her head. She carried another bleeding reaper to the dining hall.

Reapers pushed aside the tables and pulled out the emergency cots. The healers ran around, wrapping up wounds from lost limbs or putting sheets over those who hadn't made it.

Vic carried the bodies of the dead to the far wall to be cremated. Once again, their numbers had taken a large hit. Why hadn't the gates closed?

As they brought in the last survivors, Vic helped clean the injured reapers.

She tied her hair back, and the world finally seemed to calm. The other reapers sat along the wall, unwilling to leave their injured comrades.

Then a terrible scream broke the silence. Scythes clicking open echoed in the room.

Landon stormed in, Xiona in his grip. Bomrosy hit his back behind him. He turned and elbowed her in the throat, knocking her back against the wall. She fell with a thud. Vic jumped up to help her friend, but other reapers blocked her path. Though weary, she tried to shove through.

The reapers gasped as Landon held their ex-commander.

"Kai!" Veins popped along Landon's neck.

"Yes?" Kai remained calm as he left a reaper's bed.

Landon shoved Xiona forward. Even though she stumbled, she still smiled. "Care to explain this?"

All the reapers faced Kai. His shoulders sagged, and he folded his arms. "Xiona got purified in the battle with Dei."

Everyone but Vic gasped.

"You told us she was dead!" Landon's voice boomed. His gray eyes were flinty, and spittle flung from his mouth as he spoke.

"I did it to keep up morale. What Xiona did was wrong, and the purification was an accident." Weariness coated Kai's voice as he tried to explain, like he knew it was too late for excuses over being dishonest with the reapers under his command.

"We had a right to know!" Landon shoved Xiona aside,

and Bomrosy grabbed her to keep her away from Landon. "Who did this? Why are you protecting them? Are you choosing them over your family?"

Vic stopped trying to push forward as angry reapers glared at Kai.

Kai's face fell, and all strength left him. "They didn't mean to do it."

"They broke the law." Landon searched the crowd until his gaze fell on Vic. "It was her friend, wasn't it? That radiant was here in the battle."

"Landon, what's done is done. Xiona was punished for turning people into mogs." Vic cringed at the suggestion that Xiona's purification had been justified.

Landon slammed his hand against the wall. "Then turn her in to the officers! Don't purify her."

"I couldn't!"

"Why?"

"Because GicCorp ordered her to change people!" Kai shouted.

The mood in the room shifted.

Landon raised his brows. "Are you saying GicCorp is taking people and changing them to provide more blight?"

"Yes. That much we do know." The words filled the room as Kai finally shared the truth with the reapers.

"Why didn't you tell us?" Landon actually looked hurt.

The room waited for an answer. Kai looked away.

Landon flexed his fist. "Did you think we'd take their side and want to change people for money? Is that all the faith you have in us?" The hurt in Landon's voice was new to Vic. He was a prat, so she'd forgotten that he loved Nyx, even if he didn't like her.

All the reapers turned away from Kai. He stayed alone in the middle of the injured reapers.

Vic stood next to him. "Xiona broke his trust. He wanted to tell you but didn't know how."

Landon snorted. "It looks like he told you." His jaw clenched. "I'm leaving." He glanced at the wounded. "Who wants to leave with me?"

Vic hoped they would ignore Landon, but the wounds ran too deep. The uninjured reapers helped their comrades who couldn't walk. In minutes, the room had emptied except for Bomrosy, Xiona, Ivy, Freddie, Kai, and Vic.

Freddie walked up to Kai, and Ivy glared.

"Since you can't trust us, we can't trust you." Ivy crossed her arms.

Vic stepped forward. "Ivy ..."

She shook her head. "I tried to believe the best, even when everyone else believed Landon. But since you don't think of us as your team, we might as well be on our own."

Her heart hurt as she watched them walk away. There was nothing Vic could say as they left. They were right. Since the start, Vic had kept them at a distance.

Kai's expression was blank.

"Kai?"

His weary eyes focused. "I'm sorry, I need a moment. Thank you for trying."

Vic watched him go and went to Bomrosy. "Are you okay?"

Bomrosy nodded. "Yeah. I sent Maddox home."

"Good." She drew in a deep, shaky breath. The rage bubbled inside her over the constant warnings she'd given Bomrosy about Xiona. "What were you thinking bringing Xiona back here? I explicitly told you to leave her at Kai's house. Do you understand what you did?" This entire scene could have been avoided had she listened. "What makes you immune to what Kai told you to do? He's your commander too."

Bomrosy swallowed. "Everyone was already thinking of leaving before this."

"This didn't help any! Kai was trying to find the right time to tell them about GicCorp. You tore apart the whole Order!" Vic knew there were more problems, but she couldn't think clearly anymore.

"It wasn't only me. Stop blaming me because Kai didn't trust them." Bomrosy glared at Vic. "I messed up, but if Kai had been honest from the start, this wouldn't have happened." Tears fell down her cheeks. "Why are you always defending him? Shouldn't he be the one admitting his own mistakes?"

Vic clenched her fists. "Why don't you take Xiona and leave? You care more about her, anyway."

"I guess I do." Bomrosy led Xiona out, and as soon as Vic heard the steps fade away, she fell to her knees. The Order was now dark and empty, mirroring how she felt inside.

🕊 13 🕊

AMAYA

maya moaned as she shifted in her bed. She slowly
rotated her toes and fingers. Next, she moved her
wrists and ankles until she felt comfortable sitting
up. She eyed her slender body with appreciation. Amaya
had always preferred to be petite instead of muscular, even
though it sometimes gave her a disadvantage. Others could
partake in hard labor for her.

On her nightstand, the wand waited for her, and she
picked it up and cradled it like a long-lost child. It warmed
in her hands, and she stroked it. The delicate lines of the
wand twirled down the stem and met at the jade-colored
gem, almost like a flower waiting to bloom. The wand knew
her body, and she took it as a sign of acceptance. The magic
thrums always felt like coming home.

The surrounding room didn't seem much different from
before, the large bed and windows still the same. The
bedding had changed, but she might have slept for a few
years, so it was only healthy. Everything was still in crisp

grays and blacks. She smiled. Her husband's taste never changed. With so many years to live, he could try to be adventurous, but it also kept him loyal to her.

The solid onyx doors stayed closed, and she frowned at them. It was strange that he wasn't waiting for her to awaken, but maybe she'd slept too long for him to stay by her side.

She flinched as her head throbbed, sending errant thoughts through her head. "This one's a fighter." How bothersome. The body seemed weak enough, but the will was strong. She should have known by now not to let a delicate body deceive her.

The door clicked open, and a youthful man entered. Every hair remained combed in place, and the light brown strands contained a slight curl to them. The fitted suit complemented his frame, from the broad shoulders to the narrow waist. As his lips curved in an excited smile, a yummy dimple appeared in his cheek. His clear blue eyes brightened when he saw she was awake. Every time was different, but beyond the color of the eyes, they recognized each other. Comfort surrounded her, and she knew he was her home.

"My love, you're finally awake." He strode to her side.

"Tristan." Amaya rose on shaking legs, and he rushed to stabilize her. She snuggled into his embrace, enjoying his firmness under the tailored suit. She tugged at his sleeves.

He laughed. "Always impatient."

Amaya pushed her bottom lip out in a pout. He bent over her face and pressed his lips to hers. She moved her mouth with his. Nothing felt right until he kissed her. He pulled back, and she parted her lips in a frown. Even though pain lanced through her head, she still wanted him.

Tristan softly kissed her forehead. "I'm sorry, but there's a bit to go over before we can get lost in each other."

Amaya groaned. "Don't tell me this is the uprising of the cycle."

He sat down and pulled her onto his lap. "I thought it was your favorite."

She smacked him lightly and kissed the addictive dimple. Maybe she would request for him to always have dimples. He always got to pick what he liked. "So this body must have been running in the sewers at all hours of the night? Why don't you ever have to do that?" She wrinkled her nose.

"Luck of the draw. I'm afraid I brought you back too soon, and the others aren't happy with me." His brows furrowed. "They've been making deals they shouldn't be making."

Amaya pressed a finger between his eyebrows to smooth them out. He would get wrinkles if he wasn't careful. "What else is new? They don't like us being together too long. Makes them nervous." When you grew too old for too long, bonds broke and reformed over and over. That she and Tristan had never broken made them nervous because it made the couple stronger. In lifespans, you needed at least one person to trust. Otherwise, you had a miserable cycle and would have to start over again.

He kissed her again. She enjoyed it until he pulled away. "Unfortunately, you can't leave the property in your normal capacity."

Amaya shook her head, brushing away the cobwebs from his kisses. "Wait, how soon?"

"Sixty years too early."

"Tristan!" Amaya jumped out of his lap. "Why would you do that?"

He pulled at her hands to make her sit back down, but she didn't move. "I hate to say it, but I need you. Things aren't going the same as before. When we introduced the new relics, it added an issue."

"You mean the rings?" Amaya plopped down. "Ugh, I told Ethan it was a terrible idea, the idiot. Now I have to fix his mess? Or is it past that point?"

Tristan crossed his legs. "Way past."

"I'm stuck behind these walls. What am I supposed to do?" He should have used someone else's body. Her brain throbbed. She loved him, but she knew he had a type.

"Gather information."

"Oh, with spy pigeons?"

Tristan kissed her ear. "Don't worry. There's something much better than pigeons." He traced her arm, making her shiver.

"I will have to use this body, won't I?" She pouted. Amaya hated trying to act like others. She never pulled it off. "Can't you get someone else to do it?"

Tristan shook his head. "No, the family member belongs to you, and I have a feeling only you can do it."

Amaya pursed her lips. "Fine. I guess you have to give me all the information now?" She doubted her acting skills. Her strength was better suited for direct attacks than sneaking behind the scenes. She glanced at her hair color. Yep, the color confirmed why he'd put her in this body. His type was so predictable.

"But you love to study."

"Not really." She twisted her hair over her shoulder.

"What rebel has you so scared this time around? Normally, things don't get out of hand."

"I'm not scared."

Amaya made a face when Tristan looked away. He seemed more bothered than normal. There had to be too many people in power moving against them this time. Interesting. Normally, the founders were too busy looking out for themselves to worry about GicCorp. She'd have to give props to this cycle. Maybe they would be one version she would remember later. It never mattered, though. History always repeated itself. They knew each cycle and how it would end.

She grinned. The higher they rose, the harder they would fall. If they crushed too many bodies, though, they would be back where they'd started, and she didn't want to build anything or grow plants. Tiresome.

Amaya pulled his face back to her. "I need a bit of motivation before I have to study."

Tristan bent his face down toward hers. As he pushed her down on the bed, her toes curled. She really liked this body. Her fingers bent without her control, and she reached for Tristan's eyes. Amaya pulled back the attack, but she still slapped him across the cheek, leaving behind fingernail scratches.

He backed away. "See, her will is strong."

Amaya huffed. "It won't take long. I'm stronger." In the meantime, she shouldn't rile her up by kissing her husband. She found it was better to squash the soul slowly than to provoke it.

A knock sounded at the door, and another man entered. He was older, with gray at his temples, and he gave them a dour glance. Dull eyes with an expression to match. Even though he wore tailored clothing of the latest fashion, his personality didn't pull it off. He remained a hanger for the items instead. Centuries later and he still made the same face at them. Everything about the man was dull compared to Tristan. They could put the man in the best body and he would still make it fade into the background.

"Ah, Ethan, I thought you would come in and spoil the fun." Amaya pushed off the bed. She bowed slightly to the old fuddy-duddy. Just once, she would love to be in a cycle without him. His slow creep for power annoyed her and made their lives more difficult. "I hear your latest pet project is getting out of hand?"

Ethan stiffened. "As a matter of fact, it isn't. Having fewer people in the city is always better in the long run."

Amaya smoothed out her gown and flipped her hair. "You would think so, but people make this world run." He always wanted a cowed nation. This world stayed in the dark ages, even with magic. If she had a choice, they would leave Ethan behind with everyone else. She and Tristan could manage better.

"Don't push your luck, Amaya. You aren't even supposed to be here." His nostrils flared. "Someone picked a body that wasn't his to take."

Amaya bounced back to her husband and put her arms around his neck, kissing him on her dimple. "Awe, he knows what I like."

Stop.

Her arms stiffened. "Apparently, a body that doesn't like you?" She raised her eyebrows at Tristan.

He rubbed her back. "Nothing you can't handle."

"Hmm." Maybe she should give him a headache for every time this body caused her one.

"Tristan, I came to get you for the meeting." Ethan the Dull as Paint said.

"I take it I'm not invited."

Ethan pursed his lips. "You aren't supposed to be here."

"I got it. But I am here." Amaya stabbed him in the chest with her finger. "You have one day to get used to it. I hate meetings anyway."

Ethan's face grew red, and she assumed the old fool was mad or something. Tristan laughed and kissed the top of her head, then followed Ethan out the door.

Amaya glanced around the sizable room. She should paint it brighter colors while Tristan busied himself with horrid meetings. A mirror sat in the corner, and she approached it cautiously. She trusted Tristan with her preferences, but there was always something missing.

In the mirror, the slender figure stood upright. Amaya appreciated that they had good posture. Shorter than she was used to, though. Her lips curled in a smile as she took in the lovely red hair. Tristan liked a redhead. The lighter color accented the green eyes. Amaya traced her face and appreciated the well-set lines.

"You were a beauty."

Stop.

"Sorry. I can't." She turned in the mirror to check out the back of her body. Lovely. "It will only hurt for a bit. You shouldn't fight it." Some left immediately after the new soul came in. Others thought they could fight. This one thought she had a reason to stay. It would only permanently destroy her. She'd made her choice without knowing it, but Amaya always won.

Stop.

"Hush now. Let go." Amaya went to her wand. Using

her magic quickened the ownership process. Her wand warmed in her hand, and she enjoyed the feel of the surrounding air. The Nordics had always held their secrets close. The imbs focused on one aspect of their magic because that was all they knew. The still air moved around her crawled up her veins. Close to painful but the power made it worth it. Her body now saturated with the air, she pushed it down to her wand. Like breathing, the magic came back to her.

Then a wall came down and cut her off from the air before she could release it. The trapped magic stung her insides, and she screamed. Warm blood flowed down her nose. The sound of glass cracking cut through the room, and with a boom, it shattered.

Amaya faced the broken window. The shards stayed poised in the air.

Her breath came in gasps as she tried to take control of her wand. "It's not yours to control!"

The glass shards inched forward painfully. Frozen in place, Amaya struggled to regain her magic. The first shard reached her and cut down her arm. She screamed as blood oozed out of her body.

The doors slammed open, and the glass turned to sand and fell to the ground. Tristan leaped forward and pried the wand from her hand.

"What in the blight happened?" He ripped off his jacket and put it over the long cut down her arm to stop the flowing blood.

I told you to stop.

Amaya sneered. "This one thinks she will win."

I will. If I die, I will take you with me.

Amaya trembled and hoped Tristan didn't feel it. "I

messed up with imbuing the air and broke the window. I guess I'm rustier than I thought."

Tristan frowned. "Don't use your wand yet. Get adjusted first."

Amaya nodded, and her blood froze as laughter sounded in the back of her mind. Let her think she'd won this battle, but for the first time, a tiny shred of fear appeared in Amaya's thoughts.

Let it begin.

14

VIC

After Bomrosy left, Vic wandered the empty halls of the Order. The smell of drying blood grew thick in the abandoned halls. With all the mog bones and bodies in the courtyard, her home had turned into a tomb, reminding her of when she'd learned in school that they used to bury their dead instead of burning them. All the reapers had gone, leaving her and Kai to take care of the bodies. She waited outside Kai's office, but she didn't feel like talking to him. In a few hours, she would see him about building the funeral pyres.

She dragged her weary body to the courtyard and went to the small shed where they kept a supply of wood for pyres. To her surprise, Nyx reapers trickled into the courtyard. One by one they came. They didn't speak to her or each other. Ivy and Freddie worked silently and avoided her. They'd all come back to honor the dead. Vic swallowed repeatedly as the reapers worked together for their fallen comrades. Even though the task was horrific, they showed her the bond she'd cut out. Was that what Landon saw in her? She didn't doubt he was a jerk, but in her mind, she had held herself apart from them.

Once they'd finished building the pyres and placing the shrouded dead, they lit the fires and faced their fallen. Vic hadn't realized there were so many of them. The crushed bodies had made it hard to count, but there were over twenty from what she could tell. The Nyx numbers had dwindled to under forty. They'd already had the fewest members of all the Orders after the battle, and now they barely filled one hall. Not that it mattered since they'd all left.

Vic glanced at the window to Kai's office, and he looked at them, his face blank. When the fires died, they swept the ash into large sacks. The reapers went to gather their belongings. It didn't take them long to pack up their lives in the Order. They left as silently as they'd come, with their packs and scythes strapped to their backs. The brands on their necks held no more meaning than a regretted tattoo.

Vic didn't want to stay in the battle's graveyard, so she walked outside. The sun rose, and the streets remained quiet. Paying no attention to the direction she walked, she recognized the path that led to William. She didn't want to sleep at the empty Order. If she were being honest with herself, she barely slept there anymore. Even though she'd worked most of her life to get into Nyx, she wasn't one of them. Her mind twisted with thoughts that this was her own fault.

"I don't blame Ivy and Freddie," she muttered to herself. They'd done nothing but help her and trust her, but she hadn't returned the favor. If they really wanted to make a difference in Verrin, they'd need to reach out. Tristan already knew their plans, so what was the risk of bringing others in? Who else could fight the mogs GicCorp created? The reapers had deserved their trust, and they'd blown it. As long as they let fear rule their choices, Tristan would win.

She reached Kai's house, and she frowned at the door locked from the outside. Had William already left for work? It was too early yet for him. She unlocked the door and found Samuel alone inside.

"Where's William?"

Samuel smiled at her. "We need to find him."

"Huh?" This was the most Samuel had spoken to her since he'd gotten purified. She'd only heard the same response to William. He'd claimed Samuel seemed off, but Vic didn't know what the radiant did on a normal day so she couldn't judge his behavior as weird. Radiant all felt strange to her.

He got up and took her hand. "He's gone. I need to find him."

"Okay, then. He didn't come home last night?" How would he know what was going on?

"He didn't come home. I need to find him."

Vic tried not to flinch at his constant smile. "I'll help you." Had Tristan caught William? "I hope he hasn't done anything foolish." Something might have happened to him. Worry blossomed inside her. What would happen if they caught him snooping around? They might take away his relic. "We'll check his workplace and see if he's okay."

"I need to find him." Samuel's blue eyes blinked steadily.

"Right." Vic debated taking Samuel. The smiling radiant seemed frustrated. She didn't think she should leave him alone. Could the radiant hurt themselves? "But you need to stay with me, okay?"

"I need to find him."

"I'll take that as a yes. I hope I don't regret this."

She left Kai's house with Samuel, and they hailed a water taxi. Samuel smiled, but Vic didn't know if he was content or not. The eerie thing about the radiant was the constant smiling. It was hard to tell their actual feelings about any situation. He shouldn't cause her any problems —maybe.

The water lapped against the boat, and the comforting musty smell of Verrin wove around her. People chattered in the streets. Even though her world had fallen apart, the rest of the city continued on with life. Would there be any news of all the mogs in Nyx Order, or would it pass by like most of the news nowadays? Would these people get taken from their homes and turned into mogs "for the good of the city," or would they be one of the lucky ones and survive the creation of blight? A person's future was set from the day they were born in this walled city. The daily life of trying to survive kept thoughts away from what GicCorp did. Vic felt the endless frustration build. Keep the people struggling and they'll never have time to look behind the walls. When you went to bed hungry every night, how did you find time to care about anything else?

Vic faced the sky, and the blight swirled a dusky rose color. "It's almost pretty today, isn't it, Samuel?"

Samuel followed her line of sight. "I need to find him."

Vic chewed on her lip. William had mentioned that Samuel didn't act like most radiant. Didn't they forget their attachments? Samuel remembered William and showed concern for him, even though he continued to smile. They weren't supposed to worry, right? Wasn't that the whole attraction? Get rid of your worries by becoming purified.

Now that she and Bomrosy weren't speaking, her one source to look at William's relic had disappeared. The water taxi came to a halt, and they got out, stepping on the slick stone steps. Algae crept up the sides.

"Strange that so close to the nice part of town it isn't maintained." Vic stepped onto the street.

"A lot is falling that way, miss," the water taxi driver answered her. "Not enough imbs to keep up with the repairs of the city." He nodded and pulled into the dock to wait for another customer.

Or GicCorp turned them into mogs.

They walked to GicCorp. Unlike Nyx, with its streets getting emptier by the day, near the factory and shops, people crowded around them. Some, once seeing the smiling Samuel, balked and stepped out of their way. Even though he didn't wear white, his blank features gave him away. Maybe if people cared less about radiant smiles and more about the missing people, they would have more people to fight GicCorp. Bitterness didn't look good on her, and how would they know about GicCorp unless someone told them?

The massive factory loomed ahead, and she stared blankly at all the doorways. "I don't know where he was assigned."

Since she was never assigned to patrol the center of the city, Vic didn't come to the heart of Verrin often. A loud bell clanged, and workers dressed in jumpsuits of various colors emerged from the building. It might be lunch. Vic had a hard time keeping track of time. It's not like she got out much to do anything but hunt mogs. If she ever got more free time, she would sleep.

Samuel stepped in front of her and walked with purpose to a door with a large C above it.

"Here?" No one had told her about radiant radar.

"I need to find him."

Vic shrugged and went in the door. A sizable woman barked orders from the center of the courtyard. A jumpsuit clung to her thick frame, and although loud, she wasn't harsh. When Samuel tried to go to a door in the back, Vic pulled him back. "Wait a second. We can't go where we want."

Samuel smiled, but the corner of his eye twitched. Vic tilted her head. Was the Samuel she used to know still in there? If the soul got purified, as they claimed, it must stay in the body. He took in more than others thought.

"Sorry, but they'll stop you before you make any progress. We should ask about William for now, and if we need to, we can break in later," she whispered.

That strangely seemed to calm him down.

The large woman faced them. She finished talking and strode over to the odd pair. The jumpsuit made a loud swishing sound as she walked.

"Never thought I'd get a visit from a reaper and a radiant. Are you lost?" Her thick brows furrowed, and her topaz eyes said little surprised her anymore.

"I guess you could say that. I'm looking for my friend William."

"William? Oh, you mean bait?"

"Sure?" One day and he already had an affectionate nickname. Vic couldn't even open up to the other reapers. This woman must barge in and force a connection.

The woman frowned and pulled Vic aside. "I thought he didn't have a place to stay."

Vic thought she should play along. "They kicked him out of his home, but I didn't see him this morning and worried something might've happened."

"I let him stay here last night, but this morning, he was gone. The door was still locked on the inside."

Vic glanced around the courtyard filling with people in unflattering red jumpsuits. "What exactly do you do?"

"We repair the lines into Haven from the sewer." The woman crossed her arms and squinted at the pair. "If you see him, let him know I'm looking for him." Then she left.

It's not like she'd given anything away besides basic knowledge that Vic could have found out with a bit of digging. She walked to the door, but Samuel didn't follow. She ended up having to pull him behind her. "Samuel, we can't go down there."

"I need to find him."

Vic let go of him. "I know, but they'll stop you, and you'll probably get arrested. We need to wait until nightfall." She didn't say that walls cut the sewers off from the rest of the system near Haven. Inside might be the only way in or out. They might have lost William down there, or maybe he'd gotten caught.

"We may need help." Vic stared at the wall surrounding GicCorp. Officers patrolled the wall night and day. They would need to scale it or break in through the door. William might have found something connected to Haven.

"Let's come back later, okay?" There would be fewer people to spot her at night, even though she wouldn't have backup. Samuel would need to stay home, and she doubted he would like that.

Samuel said nothing, and Vic found that more unnerving than his repeated phrase. She didn't talk to him as they took a water taxi back to Nyx. She might as well talk to Kai. Samuel followed her, but she couldn't help glancing at him to make sure he hadn't run off.

They walked through the ashy courtyard, the bags of ash now gone. The floors smelled of cleaner, the spatters of dried blood gone. She went to Kai's office. She knocked and heard a soft, "Come in."

She opened the door, and Kai sat in his chair, facing the window. "Kai?"

He turned the chair, his eyes bloodshot and face drawn. "I thought you'd left with the others." He turned back to the window.

"No, I went to check on William."

"I guess he's more important."

Vic held back the words she wanted to say. "No, I only wanted to make sure he was okay. Is that a problem?"

"No."

Vic walked to the window and stood in front of Kai. "I'm here to help."

"Help with what? There isn't anything left to help with."

Vic growled, "I'm not here to fight with you. This isn't over yet. If you could get your head out of your ass, we could use your help."

He turned to face Vic. "I'm so tired, Sparks."

It hurt her to see him so defeated. The confident Kai had disappeared when he'd become the commander. Vic wrapped him in a hug. "Me too."

He relaxed in her arms, and they stayed that way for a while. When they finally broke apart, Kai started as he saw Samuel in the room. "Why is he here?"

"William went missing after his first day on the job. Samuel is worried about him."

"I guess we need to go find William?"

"Yeah."

Kai stared out the window at the empty courtyard. "I messed everything up."

Vic gripped his shoulder. "No, you did what you thought was best."

"So did Xiona."

The mogs' attack on the Order had provided Landon with the chance to find Xiona. Bomrosy claimed no one else could use her tech, but the doors had opened on their own. "Do you know why the latches and hinges opened?"

Kai shook his head. "When it happened, Bomrosy ran up here to inform me. Something messed with her transmission. She didn't have time to figure it out before we heard the mogs coming. We assumed she was the only person who understood tech and didn't rely on magic."

Vic paced the room. "You don't think GicCorp did something?"

Kai got out of his chair and put on his harness with his scythe. "Tristan knew about the tunnel. I don't think any of our reapers would know how to mess with Bomrosy's system. I didn't trust them enough, and they left. I don't want to think any of them would have loosed mogs on their own Order."

Vic snapped her fingers. "Oh, and the pile of bones outside the sewer. Only GicCorp has that kind of access."

"Sadly, I don't think Tristan will tell us anything."

"I can do my best." The smooth voice sounded from the door. Tristan, in a freshly pressed suit, strode in like he owned the Order.

Kai reached for his scythe but didn't flick it open. "Make yourself at home."

Tristan's eyes gleamed. "I don't think you can say that anymore, *commander*." He folded his hands together behind his back. "I have never seen an Order fall so far or so fast. I commend you for your record-breaking efforts to destroy something."

"Did you come here to gloat? We have other things to do." She kept him in her sight but moved so Kai's desk stayed between them.

"If it were only that simple, but you see, my dear, your commander broke the law even after I'd taken the time to warn him." Tristan tapped his foot. "Do you think I gave that warning lightly or didn't mean it? The officers of Verrin are behind me. For the safety of Verrin, it is forbidden to mess with the grates leading out of the sewer. The mass of mogs you baited and brought in could have killed many more people than your reapers." Tristan shook his head in false sadness. "Those poor families of the reapers who died. I went in your stead to comfort them and tell them of the loss."

Kai's hands formed into fists. "You had no right to talk to the families. They needed to hear it from me."

"Why? So you could spin more tales?" Tristan rested his hand near his wand. "I gave them a generous compensation for their loss and told them you wouldn't put any more lives at risk."

"More like bribed them. It isn't your duty to fire commanders. You don't have power over the Orders." Vic stepped in closer in case she needed to help Kai.

"You'd like to think that, but no one is above the law." The cheerful note in his voice grated on her nerves.

They heard shouts and footsteps on the stone floor leading up to the office.

"I'm not the one relieving him of his command."

The officers burst into the room and crowded into Kai's office.

Vic's throat dried. "Wow, do they really need twenty people to take one person in?"

"I told them there might be some resistance." Tristan stayed back and calmly watched the scene as though he were viewing a boring play unfold.

Kai stiffened, and Vic noticed the hand that held his scythe tremble. He would lose his scythe, leaving his family relicless.

Vic placed her hand on his shoulder. "I'll return this to Freddie. He was looking for it." She gently pried it out of his hand. "His relic broke in the fight," Vic explained to the room, pretending they would care about her story.

Tristan chuckled, but he said nothing. The officers ignored her and moved in on Kai. He released the relic to her and didn't resist as they cuffed him.

Kai said nothing as they took him out, but he glanced over his shoulder, his face downcast.

"I'll take care of this," Vic called after him.

A stocky officer held out his hand to her. With triple bags under his eyes, he eyed the relic. "I need his relic."

"This isn't his. The gem broke in his last night. This is Freddie's. He got his fixed, unlike Kai. He was returning it to him." As the words poured out of her mouth, she confused even herself. Couldn't she come up with a better lie? She'd had better excuses when sneaking out of the house as a teenager.

The officer rubbed his shaved head. "That's a nice story. Turn it in to us and we can trace the scythe to Freddie's family."

"But this is Freddie's."

"So you say. We can return it to Freddie once we prove it isn't the commander's." Even though the officer looked ready to fall asleep, he still pushed on with his duty.

Tristan placed an arm around Vic, and she shook it off. "She's telling the truth, officer. There is a shattered scythe down on the first floor that belongs to the commander. Their repair person was trying to fix it, so there is nothing to confiscate."

The officer looked between them, and Vic thought he might go against Tristan. "Whatever. I don't get paid enough to butt heads with founders." He followed the other officers down.

Vic paced back from Tristan. "You can leave too." Tristan reached for the scythe, and Vic looked down at his proffered hand. "Can I help you?"

"The relic."

Vic grinned and pulled out her scythe with her other hand. With a smooth motion, she flicked it open. The sound echoed in the office. "Come and get it." *Let him give me an excuse to fight him.* She got ready to dodge his strange magic.

Tristan reached for his wand, then dropped his hand. "I'll let you win this one. I have a feeling you'll need it."

Vic held the relic between them. "Don't get all cryptic now."

He calmly walked to the door. "If I were you, I'd make sure everything of value was out of the Order by nightfall." His footsteps grew distant until she was alone once more.

Vic leaned on her scythe for support. "Samuel, he won't lock up the building, will he?" She turned to face the brother, but he wasn't there anymore. In all the confusion, he'd vanished.

"Samuel?" Vic yelled and ran down the hall. "Samuel!

Sam!" She burst into all the rooms, but there was no sign of him. "Blight take me, did he go back to GicCorp?" She let out a frustrated scream that had no response in the empty halls. Couldn't one thing go right? Now she had to hunt down the radiant when she should have been getting Kai out of jail.

Vic sprinted out into the streets since Samuel didn't have money for a water taxi. After hours of searching the alleys between GicCorp and Nyx, Vic needed a break. She would stop by Nyx one more time and then check Kai's house again. Maybe Samuel would return there. It might be time to check the jails. If he'd tried to walk into GicCorp without stopping, he might have gotten arrested. What if they returned him to his parents? Vic grimaced. She didn't think any harm would come to him there, but William had been firm in keeping their parents away from Samuel. If they hurt him, it would be her fault.

Her body heavy, she returned to Nyx. She didn't know what Tristan had meant when he'd told her she should have everything out. She went up the stairs to her room and took out her pack from her room closet.

It only took moments for her to pack up her black clothing. Then she gently placed Scraps on top, and he purred as she scratched his ears. Vic went to Kai's room and gathered his items. With two packs and two scythes, she went down to the courtyard.

An ache formed in her chest as the empty building faced her. The windows, once bright with light, were now dead and empty. No shouting reapers in the halls or training in the yard. The friendly smell of food had given way to the fading scents of blood and the rot of mogs. The reapers had been the beating hearts of the Order, and due to a series of terrible choices, they'd been broken one by one. Vic gripped the packs and turned her back on the tragic sight.

"It's not over yet, Tristan. You can't take us down completely." She walked out of the iron gate and left the building she'd yearned to call home behind.

15

VIC

Vic stepped into the dreary house. In her heart, she knew Samuel wouldn't be waiting for her. Scraps jumped out of the pack as she set it down. He rubbed against her legs, and she went to the kitchen to find him something to eat.

"Scraps for Scraps." She placed a bowl out for him and sat down on the sofa. When was the last time she'd slept or eaten? She fought against sleep. There was too much to do.

Scraps jumped in her lap, and she stroked his fur. "I need to see Father about Kai, then wander the streets looking for the prodigal brother." Why hadn't she kept a better eye on him? She should have returned him to the house before going to see Kai. It was almost like Samuel had William radar, and now that she'd lost Samuel, she didn't know if she could find William. "Ugh, these brothers will be the death of me."

Vic didn't want to take time to sleep, not while there was daylight to look for her friends. "This has been the longest day ever."

She didn't know who she talked to, but with the loss of Bomrosy, William, Kai, and now Samuel, loneliness crept up on her. She had to make do with keeping herself company.

"It'll work out. I'll get Father to help with Kai, then I'll get Maddox to help me in the sewers." If Mads helped her move stone, she could break into the sewers that led to where William might have gotten lost or taken. She hoped for lost. At least then he might be safe from mogs. She didn't need to waste any more time waiting. If they could cut through the stone, they might find out more information, even though there might be a hundred masked people waiting for her. She could teach Mads her escape method of jumping into sewage. There was no chance that would go wrong.

She found coffee grounds in the kitchen and brewed it as dark as she could. She gagged down the bitter liquid and left Scraps in charge of Kai's house. The caffeine burned through her, making her jittery as she walked to her childhood home.

The glass home glowed in the light as it always did. It cast rainbows across the courtyard as the sunlight gleamed through. Vic leaped up the steps and went straight to her father's office. He sat back, making small figurines of glass at his desk with a contemplative look on his face. When he noticed her, he waved for her to sit down.

Vic paused at the warm welcome. She still wasn't used to working with her father. Their relationship still carried scars from last year, and she still saw him in a different light. As much as she wanted to get over it, the nagging feeling remained that he was playing a different game.

"I was about to come see you and Kai. I have good news." He placed his sand to the side of the desk.

"Em?"

Her father shook his head. "Not that good, I guess, but more and more founders are coming to our side." He leaned back in the chair, and it creaked with the movement. "They're moved more by greed than the vital story, but we can work with what we have. Clear lines are being drawn amongst us, and it looks like we may have the numbers to vote out the Nordic family."

Vic leaned against the armchair. "That was quick." After all the deaths, they could just vote the problem away? Would another greedy founder take the Nordics' place?

Her father rubbed the wrinkles on the sides of his face. "Not really. I've been working on this since before Emilia left us. The Nordics are making bolder moves, and that's what's drawing the other founders to our side. They're slipping." He stretched. "Sadly, at the cost of your Order. It upset many founders that they're pooling their power in a place where founders don't belong. Tristan is upsetting many traditionalists. Also, Ethan is making friends with the radiant leader, which is also good for us. Most founders don't care for radiant."

Vic sat on the arm of the chair and placed her feet on the seat. "I guess you already know that Kai has been arrested?"

He came around his desk and tapped Vic's knees to move her feet back to the floor. "I'm working on that. There's a firm case against him."

Vic couldn't help but be impressed by her father's network. Only moments before, she'd felt alone in this fight, but she'd forgotten about the ones who worked behind the scenes of the battle.

"I've lost contact with Maddox Stone, however, but she's

been more your contact." Her father pulled out a pouch of sand from his inner suit pocket and began to form small glass beads. Vic eyed the glass and knew this helped her father concentrate.

"I wish I would have known how much you'd accomplished. That would've made Mads feel better about joining our side."

He let the handful of glass meld into one large mass. Vic thought she could see a face. "We can make no promises. The danger of this game is that the founders can be fickle. They may say they'll vote out the Nordics, but we'll never know until the vote happens."

Vic didn't tell him she'd promised to help get Maddox out of Haven. "I know. I'll check on her now, though. I wanted to stop by and ask for help with Kai." She pushed herself to her feet and inspected what her dad had made. Before she could figure it out, he let it fall out of shape.

"Their case hinges on bones and the grate. They don't have any proof that Kai brought the bones, and the latch on the grate is different from the others they found. I think there's a chance he will get out." He set the lump of misshapen glass on the desk next to his other creations.

Vic drooped. "I'll take any chance."

"When did you last sleep?"

Vic waved him off. "I'll sleep after I go see Maddox." He opened his mouth to speak, but Vic cut him off. "I need to see her tonight." She'd already waited too long, and on the way, she could look for Samuel. Maybe she would need to warn people before they got near her since everyone around her disappeared.

Her father rubbed his jaw. "You look like the walking

dead. You'll be no help to others if you collapse on the street."

"I know, I know." Vic turned to leave but paused at the door. "Thanks, Dad, for doing all this. I understand how dangerous this is. Please look out for yourself." Another time, when her brain worked, she would talk about what a change in leadership would mean for all those who weren't Verrin founders. She had a list of missing people and needed to check off the other two before she could pry into her father's mind.

"I am." He traced the rim of an empty glass. Vic worried he drank too much these days.

They both let unspoken words pass between them. They would go down fighting if they had to. "We'll find her." She believed he wanted Em back, and that kept her going.

"I know."

Vic left his office feeling lighter. The power of the founders gave her more confidence. The problem of who would be in charge next could be left for later. Losing Nyx hurt, but if it caused Tristan to mess up, she could handle it. She couldn't tell who was winning, but it seemed like either side was one move away from causing the downfall of the other. GicCorp hadn't yet shown its hand to the city. She feared that when they did, it would be too late to stop them.

Vic got in a water taxi, and it rocked her to sleep while she rode it across the wide city to Maddox's house. The driver nudged her awake, and she stumbled out of the taxi and wiped the sleep from her eyes. The cool evening air helped wake her up. After she got Mads and they found Samuel, she promised she would sleep.

The Stone house sprawled over acres of land that Verrin couldn't spare. Since they'd built most of Verrin with stone, they were second in power to the Nordics. Vic had a feeling the Stones had sided with GicCorp. They benefited too much from them and vice versa. Unless they wanted to be in charge, there was nothing the founders could offer them that would be more attractive than what they had now.

Vic rang the bell, and after a moment, the stone gate slid to the side. The extensive building rose from behind the gate. Where her house was filled with light, the stone house basked in darkness. The gray walls made Vic feel small. No fountains or statues graced the courtyard. The blank void of stone sucked in all the darkness.

Maddox had hated going home after school, and Vic could see why. The bleakness of the house was overwhelming. Even though she couldn't see anyone, she felt eyes on her as she walked to the front door. The Stones employed security for their home. She didn't know any fool who would attack them, but maybe they were the smartest of them all. They might know the Nordics better than anyone and had thought ahead to protect themselves.

The door opened as she approached, and Vic nodded to the butler as she entered.

"Mr. Stone is expecting you."

"He is?" Vic could count on one hand the meaningful interactions she'd had with the man—the interesting drunk at a party and the standoffish father to her friend. She had to admit she'd enjoyed him always causing a scene at the boring events, even though he was a jerk to his daughters. Maddox didn't have the desire to hurt her sister. Vic assumed that might be how she'd "lost" becoming the heir.

The butler led her through the cold stone hallways. Barely any light from the outside came in, only the flickering magic behind the glass lamps. A thick carpet dulled their footsteps, and he directed her to an office. Different stones could have been used, but only bleak gray graced the halls. The feeling of being buried alive in the house overwhelmed her. She breathed better in the sewers. Stone could stand to put in some windows to let in a breeze.

They came to another stone panel that blended in with the wall. It swung open to reveal Mr. Stone's office.

He sat at an enormous marble desk molded into the floor. It would seem strange to have something placed with such permanence, but with his skill, he could move the desk at a whim.

Many said his imbuing with stone had yet to be matched. He cut through it like soft cheese and barely used any of his relic's power. In his office, another thick carpet lay on the floor, but the entire room only had the desk and his chair. The wide chair fit his vast frame and was likely molded for comfort. Sitting on stone couldn't be that comfortable. From the lack of other furniture, Vic guessed he wanted others to stand. She admitted the walls, with unique types of stone molded together to create vibrant swirls, impressed her. So he appreciated colors other than gray.

"You came to see Maddox, but she isn't here." His wide face didn't look up from his desk. He could have used his head as another block in the walls of his fortress since it was square enough. His face was flushed red, even though the room felt like an icebox, so he might be running hot or enjoying drinks while he worked. He finished counting what looked like credits figures and put them in a stone box, which he sealed with magic. "She said you would stop by, and I waited for you like a messenger boy. I will meet her at your famous Order."

"Why?"

He waved his flabby hand. "Something to do with tunnels. I agreed to help."

Vic cleared her throat. "You agreed to help Nyx?" That didn't seem right. Her father had mentioned nothing about Maddox's father being involved. He hadn't exactly told her which founders were involved, but if Stone had joined their side, he probably would have mentioned it. His eyes shifted rapidly. He must be lying.

He pushed his thick frame up and tucked his wand in his holster. "She wanted one favor before her ceremony." Vic doubted he would dote on Maddox, even if she'd asked for a last meal.

"Why didn't she wait for me here?" Vic's fingers itched to grab her scythe. Had she walked into a large stone jail? Did Stone know about the masked figures that had chased her in the sewers?

His beady eyes glared at her from under bushy eyebrows. "You can come with me or not. I'm doing you a favor, and I don't have time to deal with you."

Stone threw on a jacket and brusquely walked to the doorway. The stench of stale alcohol followed him as he brushed by her. Vic jolted after him. Even though she didn't trust him, she wanted to get out of this house. It felt like a giant jail cell. With the constant running from danger in the sewers, she hadn't thought about the danger above ground.

He trudged ahead, and after they'd gone out the door and through the gate, Vic breathed normally. They went to a water taxi. The boat teetered from his weight when he stepped inside. Vic went to the one beside his.

"What's wrong, girl? There's room for you."

"I think I'll go home since Maddox is gone."

Stone tapped his side. "I'm not one for subterfuge."

"Obviously." He should have known that Vic knew he would do nothing to help Maddox. Even tired, her brain still worked that well, at least. If they'd trapped Maddox in the house, Vic didn't know how she would go about getting her out.

"There is something you need to see." He rested his hands on his large stomach and relaxed back in the boat. The driver waited, glancing between the two founders.

A sheen of sweat appeared on her forehead. "Is Maddox okay?"

"Let me show you the thing first, then we can talk about my daughter." He shifted, making the water taxi rock.

She could run away now that she'd escaped the stone walls of his house. "Fine."

It might be something she needed to see. She worried about Maddox.

On the way, she tried to think of ways to break Maddox out of her own home. Each idea seemed more impossible than the next. Maybe Maddox could stay at the Glass house. Maddox worried about losing her wand, but that might be the price she needed to pay to stay out of Haven.

At their stop, the taxi bucked as Stone got out. Vic followed him at a distance. She monitored the alleyways. If the masked figures were around, she'd need to run. She had yet to see them outside of the sewers, so she felt a tad safer. If she couldn't find Maddox, she would have to locate William some other way.

They approached the abandoned Order, and Vic's heart hurt to see it so empty. Soon, it would be teeming with life again. The reapers, maybe besides Landon, were good people. They would forgive Kai and come back. They might not want to fight GicCorp, but they wouldn't turn people into mogs. Vic held on to her uplifting message. She could believe it if she had to. She had to believe in something.

Stone paused at the Order. He said nothing, staring at the building. The surrounding stench grew stronger now that they'd stopped moving. Didn't the man ever shower? "Credits matter these days. There's little that happens without credits to back it up."

Was he talking to himself? "Okay, then. Are you giving me a loan?" She tapped her foot on the cobbled ground outside the Order.

Stone grumbled, "Some may think I have little power since I do what others tell me." His face reddened. "I could buy out every factory if I wanted. I could buy out GicCorp."

"Why are you telling me this? I get it, you're rich." He could buy them out, but he couldn't run them all. He would still need the other wands to imbue materials.

He rubbed his pudgy jaw. "I don't know. I never liked you."

"Fine, I'll go." He'd dragged her all this way to tell her that? Where was Maddox? He was a waste of time.

Stone grabbed her arm and squeezed. "He wants you to know there's no going back."

Vic jerked her arm away, and it smarted where he'd gripped her. "Why come all this way to say this? He shut it down. I get it." She stepped away from him and pulled out her scythe. She didn't like him touching her. He was fast with magic, but she would cut off his hand if he grabbed her again.

Stone's lips parted, then the air felt heavy. The light breeze stopped, and the crisp scent of rock surrounded them. Stone placed his wand on the wall of the Order. Vic thought he would seal up the gate with stone, but then the wall sank into the ground in a blink. One moment it had stood strong, and the next it had disappeared.

"No," she whispered. She pushed at Stone, but it didn't matter. The large, proud building of Nyx had sunk into the ground. Only a large patch of cobbles remained.

"Why?" She'd become a witness to the rumors of his power. She had never seen anyone imbue that much in one go. When Tristan had told her to leave, this was what he'd wanted. Stone's gem didn't gleam, but he shouldn't have been able to level an entire building. That was impossible.

Stone put away his wand. "I think he likes to make a show. It hurt, didn't it?" His jowls grinned at her, showing small teeth.

Vic swallowed. Even though she'd recently found her way into the Order, the empty space felt wrong. When the other reapers saw this, their hearts would break. Bomrosy had found a place and acceptance here without a relic. Kai had lived here, and the Order had helped support his family. For many, it had meant safety from Verrin, if only in the form of a hot meal. She tried to tell herself it was only a building, but in Verrin, walls kept you safe, and now there was nothing.

"Destroying the building won't destroy me." Vic squared her shoulders at Stone.

He knew it still influenced her. "Fine. I'm the messenger today." He whistled. "I even impressed myself with this."

"Glad you're happy." Vic turned away from him.

His annoying voice called after her, "Don't you want to know where Maddox is?"

Vic really didn't want to know. This man had nothing good to offer her. She faced him once more.

Stone's jowls wobbled. "Tristan generously offered to

take her to Haven early. I'm thankful for the honor I can give to the city. We sent her off this morning." He tapped his pudgy belly while delivering the final blow.

Vic's body grew limp as she tried to accept the reality of his words. She wanted to scream at him that he was lying. She flicked open her scythe, and the smugness on his face vanished.

He backed away. He'd probably thought she wouldn't react this way in daylight.

Vic lunged forward before he could move for his wand. Fat meant slow, no matter how much magic the man had. She pressed the blade under his double chin.

"Try to lower your arms and we'll see who is faster. You used up your magic, didn't you?" Her voice came out flat.

The confidence in his stance vanished. When he tried to move, she pressed harder. A cut formed, and he stopped moving. He whimpered.

"Do you think this is some cute little joke to me? You bring me here and destroy my home and then tell me my friend is gone?"

Stone didn't talk, but he shook his head almost imperceptibly so he wouldn't cut himself on the blade.

Vic leaned in and grinned. "Where are your guards to protect you?" A bit of madness overcame her. She could slice his neck and might not even care. Then the smell of urine came from him. Vic sneered. "Next time Tristan wants you to play messenger, I'd decline." She stepped back, and in a flash, she flicked the tip of her scythe across his flabby cheek.

He cried out, and his hand smashed over the wound.

"A reminder. Now you should run."

He waddled away and glanced back to see if she

followed. When he turned the corner, Vic sank to the ground. "I'm sorry, Mads."

The heavy burden settled on her shoulders. Even though it grew dark, she didn't move.

"I need to gather my thoughts, then I can leave."

But her mind raced, and her body remained limp. Night fell.

16

WILLIAM

William shifted in the hard wooden chair, but his arms stayed tightly tied to his sides. He blinked, wishing he'd fallen into a dream and this wasn't his reality. In his foggy mind, he remembered seeing masked figures, then trying to get out of the doorway. Even though it smelled of wet dirt, the floors were stone. The room was made from the same black stone as the Haven sewers. He was the only thing in this room and couldn't see any doors. Small pockets in the ceiling let in the stagnant air. At least they let him breathe. There was no breeze to speak of, and moisture clung to his skin and clothing. William had heard of steam rooms, which those with money sat in for pleasure. If it felt anything like this humid box, he didn't see the appeal. If the rich wanted to feel sticky, it was their money to waste.

His fingers couldn't reach the rope binding his arms. Even if he untied himself, he didn't think he could fit through the small vents. He would need a wand to get out of this room, and his captors wouldn't be handing those out.

The passage of time meant nothing as he nodded off. His head jerked when he almost reached sleep. He ached from who knew how many hours he'd stayed knocked out and tied to the chair. Sam would be okay, and he hoped Vic would check in on him. She would be the first to notice he was gone, but on her list of people to rescue, his name would be at the bottom.

A loud scrape got his attention, and dust rose from the ground, making him choke as it billowed out. As though it had formed from nothing, a door opened in the wall. In the room's bleak light, he thought it had formed from magic. When the door opened, he realized it fit perfectly in the wall. Small latches covered the ridge, almost invisible to the naked eye.

Two people dressed in black appeared, with only their eyes showing from behind their masks and hoods. They stared at each other. The hall behind them was only a tad brighter than his cell, but it still made him squint from the change in light.

"This the special one?" The man's tenor voice came out muffled from behind the mask. William couldn't tell what color his eyes were since the hall light cast the two men in shadow.

"Yeah, they ordered us not to change this one." His voice sounded gravelly, like he enjoyed smoking in his spare time. He stood taller than Tenor.

Smoker and Tenor untied him but held him firmly in their grips and then retied his arms and hands behind his back. The whiff of smoke coming off the one man confirmed William's theory.

"Do we need the wand?" Smoker asked.

"Grab it, just in case. They probably want us to hand it off to them."

William shifted, and their grips tightened. "What's going on?" After hours of monotony in a closed room, he had grown more nervous about being taken outside it. They could be taking him somewhere to kill him for all he knew.

Tenor snorted. "Look, this one wants to know what's going on."

"Just like everyone else, the special one."

William cleared this throat. "If you're going to kill me, there's no harm in telling me."

They exchanged a look, then burst into laughter. "That's new."

They yanked him out of the stone room and down a hall that matched the sewers.

"Where are we?" One long tunnel stretched in front of him. If he escaped, he could run forward or backward. Not many options. His wand was tucked away in Smoker's harness. To have a better chance, he could try to grab it. The stone glowed, showing him it had recharged.

"Hush and let us deliver you." Smoker shook him.

"Yes, be a good package."

William gritted his teeth. How long had he stayed in the room? Would Vic worry about him? Would Sam notice that he hadn't come home? How would anyone find him? He could try to trip Tenor and use his body weight to get out of Smoker's grip.

On their way through the tunnel, they met more masked figures. With more people appearing, his plan to lose his two captors got more difficult. He didn't think he could take on two men, let alone four or more. William peered at their eyes.

If he got out of here, he might recognize them. He noticed that the people who escorted him would nod to some but not others. Squinting in the dim light, he noticed that those they didn't acknowledge had dull eyes in the light. He bit back a gasp. Those were radiant eyes. What were the radiant doing down here? He hoped he was mistaken. It had to be the lighting. He could barely see eye color, so how could he confirm anything? Were the masked people using the radiant to gather people to turn into mogs? Boiling anger coursed through him. The purpose of the radiant was to live and work together in uncorrupted peace. Using them like this made them no better than slaves and polluted what the radiant believed.

He'd left when he'd seen the corruption his father had started, not wanting to be part of it. He already had to deal with the guilt of forcing the change on his brother. Had these people chosen this? When they picked the radiant path, they knew what awaited them. This felt like an abuse of their bodies and souls. A sick feeling grew in him the farther they went down the tunnels.

Sam had told him once that maybe neither side, magic or radiant, had the right answer. "Then what's left, Sam?" William had whispered. Was there a third option?

"What are you muttering?"

"Leave him. We're almost there."

They came to an open room that contained piles of junk. Twisted metal formed broken statues, and stones littered the floor. A horrible smell grew stronger, and William knew they must be close to raw sewage. A burble confirmed that flowing water was nearby.

"This is where they want him?" Smoker asked.

Tenor guided them to a large scrap of metal sticking out

of the ground. "Tie him up. We're behind on our quota from dealing with this one."

They tied him to a metal pole.

"Should we leave it here for them to pick up?" Smoker pulled out the wand.

Tenor glanced across the room, and William couldn't see what he looked at. "They aren't here yet. We can't wait all night. Is he secure?" They placed his wand far out of his reach. It stayed within William's sight. They glanced between William and the wand.

"They'll get mad if we take it back. I'd rather avoid their misplaced anger."

They walked to a wall and opened another invisible door.

"Hey, what's going on?" William's voice echoed in the room of discarded ruins.

They ignored him and shut the door behind them.

William shifted against the rope, hoping for some give in the material. His gaze darted around the piles of junk. Tied like this, he felt like a sacrifice to some animal. He shivered and bent his knees, trying to rub the rope against the metal bar.

Would they go through all that trouble to feed him to something? He tried to convince himself that it would be troublesome for them to do this, even though they'd only relocated him and tied him up.

"If they wanted to kill me, they could have done it in the cells." That sounded convincing. The chilly air hit his sweaty forehead, and he rubbed the rope up and down the pole to wear it down before the next person or thing came for him.

The sound of water bubbled in the gigantic room, along with him sawing at his bindings. He couldn't see a river, but maybe if he got out, he could follow the water out of here. He hadn't adapted to the smell, and it only got harder to breathe. It might be the only way out.

"If Vic can take a sewage bath, so can I." He wanted to vomit thinking about it. He didn't know how much time had passed, but he stopped sawing and leaned against the metal pole, breathing deeply. There was no way to even see if he'd made any progress.

No joy overcame him when voices sounded over the rush of water. Then one voice he recognized rose above the others. His father's.

"Thank you for finding him. We've been looking for him for a few weeks, and I was getting worried."

Another voice replied, but William couldn't make out the words.

His father replied, "No, he will stay with us. My wife was worried about something, and I need to look into it."

Around the corner, his father appeared, followed by a masked figure and Sam.

"Sam?" William jerked forward, but the rope held him back. "What are you doing down here?"

His father's face tightened. "Someone found him wandering in the streets. It looks like you didn't do a very good job of taking care of your brother. You abandoned him the first chance you got."

William pulled against the rope. Scrapes formed on his skin and burned at his weight. "I didn't abandon him. Sam, are you okay?"

Sam didn't answer.

William's father turned to the masked man. "I'll take care of this quickly and join you. I'll grab the wand."

The man glanced between the family members. He paused, then he nodded and left them.

Their father let out a long breath, stepped up to William, and slapped him across his face.

William's head jerked to the side and hit the metal pole. A ringing sound buzzed in his ears, and he tried to orientate himself again.

"My disappointing son. You were supposed to be in charge of all this, but the false promise of magic has warped your mind." White patches appeared on his father's face from where he clenched his jaw.

The copper taste of blood ran over his mouth, and he realized he'd bitten his tongue. He spat at his father, splattering red on his white uniform. That earned him another slap, and his head banged against the metal pole again.

William took a rattling breath, then laughed, causing blood to dribble out of his mouth and onto his clothing. "All this? In charge of the sewer? Are you the shit king?"

Two more slaps and William felt his left eye swelling.

His father's face reddened. "You have no clue who holds the power in this corrupted city." His father snarled. "I did everything for you ungrateful sons, and now there's no one to leave my legacy to."

"Your legacy of forcing people into the radiant life? You made a mockery of people's beliefs in something better." The ropes cut into him, and he lunged at his father. His head throbbed as he shouted, "I believed! I believed you had honor. I chose that belief over my brother. You betrayed me and him." His throat ached, and his voice bounced off the stone walls. "We don't want your legacy. Leave us alone. You're not my father anymore. I will live the rest of my life trying to make up my mistake to my brother." His heart ached as he looked at the man he'd once called father. When had it become like this? Magic and power corrupted. How could this man not see what he had become? William stared at his father and saw the fervor in his stance. There would be no reaching him. He remained steadfast in his beliefs.

His father's mouth thinned. "Well, that won't be very long."

"You're going to kill me?"

His father held out his hand. "No. I will save you."

William stopped pulling against his bindings and pressed back into the metal pole. "You aren't serious? You're going to force purification on me? Can't you let me leave?" He shouldn't have been surprised. After all, that's what his father had demanded of Sam. Why did he still look for hope in this man?

His father twisted the ring around his finger, and it flickered slightly. "I can't let my son become what I hate. It saddens me that you don't get a choice."

A panicked gasp left William, and his father's hand drew closer to his forehead. The ring glowed as it rested on his head.

William didn't turn his face away. His father blocked his view of Sam.

What color is the sky, Brother?

William's vision blurred. The ring warmed. Something stretched into William, and instead of pulling, something tightened around his mind.

I'm sorry I failed you.

William closed his eyes and accepted his fate. A loud crack made his eyelids shoot open. Sam stood before him, holding a long metal rod smeared with their father's blood.

It took William a moment to realize what had happened.

"Sam?" He leaned his face toward his brother. "Samuel, was that you?"

His father moaned, and Sam took another whack at his head. William flinched.

"Let's not kill him."

"Do what you must."

His father didn't make another noise, but William saw his chest rise and fall. Let the bastard stay down here by himself. "Can you untie me?"

Sam stepped behind him and quickly got the ropes off. William bent his fingers and flinched as blood flowed back into his arms. He grabbed the wand from where Smoker and Tenor had left it.

He pulled his brother into a hug. "Thank you."

Sam's arms stayed at his sides.

William stepped back. "That was very un-radiant of you." He didn't want to stay down here any longer. "I don't suppose you know the way out?"

Sam walked into the pile of junk and stopped at the edge of the sewage water.

William covered his nose and took a shaky breath. "So do you have the boat you arrived on?"

Sam didn't answer.

William glanced down the dark tunnel. A tiny ledge hung over the river. "We better get moving."

The brothers placed their feet on the small ledge. William's mind raced with questions his brother couldn't answer.

Wᴵᴸᴸᴵᴬᴹ ꜱᴸᴵᴘᴘᴇᴅ ᴏɴ ᴛʜᴇ ᴸᴇᴅɢᴇ ᴬɴᴅ ᴬᴸᴹᴏꜱᴛ ꜰᴇᴸᴸ ᴵɴᴛᴏ ᴛʜᴇ murky water. He swore his heart stopped. Sam remained calm behind him, and the tiny ledge didn't seem like a problem for him.

"How are you managing this?" William asked his brother.

He only smiled.

"It's not like I'll die if I fall in." He took a deep breath of putrid air and gagged. "I'll never be clean again." No amount of showers would undo the sewage bath if he fell in. He admitted there were more important things than staying clean, but he almost didn't mind the distraction from his father's plots.

"Should we have …" He couldn't say the words. "Let him go?" He'd left his father, knowing he purified others. Was it his responsibility to stop him? Could he stop him? Maybe they could turn him in to the officers and call it good.

"I might as well go in the cell next to him." William inched along. If he turned in his father, his father wouldn't hesitate to turn him in too. The thought of going to jail for what he'd done to Sam didn't bother him as much as he'd thought. It was only right. While with Vic, they'd operated more in shades of gray, but he could admit he found more comfort in the black and white. Slowly, his stance had crumbled the more he'd seen his father for who he really was, but that didn't change the fact that forcing purification on someone was wrong. Vic would agree, and she would understand if he ended up in jail.

"That is what I'll do." After all this was over, he would turn himself in for justice.

"Do what you must."

"Now you talk?" William flinched, and he slipped again.

He swallowed. "I never heard a radiant so fixated on a phrase." They responded in simple sentences and mostly didn't communicate. Sam had stopped their father and repeated a phrase that cast constant judgment on William. "I deserve it too."

The river splashed and lapped at his boots.

"When will this tunnel end?"

His breath shortened at the thought of what coated his boots. He would burn them if they ever got out of here. Maybe he should've looked harder for a boat. His fingertips hurt from gripping the smooth wall. His entire body pressed against the cool stone, and the tension in his legs caused them to cramp, yet they shuffled on down the tunnel. If they ended up on the Haven side, who knew if they could even get out, but they pressed on. Up ahead, a black hole in the wall grew larger. William wondered if he was imagining it. As they crept closer, the hole looked like a tunnel. The landing tapered down, forming a ramp into the sewage river, like it could be a stopping point for loading boats.

"I'm not sure if this is a good thing or a bad thing." If anything, his fingers could use a break, and maybe they could find a different tunnel to walk down. They made it to the dock, and he glanced around before jumping off the ledge. He groaned as he flexed his stiff fingers and stretched out his legs. He'd lost years of his life being that close to falling into a river of defecation.

"Any clue from here?" Even though it was deserted, they shouldn't stay in one place too long. When Smoker and Tenor had taken him to his father, they'd met many masked people in the tunnels.

Sam walked back to the river like he was saying he'd come from there. William moaned and went to the other side of the entrance. This time, there was no ledge to walk on.

"We need a boat, unless we want to swim upstream." The water waste flowed rapidly. William eyed the path away from the dock. "We may have to try our luck." He pulled out his wand. The stone glimmered, and he had a bit of magic to work with. "Maybe we can make our own tunnel." He spun in a circle. "We need to find out where."

Maybe Vic could handle being coated in sewage, but William would rather take his chances in the tunnels.

The closer to an outer wall the better, if he could even find one. "Maybe a grate or window would be better."

Sam stood still, and William walked down the tunnel. "If we find a boat, we can come back."

Sam followed without questioning him.

The stone ramp led up, and William stuck close to the side. It leveled out, and crates were piled on the edges. He couldn't see inside them, but he breathed easier at having more cover. The sound of the river faded behind them, and they walked silently together. Another large opening grew in front of them, and William ducked behind the crates with Sam to listen. Only a dripping noise and the strange smell of rot mixed with sewage.

"I don't know if it smells better than the sewage or not," he whispered. He clamped his mouth shut. He should stop talking to Sam, but he couldn't help it. Part of him hoped that someday Samuel would answer. Down here, though, he was being plain stupid for making unnecessary noise.

They came out from behind the crates and walked down the wide hall, twice as tall as the small tunnel behind them. There was nothing special in this one, only more dim lights and black stone. Pillars came into view, and the rotting smell intensified. It was like that time William had forgotten the ice and all the meat had spoiled in the fridge. Had something died down here?

They passed the first pillar and discovered a huge metal cage with no lock. William couldn't see inside the dark cell. He covered his mouth and nose from the smell, and something large threw itself against the metal bars.

William jumped back and bit his cheeks from yelling. His heart pounded as an enormous eye glowed in the dark. As his eyes adjusted, a mass of black skin threw itself at the bars toward him again. A giant mog growled.

More thuds and growls echoed in the hall. William, standing next to his brother, saw rows upon rows of cells. "Why are there mogs in Haven?" Maybe he wasn't in Haven. They could've taken him anywhere. The matching stone walls might not mean anything.

His heart sank as he thought about the people he'd seen getting dragged in before he'd been caught. It didn't make sense. If Boreus was now turning people into mogs, why would they bring people here? Was GicCorp letting Boreus in to drain the mogs? William shook his head. No, when he'd seen the masked figures entering Haven, he'd known it wasn't Boreus. Why did Haven need mogs? He could barely see, but they were huge compared to what Vic had described. GicCorp must have decided to do the draining themselves and skip the reapers. How did they do it without scythes? Questions piled in his head. He needed to get out of here and talk to Vic and her father, then tell Kai they might have the wrong target for who was putting bones out for bait.

The mogs groaned louder as they walked. William didn't want to get too close, but they shouldn't walk down the center. If they had to duck behind a pillar, they'd have to hope that the mogs' hands couldn't fit through the bars of the cage. They continued to throw themselves at the brothers, getting more and more agitated as their meal walked away from them. The cages finally ended, but instead of more tunnels, twilight glowed in the distance beyond another large entrance.

They went to the corner and peeked out. He ducked back quickly and pressed his back against the wall.

An army. His heart beat rapidly. People waited at attention in the arena-like structure. It was miles long. How could they get by all those people?

He squatted and pulled Sam down too. They could go back to the river. Maybe he could use his wand to make a raft out of the crates? But how would he propel it with magic like the water taxis? He would also need magic to keep whatever he built afloat. At that rate, the boat would sink within minutes.

William drew another breath and peeked out from behind the wall.

Rows and rows of people stood in black clothing and masks, all facing the same way. His breath came out louder as he took in the sight. Something was off. They didn't even shift. Too still.

He took a chance and poked his head out farther. The large structure didn't look familiar from the inside. His vision traced along the open arena and saw the tower from GicCorp. He was right. This was Haven. William wanted to see what the people were looking at. No one was at the front, and he ducked back. They were awaiting orders. Or they'd already gotten their orders to stand. Radiant.

"No, no, no, no." There were so many. How could there

be this many? "Is Father in charge of this?" William glanced out again. These radiant weren't taking part in a peaceful community; these people had been ordered to go get other people. They weren't being turned into mogs. GicCorp had turned them into their own obedient radiant army.

"Why?" William looked for answers that his brother couldn't give. "How could they pollute the radiant this much?"

When his father had mentioned forced change, William hadn't understood the scale. Now he truly saw what was inside Haven. He couldn't even count how many people waited there in silent attention. There were enough to fill the Nyx district.

William swallowed and stepped out. The last test. No one even glanced in his direction.

"Come on, Sam."

He stayed to the side to avoid the eerie eyes of the silent warriors. He didn't want to know why GicCorp needed an army, but it couldn't be good for Verrin.

Darkness grew, and the lamps around the giant arena glowed. They turned so the dimming sunlight was on their right. They needed to head south toward Verrin. GicCorp must trust that no one could get in or out. That worked well for them now that they were above ground. Dare they head toward the gate?

If he had to guess, that was where they brought in the actual vitals. The rest they took through the underground like he'd seen. Did the vitals get purified as well? He ached at giving this news to Vic and her father. There was no proof of that. He couldn't even see their faces. He was too lost in his thoughts and jumping to too many assumptions.

What he hadn't seen so far was a giant relic that purified

magic. A large tunneled doorway with onyx doors sat open. They entered, and a metal gate was within view after a few feet.

He could see the familiar building of the Nordics' home through the metal bars.

Sweat dripped down his face. No one guarded the gate. He took another deep breath and went to the side of the metal gate. He needed to bend the bars slightly so they could fit. They were so close to getting out. His heart raged in his ears as he held the wand in his sweaty hand. When had he ever sweat this much?

He pushed his magic against the iron and swallowed the metallic taste in his mouth. The bar bent, gradually widening to allow a body to fit. "Go, Sam."

Sam squeezed out, and William followed. He pushed his magic again, letting the bar settle back into its original shape.

William drooped in relief.

They practically hugged Haven's walls as they made their way between the buildings. Every slight sound made him jump, and every shadow became a guard. William could see the GicCorp factory walls ahead.

"Stop."

William turned with his brother. His heart tried to break through his ribs. A security guard for GicCorp stopped with his wand out.

"Yes?" *Play it cool. You're out.*

The guard took him and Sam in. "Why are you wandering around this area?"

"Sorry, sir. I had job testing earlier, and I was so worried I didn't pay attention." William didn't even know if there had been job testing today. If the guard asked him what day it was, he wouldn't know that either.

"And him? What's a radiant doing with you?"

This guy took his job too seriously. "My brother got purified, and I asked if he could come with me today since I was nervous." William made his lip tremble. It wasn't hard since his entire body wanted to shake. "He tried to support the entire family, but we couldn't bring in enough credits."

By some miracle, the guard relaxed. "I get that." He waved them off. "Get out of here before someone else comes along."

He didn't have to be told twice. He nodded at the man and briskly walked into the city. He hadn't taken a breath that whole time.

His hands shook as they got farther into Verrin. He worried he would wake up and still be in that cell. Somehow, he'd made it in and out of Haven. Now he needed to tell someone.

※ 17 ※

VIC

"Let's get out of here," Vic's father said from behind her.

Vic sat on the ground outside of what used to be Nyx.

"They took Maddox to Haven."

"I'm sorry." He reached out his hand.

Vic gripped the familiar hand, smooth from constantly touching sand. He pulled her up and raised his brows when she didn't let go. He blinked a few times and turned his face away from her.

"Your men are at the house."

Vic jumped. More than one? "William? Kai?"

Her father's lips twisted. "Yes, and a radiant."

"Samuel!"

Vic let go of her father's hand and ran toward her childhood home. She thought she might have heard her father laugh behind her, but she didn't slow down. She burst inside the house, and there they sat drinking whatever her mother had served them.

Vic stilled in the doorway and took them all in. William rose, and she yanked him into her arms. He dropped his glass to the ground.

"Your mother won't be happy about that," he murmured and squeezed her back.

Vic released him and punched his arm. "Do you think I care?" She turned to Kai and lunged at him as well, but he had time to put his drink down. "You got out?"

Kai brushed back her hair. "There will be a trial, but somehow, I don't have to wait in jail. I'm not sure what strings your father pulled."

Vic grimaced. "Loaned a bit of founder privilege."

"Since I'm the one benefiting, I can't complain about the injustice of it."

Vic pulled away and grabbed poor Samuel in a hug. "Where in the blight did you run off to?"

Samuel smiled.

Vic ran her hands through her hair. "I'm so sorry, William, that I lost your brother."

William sidestepped the broken glass on the floor. "Actually, it turned out to be a good thing."

Her father stepped into the room and imbued the broken glass together again. "Now that you're here, I'd like to hear William's story. We wanted to wait for you."

Vic sat, and William told them about the masked figures taking people. Vic swallowed when he mentioned that his father had tried to purify him.

"And Samuel stopped it?"

William nodded. "I'm still not sure what that means. But while escaping, we came across hundreds of people standing in the middle of Haven."

"An army?" Kai asked.

"They were all masked like those who chased you down. A first, I thought they were normal, but they were all radiant."

The group sat in shocked silence.

Vic's broken voice sounded like it didn't belong to her. "You mean they aren't turning people into mogs like we thought."

"That's my theory. There are too many to be vitals."

Her skin grew cold. "You think they're purifying the vitals too?" Was that what Tristan had meant by *alive*? Her sister would be alive in body, but not in mind.

Her father broke in, "I don't think they would go through that trouble. Taking people is a recent development. They're using the vitals for something else. We need to keep in mind that the vitals are needed because of their first-generation relics." He eyed William. "William's an imb now, and he safely left Haven. He proved that what the Nordics say about the relic in Haven is a lie."

Vic jumped out of her chair. "That means I can go get Em."

"Yes, but not yet."

She frowned. "What do you mean, *not yet*? What if they purify her? You think they won't, but we're shooting in the dark."

"We are, but how are you going to get inside?" He poured himself a drink from the cart and took a long gulp.

Vic crossed her arms. "William described a room like the one I saw. This time, I can take a boat in. Get off at the first dock—"

"—and wander around until you get caught?" Kai asked.

"I won't leave her there for another day. I want to get her and Maddox before something happens to them."

"You're being foolish. You might not make it out without them noticing you."

"William did!"

Kai stood and faced her. "By pure luck."

"He said the doors aren't guarded very well. And I think he's right that GicCorp is too confident that people won't go in. If I take the same path he did, I'll have a chance." Vic tightened her hands into fists. "You would do the same for your sister."

"Vic, think about this. I know how you feel, but we're at war with a massive corporation that runs the city. You don't know what's going on behind those doors. I hate to say this, but sometimes, there are casualties in war. You may have to let go."

"Let go?" Vic's voice deepened. "How dare you tell me that my sister and Mads are casualties. We have a chance to get them out. I'll take it with or without you."

Her father stepped forward. "Victoria, give us time to plan."

"Plan? So we wait until it's too late. Am I the only one seeing this?" Three pairs of eyes looked at her with pity, and she turned away.

"Vic, they aren't saying to leave them," William whispered. "Let your dad gather allies. Then we can go in after them. This way, we can maybe pull out more people. The other founders would like their family back too."

Something in Vic told her to move. She glared at Kai. "Never assume what I'm feeling." She tensed as she spoke. "Don't you get it? Ever since Em left, I've had this sick feeling that I need to get her. It pulls at me. Even though people told me I was being ridiculous, I've been fighting Haven since the beginning." She tensed. "I've been patient. I've waited. But there's something that connects me to her, and she needs me." Her arms fell to her sides. "I know I'm reckless, but I'll only wait so long, so make your plan. I'm going in within a week, plan or no plan."

Her father nodded, and William brushed her forearm lightly.

Her feelings jumbled together. The never-ending ups and downs went still inside her. She needed to do something, and she hated depending on others.

"I need some time alone." She left the room. For the first time since Em had left, she went up to her sister's room. The glass statue still stood in the middle, glowing with life.

She felt a tug in her heart as she stared at her sister's likeness. Vic sat on the bed, and tears fell down her face as a soft lilac smell comforted her. She gripped the blanket in her hands.

"Let them make their plans."

She didn't care. She would need to solve how to get the vitals free. They'd gotten William in, and he'd told her how he'd gotten out. Now she knew a way in from the sewers. There would be no more waiting. Tristan's eyes haunted her. What he'd left unsaid worried her more than what he'd told her. There was a ticking clock, and she might already be too late.

⊗

A FEW HOURS PASSED, AND VIC TURNED AWAY WILLIAM AND her father when they came in to talk to her. She played her part well, or so she hoped. In the middle of the night, the house quieted, and Vic made her move. She waited until her father had left his office and snuck in to grab a handful of cash credits. She debated going out the front door, but it was right under her parents' room. With soft footsteps, she ducked back upstairs to Em's room.

She tucked her hair under her hood, grabbed a spare lamp used for magic outages, and put her scythe in her harness. Vic opened Em's door to the balcony. Her balcony extended next to Em's, and there had been many nights when Vic had jumped over to her sister's balcony since it was closest to the wall. Vic eyed the empty yard in the darkness. Only the trickle of water from the fountains spoke in the night air. She jumped down to the wall and gripped it, letting her body hang from the edge. She bent her knees and let herself drop. Her feet smarted as they hit the stone street. The quiet streets greeted her as she headed toward GicCorp. She didn't worry about people seeing her since they could assume she was on reaper business.

She ran through the city to the last water taxi stop closest to GicCorp. Luck was on her side when she saw a driver locking up his boat for the night.

"Brave being out so late." Vic nodded to the man.

A bald spot on top of his head gleamed in the lantern light. His hunched form spoke of sitting for many years at the helm of a water taxi. "Some get off work late, and we need the credits. I trust the reapers to do their job."

"Can I buy your boat?" She didn't waste time and held out the wad of money to him.

His mouth dropped open. "It isn't worth that."

"I know. You'll go through the trouble of making another, and I want it to be worth your time."

The man glanced between her and the narrow boat. "You could get a better one."

Vic shook her head. "I need one that floats. If you don't

mind, could you add on a couple wheels and make it thinner, if you have any magic left?"

Together, they pulled the short, narrow boat out of the water. He did what she'd asked of him and included two long poles with flat ends. "So you can steer it."

Vic thanked him and pulled the light boat behind her toward William's testing area. The wheels clattered against the cobblestone, but the streets were empty, and she doubted anyone cared. She could try to get in from the sewers, but the boat might not survive the drop into the lovely sewage river. She thought the large grate would be easier, as long as she could navigate. This time, she'd brought a lamp with her.

Vic left her boat in the alley near the testing area and waited for the guard to pass by. After he'd turned the corner, she used her blade as leverage to pull on the lock until it broke. She ran back to her boat and went inside the testing building. She kicked aside the broken lock and shut the door, hoping the guards wouldn't look too closely or that she would be gone by the time they got back.

She racked her brain for the door her and William had come out of after his test. She turned her back to face the door to get a sense of the location. Vic chose the door to the far right. Darkness coated the room, and she turned on the lamp. The grate had the broken latch. This had to be it. She pulled open the large grate and carefully slid the narrow boat down into the tunnels. She hopped down into the tunnel after and shut the grate with a loud clang. She flinched.

The lamp glowed in the bleak area, illuminating the path she must have stumbled out of. In the wide room, there was no other path. She sighed in relief since she hadn't been able to see anything the last time she'd been there.

The boat's wheels creaked as she pulled it along in the dark. Her father and Kai would be furious when they found out she'd left. William might understand the most. Vic didn't want to give herself time to regret coming alone. If the founders wanted to rescue the other vitals later, she would help them, but she needed her sister now. Nothing was as it should be, and she would not let her become a casualty. Maddox was in this situation because of her. Vic lived with enough guilt. She didn't need more when she could get them out. If she needed to live in the tunnels and search for them every day, she would.

The sound of water grew louder, and the familiar smell of sewage greeted her.

"Here we go. Let's avoid the swim tonight."

She found the room of twisted metal and gems—where William had almost become a radiant. She wondered if Bomrosy had found out anything about the gem. She went to the river. The hardest part, for now, would be pushing the boat upstream. She thanked the man's foresight for the poles. She'd forgotten that detail in her hurry to get down here.

The current wasn't strong, and Vic got in and used the poles to push herself off the shore. She thought the boat might sink without magic but relaxed when it floated. Imbs wouldn't want to waste magic making the boat float. They would build it right the first time. The poles were long enough to reach the bottom of the river. She stayed close to the side where William and Samuel had walked. In the dark lighting, she didn't want to miss the dock.

The entrance turned out to be easy to spot, and she

pushed the boat toward it. The bottom of the boat scraped against the stone ground when she landed on the ramp. It only took a moment to pull the boat out and tuck it behind large wooden crates.

"I hope we can all fit in it." Vic worried her lip. Em and Maddox were more on the slender side, so it should be okay. She huffed. "If I have to swim out of here, I'll swim out." She grinned at the thought of William trying not to fall into the water. He'd probably had a panic attack over it.

Vic didn't hurry in the dark halls. She unharnessed her scythe, keeping the blade ready in case someone attacked. In the area where William had found caged mogs, the silence bothered her. She swallowed when she noticed the first empty cage.

Surely they didn't let them wander around? Maybe they relocated them at night? It seemed like too much trouble to move around mogs constantly.

The mogs that attacked Nyx had all mobbed in at once. Had they come from here? How did GicCorp control that kind of release?

Vic made her way down the long hall of cages. Her steps were silent, and at any noise, she scanned the area.

A wide opening appeared ahead, and she peeked out into the extensive field. Empty. The radiant were likely out gathering people now that it was dark. She walked into the open area. The bottom of the structure had many large openings. Maybe more mogs or supplies? Vic focused on the upper floors, which contained rows and rows of doors with small windows. Did the radiant or the vitals sleep there? Was there a difference? She would pull off every hood and mask from every radiant if she needed to, but for now, she could check the rooms.

Her hand curved around the edge of the wall, and she spotted a flight of stairs to her right. Even though the area was empty, she rushed to the stairs. The open area let in the night breeze, and it was enjoyable not to smell human waste for once tonight.

Light flooded the large arena, and she narrowed her eyes against the sudden brightness.

"You're an interesting woman, Victoria Glass," a voice echoed throughout the arena.

Vic turned to see Tristan standing on the second floor. No one else was with him.

"Glad I can entertain. Why don't you save me some time and tell me where my sister and Maddox are?" She couldn't turn back now that she'd come so far. She could go through Tristan, maybe. He'd come out alone, confident in his power to beat her. That thought worried her, but something in the tunnels had attacked and weakened him, so he could be wounded.

"The call to be a vital is noble. Why would you separate them from their duty?" A sarcastic edge tainted his voice.

Vic swung her blade in front of her. The swish of her blade through the air comforted her, and she rolled her shoulders. "You already know I don't believe it. Your lies smell stronger than the shit river I took to get here. Where's my sister? I helped you once. Give her back to me."

He wagged his finger. "That wasn't the deal. I said she would live."

Too smug at her expense. A question burned in her throat, but she didn't want to ask. "Did you keep your word?" The words hung in the air between them.

Tristan stared down at her. A slow tilt to his head, but she could still see his damn smile. "No."

The world closed in around her, and all she saw was the man who'd killed Em. An animalistic screech blasted through the air, and it came from her. Vic's body blurred as she ran to him. Her ears rang, and with every heartbeat, she felt her blood coursing through her. There would be no more peace in her world. Her scythe would cut through the flesh of his neck, even if it meant her life.

Vic vaulted up the steps, but near another side entrance next to the stairs, a large mog stuck out its arm, ramming into her.

Vic flew back and gasped for air. In her rage, she'd paid no mind to her surroundings. She pushed up and cut blindly at the mog, but more surrounded her. She spun around, and they closed in, leaving no gap. The black creatures stilled, making a cage of rot and bone, and watched her.

She jerked her head to face Tristan as he looked down at her and screamed, "What's this?"

"Your funeral."

Vic's body burned. Even if she could take down one mog, it would fill her gicgauge. With another scream, she raised her scythe in the air. She glared at the man who only knew how to take.

"I may have failed today, but others will come." With all her force, she slammed the gicgauge against the stone floor, and it shattered off her relic.

Tristan's eyes widened.

Vic wasted no more time. Once the stone got overwhelmed, it would shatter too, but she didn't have to die lying down. Holding her blade in front of her, she dove under the mog with the longest legs. Breaking out of the circle, she tried to gain some ground against them.

Her reprieve didn't last long, as the mogs came at her in a

rush of crunching bodies. She took a deep breath to calm her mind. In her anger, she would make too many mistakes, but grief overwhelmed her, and all she could see was her sister's face. She met the first mog, a stubby thing that had broken away from the rest.

She dodged its attacks and sprinted out of the room. Her scythe burned in her hands as she slashed it, almost too hot for her to hold on to. Power flowed like a wave of pure fire crashing down. For now, there was no limit to her relic. She would use it until the stone shattered.

The blade glowed a brilliant red. The stubby mog fell in a pile of bones, as did the one next to it. She didn't even need to touch it. Wild power coursed through her as she planted her feet and let the fire of her scythe flow through her body. Tears left her eyes like lava scorching down her cheeks. She would burn to ash as flames licked her insides.

She ignored the mogs melting around her. The fire burned and fueled her body.

Vic pushed her consumed body toward Tristan. Ash swirled through the air. She opened her mouth, and fiery blood dripped from the corners and onto her chin.

"Burn with me."

Tendons popped from Tristan's neck, and his lips trembled. He opened and closed his mouth, but no words came as she strode toward the stairs, the mog bones aflame behind her.

"Scared?" More blood poured from her mouth and burned her skin. The relic turned white-hot in her hands, but she didn't let go.

Tristan pulled out his wand, and a force hit and crept through her.

Numbness from the orb in her neck branched out in her

body. Vic flinched as her fire dimmed around her and the orb's coolness took control.

"This is how you control the mogs?" Vic rasped.

Blood splattered the ground in front of her. She let out a low, hoarse laugh and raised her hand before the orb's power overcame her. Her fingers dug into the flesh of her neck. Her scorched skin pulsed as she gripped the orb. With her bare hands, she ripped out the orb. It dropped to the ground without a sound and fused into the stone. More blood traced down her body. She became the fire that burned inside her.

The control Tristan had tried to gain over her vanished, and her magic reignited, but her body couldn't take much more.

In desperation, she pushed forward but fell to her knees, reaching out for him. She didn't understand, but Tristan blurred under her magic, and an echo of someone else shadowed behind him. Someone faceless and empty.

"No," he yelled. More mogs surrounded her as Tristan hunched over.

The mogs tried to use up her magic, and she screamed. She would die and take him with her. Vic reached within herself but found nothing more. The fire dimmed inside her. The point of no return had arrived. She would use everything in her last moment and join her sister.

Vic focused her relic, not on the mogs but on Tristan. "Die."

She was close enough to see sweat pour down his face and death reflect in his eyes. Maybe now her sister would be at peace.

I'm sorry, Sister. I couldn't save you. Vic pulled the magic through her with one last tug from her own body. *I'm ready to die.*

❧ 18 ❧
VIC

"Vic, stop!"

A voice pierced her tired mind. No, she couldn't stop. She needed to kill him.

"Vic, we're here. Don't do this. We need you."

The smell of clean linen surrounded her, breaking through the ash and calming her.

"He ... killed ... her ..."

"We'll get him. Let go of your magic. Let us help!"

She paused at the desperation in his voice, and the flaming magic around her stilled. Vic reached for it again. "No. No. No. No!" She coughed, and blood spattered William's clothing as he held her on the ground. "Why? Why did I stop? Why did you stop me?"

His blue eyes searched her. "It's not time to go yet."

"I could have killed him." She wanted to see his body dissolve into ash.

"I know, but I couldn't let you go. I'm sorry." His hand brushed her sweaty hair from her forehead. The coolness of his hands soothed the burning inside her.

Tristan's voice sounded from down in the arena. "If you go now, I'll let you live."

Vic looked past William. Rows of black-clad reapers filled the space. The leaders from each Order stood in front of them.

Kai stepped forward and pulled out a piece of paper. "Decree number twenty-eight: If a reaper should see a corrupted soul or mog enter into a building, the reaper shall not be hindered to enter and contain the blight." Kai tucked the paper back into his pocket. "I see a lot of mogs in Haven." He turned to the other leaders. "Don't you?"

The Boreus and Dei leaders nodded, and Tristan's face turned red. "Leave!"

In unison, all the reapers drew their scythes and flicked them open.

"We will, as soon as we clear out the mogs." Masked figures joined Tristan, and more mogs appeared.

Tristan voice grew icy. "Fine."

With a roar, the mogs and reapers collided on the open field.

Shouts of battle reverberated in the arena. More and more mogs came from the tunnels. The flood of reapers met them. Boreus and Dei had brought hundreds of reapers, and the mogs formed a black wave of flesh as bone clanged with metal.

William pulled her up and held her as she regained her footing.

"Let's get back. You can't fight in this condition. We can find Maddox and the other vitals."

Vic stumbled as he pulled her to the other side of the arena. The reapers held the line against the giant mogs. More people joined Tristan, but she couldn't see who from this distance. More mogs appeared, but the reapers met them head-on. The bones of drained mogs fell to the ground.

"How did they all come together?"

"Thanks to Kai and a guy named Landon."

Vic balked. Landon had helped?

"Can you walk? I can go look for your sister and Maddox after I get you to safety." William's arms gripped her, and Samuel came up to support her on her other side.

Vic turned to the battle, and he held her back. "Kai told me not to let you fight. Your gicgauge is broken. You'll lose your relic and your life. Trust them."

His words came out in a rush as he led her toward the tunnel to the sewer. She had many questions, but they didn't have time. "I can walk. I want to find Maddox."

William's brows rose, but he didn't question her. "We don't have much time before we have to go."

Vic's body ached as she forced her legs up the steps. She felt heavy and needed sleep.

Samuel stayed under her arm, supporting her as they shuffled to the second floor. "Why's Samuel here?"

"He didn't want to be left behind."

Vic shrugged, and they reached the second floor. The doors faced the arena, with only a small barred window to see inside. Slats on the bottom were where they got their food delivered.

"Like a prison. If the radiant do what they want, would they need to be locked up?"

William peered into the barred window. "I have a feeling this isn't for the radiant."

Were the vitals locked up until GicCorp turned them? Or did they use them for something else? Was there a fate worse than a radiant life for them? Vic hoped that Maddox would still be herself.

They rushed through the halls, but the rooms were empty. William stayed ahead to look inside while Vic limped behind him.

The battle raged on below, and all the reapers' gicgauges would be full before long. Then they would need to retreat.

"Maddox!" Vic yelled down the hall.

William caught on to her idea and ran forward, shouting her name. A faint reply answered from ahead. They exchanged looks, and William darted toward the answering call.

He reached the door first, and by the time Vic arrived, William was muttering with his wand out, "What in the blight is locking this?"

Maddox stood at the door, peering out. "Vic!" Her fingers reached through the bars.

"What are they doing to you?" Vic asked and touched Maddox's icy fingers.

"I don't know. The masked people brought me here and shoved me in this cell. No one is telling me anything. After a few days, it got quiet around me. I can't even sense how they locked me in. The door is sealed. The latches don't use magic."

"Will, can you open it?"

He clenched his teeth. "Give me a second. It's a bit of everything. I'm not as experienced as I should be. If they used what your friend calls tech, I won't even know where to begin."

Vic held on to Maddox's fingers. "Hold on, okay. William's the only imb here, and he just started using magic."

Maddox snorted. "Pulled out all the stops, huh?"

Vic smiled, although it was a bit wobbly. "Yeah, nothing but the best for my friend. I don't suppose you know where your wand is so you can help?"

"Not a chance." She paused. "I saw your sister."

The hollowness returned in a crushing wave. "She's dead." The words sounded like they'd come from someone else.

"What? When? I saw her before all the shouting started. Those who carried her took her farther on. I couldn't tell which room, though. I was trying to see what was happening down there when I heard you say my name."

As Maddox spoke, Vic allowed hope to live in her. Tristan could have lied to mess with her, but she'd believed him. "Are you sure?"

"Not that many redheads, Vic."

Footfalls thundered from behind them. Masked figures stormed toward them as William tried to unlock the door. She dropped Maddox's hand, and her heart pounded as she flicked open her weapon.

The path was narrow enough for her to hold them back. It became a matter of how long her body could hold up before she dropped.

William cursed. "I can't even make a dent." His fist hit the door as he worked.

"What's going on?" Maddox asked.

"Masked radiant," William answered. "You can't kill them, Vic. They didn't choose this."

Vic let out a frustrated sigh. "Are you kidding me? They'll probably try to kill us."

"He's right, Vic. Get your sister."

"What are you talking about? I'm not leaving you here."

The first radiant approached, and they were right. Their faces were blank as they fought Vic. She kept her blade away from them and hit them back. They weren't trained fighters, so she had the advantage. GicCorp could tell them to fight, but it didn't make the radiant fighters.

Too many of them built up behind them, and Vic couldn't hold them back much longer.

"Vic."

"Don't tell me to leave you again, Mads." She'd come this far to find her friend. She couldn't leave her behind now. Sweat mixed with the drying blood on her. Her legs shook, and the masked figures piled on, using their weight against her scythe to push her back.

"Vic."

"I won't." Vic held her scythe across the path. She could push them back. She was strong enough to do this. She couldn't leave. Samuel tried to help by holding the relic so she could defend her face from the radiant.

Her feet slid back. Soon, they would be by Maddox's door.

"Vic, you're done here." Her friend's voice, even though quiet, cut through the noise. Acceptance of what Vic had tried to do filled it, but she could hear that Maddox had quit.

Maddox was right, but she was tired of losing.

"Why can't I save anyone?" Vic choked.

A sad sigh sounded. "Get her out of here, William."

Two hands grabbed her upper arms and pulled her back before she got crushed under the weight of the radiant, who fell forward without the staff of her scythe in their way. Vic's eyes met Maddox's. Her friend's blue eyes contained unshed tears.

"I'll come back," Vic rasped.

"I know."

Vic held back tears as she ran with William and Samuel. Her shoulders slumped, and she took a chance. "Emilia!"

No answer. William looked through the barred windows.

"I can try to block them now that we've gained some ground. But I might not have enough magic or be able to make a barrier fast enough to stop them," William panted.

The radiant stayed on their heels.

"If you don't, we won't be able to take a chance on her door," Vic answered.

He nodded. Vic spun around, her relic hitting the radiant in front in the knees. They toppled to the ground, and the others didn't have much stopping power and tripped.

In that brief second, William pulled stone from the side walls. He made four wide panels to block the path. The horizontal bars left no space for a human to squeeze through. There would be no returning that way for them either.

The blockade would buy them time, but the shouts in the arena grew louder. The reapers were getting pushed back, and they would get trapped here if they didn't escape back down to the arena.

"We can't look forever, Vic."

"I understand." Her feet throbbed, and she kept moving.

William froze. "She's here."

Vic plastered herself to the door. A body lay prone on the bed, unmoving. She pounded on the door while William got to work. The radiant behind them had already broken through one of his side pillars. The bars William had made were too thin to hold them forever.

With strange ease, the crack in the door grew.

"This is odd," William muttered. "The latches aren't locked."

Vic ignored him and yanked on the handle, throwing the door open. "Em!" She went to her sister's side and touched her face. Emilia's skin was cold to the touch. "No. Em, wake up." Panic rose in Vic, and her world shrank.

"It's okay. She's breathing," William's voice cut through her panic, and she could see the slight rise and fall of her sister's chest.

Those words brought her back, and Vic tried to lift her sister's still body. Her arms gave out, even though her sister wasn't that large, and she fell to her knees. She almost screamed in frustration.

"Let me." William eased her aside and lifted Emilia. "Can you run?" He took in her kneeling form.

"Yes." There was no other option. She would get her sister out of here with William.

Samuel took her hand, not saying anything, then they burst out of the room. William stayed in front while they ran to the other set of stairs. Samuel helped pull Vic, giving her the energy she needed for their last retreat.

"They blocked off the stairs!" William shouted.

There was no way they could fight them.

Vic looked down at the arena. The reapers' backs were to them. The last person she wanted to see noticed them: Landon.

He ran toward them while the other reapers held back the mogs.

Landon took in the four people on the second floor. "Jump. I'll catch you."

Not that far to fall, but they could break bones if they landed wrong. William shifted Emilia to the railing to drop her into Landon's arms. Vic held out her hand to stop him.

"Don't." Vic stared down at the man who'd harassed her.

He'd come to help them fight. Could she trust him?

William glanced between them.

Landon spat on the arena ground. "I hate you, founder, but I'm on your side."

Vic swallowed, and her shoulders stiffened. "Don't drop us." If he broke any of her sister's bones, she would break his leg.

With a nod, William carefully let Emilia drop, and Landon caught her. His knees bent with the momentum.

William gestured for Vic to jump, but she shook her head. "Samuel, go next."

To her surprise, Samuel listened. He put his legs over the ledge and held on with only his hands. Then he dropped into Landon's arms. Landon grunted from the radiant's extra weight.

Vic followed him, knowing William wouldn't go before her. She landed in Landon's arms, and he quickly placed her on the ground to catch William.

"We can't drain them all. The last line of reapers are at the front, and they'll be full soon," Landon shared before running off to the exit, expecting them to follow.

They ran with the other reapers to the sewage river. The ones in front caused the rest to pause as they loaded into boats. A loud call went out, and they all broke into the tunnel. The reapers with empty gicgauges stayed at the back but pushed forward. Vic and William stayed toward the back since she couldn't run as fast and Emilia's body impeded William.

The turn to the ramp approached, and reapers loaded into boats and pushed off down the water. Only three could fit on a boat.

They were at the end, and moans from the large mogs

came from the tunnels behind them.

"Go with Em." Vic pushed William toward a boat with only one other person in it. He opened his mouth to argue. "I'm trusting you, Will. Please."

He shut his mouth and got into the boat with Emilia. "Samuel, keep her safe."

The reaper pushed them down the river. They disappeared with the other boats around the bend.

In a flash, the boats took off, and the last of the reapers jumped into the water, holding on to the sides of the departing boats. Vic grabbed the small boat she'd stashed earlier, and before a mog could grab them, they hopped in. She pushed off with her pole.

The mog swiped at the boat, making it rock, and she dropped one of the poles. The water swallowed it instantly. "Blight."

She pushed forward, the other boats already too far ahead to notice her and Samuel.

The mogs entered the water, and she frantically shoved off the ground. The waves from the mogs pushed them forward.

"Samuel, look out for piles of metal and stones," Vic called behind her. She focused her gaze on the mogs and didn't want to turn around. Sweat dripped into her eyes, and the stench, as always, made it hard to breathe. She didn't know how her arms still functioned, and they shook from the effort.

"Here," Samuel called, giving her hope.

She looked behind her and shoved the boat onto shore. The familiar twisted metal and dead stones were a welcome sight. They jumped out, the mogs not far behind them.

The reapers had already gone ahead.

Vic glanced down the tunnel. "Samuel, run."

He stood there.

Vic pulled out her relic. "I can see why William's frustrated with you."

The stone told her she still had magic, which didn't make sense, but she didn't question it. There was no gicgauge, and she could buy William time by taking out the first few mogs. It didn't take much for the fire to burn through her once more. It molded to her like an old friend.

Pain bloomed, and she knew she wouldn't need to touch the mogs. She would take out the first line of mogs, then they could run. Vic stamped her relic on the ground. The magic, alight with power, burst out and incinerated the mogs. In her blurred vision, faceless forms separated as they fell. Ash burst into the air, and a feeling of joyful release moved inside her. The feeling wasn't hers, and she didn't understand it.

The power consumed, and Vic found it impossible to stop the flow as she burned through the mogs. Her body burned with them as magic flames licked her hair. The metal and the surrounding stone heated, and something foreign came alive inside her as the dead relic stones in the twisted metal graveyard came back to life.

Once the mogs had burned, she couldn't stop. Vic had lost control as soon as her magic had touched the dead stones, which she'd thought were useless junk.

Her scream reverberated in her ears, and something dripped from her eyes that wasn't tears. Then she burned out. Ash coated her tongue. Blood dripped from her mouth. "I think I stopped them."

Blackness clouded her gaze, and she dropped to the ground.

❦ 19 ❦
WILLIAM

With the help of other reapers, William pulled Emilia out of the grate entrance and into the room where he'd taken his disastrous GicCorp test. In the mayhem, he'd lost track of Vic and his brother. They wouldn't be far behind him. When reapers stopped coming out of the entrance, he reached to tug on cuffs that weren't there.

A reaper covered in dirt and smelling of sweat stopped next to William while he waited next to Emilia's sleeping form. "You better get moving. The news will stay ahead of this, but you don't want to be caught here."

Thanks to the founders and Conrad, the Verrin Daily News would report that mogs had broken into Haven. The reports would skew the story so the reapers would be the heroes, which they were, but not for the reasons the public would think. William was in favor of telling the truth about the radiant army, but the other founders thought it would lead to panic. They wanted more information and were slow to take action.

"Are there any more people behind you?" William asked.

The reaper frowned. "Honestly, I don't know. Once we all got in the boats, we got separated in the current. Is there someone down there? Do I need to go back?"

William was about to say yes—he didn't want to leave Emilia behind with someone else so he could go look—but then a scuffing sound came from the tunnel and a blond head popped up from the grate. "Sam!"

Sam went back down and then returned, holding up Vic's limp body. The reaper helped pull her out. William checked for a pulse and breathed a sigh of relief when he felt it. Her breath came in shallow gasps, and her body felt hot. A thick layer of blood had dried around her neck, but the wound didn't look too deep.

"Thank you for your help," he told the reaper. "Sam, were you the last ones?"

Sam picked up Vic and didn't answer. Taking that as a yes, William went over to Emilia and lifted her in his arms. The brothers followed the reaper out of the building at a fast clip. Kai waited at the dock by GicCorp, and the tension left his face when he saw the group.

"I thought I'd need to go back and look for you." Kai helped load them into one of the last automated water taxis. The other reaper saluted Kai and ran off. They placed the sleeping sisters side by side. Before William could ask about the reaper, Kai continued, "All the reapers are separating into founder homes for safety. I got word from Conrad that they would do that much."

"I'm surprised they did anything." When they'd realized Vic wasn't in her room, her father had practically dragged the founders into his home to get their support in putting pressure on the news. Kai had called in the Order leaders, and the Boreus leader's shocked face had told them he'd known nothing about the bones left for mog bait.

The Boreus leader had called in his reapers. Dei had been more reluctant to join in. All the leaders had asked for volunteers, and the turnout had been shocking. The biggest surprise had been Landon returning with Nyx reapers. Most of them had doubted the news until they'd seen the mogs attacking Vic in the middle of Haven. They hadn't gotten to the part about forced radiant changes. He thought they'd avoided it for his sake.

The farther the boat took them from GicCorp and Haven, the easier William breathed.

Kai placed his hand on Vic's forehead. "Does she have a fever?"

"I'm not sure. She felt hot when we got to Haven. Do you think she used her magic again?" William told himself that Kai's hand on Vic's forehead didn't bother him. He felt like a jerk for thinking that way, with Vic and Emilia both passed out. They needed help, not jealousy. "Sam, did Vic fight the mogs?"

Sam stayed silent.

Kai gently brushed the hair away from her sweaty forehead. "Knowing Vic, she must have. She'll shatter her stone if she isn't careful. There's no gicgauge to protect the flow of magic or stop when it gets too full. Once the stone is broken, it'll use up her body. I only know of one person who survived that kind of magic flow, but she lost her relic."

William placed a hand on Emilia's forehead, and unlike her sister, she remained cold. They didn't have any blankets. He shifted the sisters closer together and tucked Emilia's hands under Vic. "Can we go faster?"

Kai shook his head. William knew the boat was automated, but he still shifted nervously. He sat on Emilia's other side to share his warmth. Maybe some heat from Vic would seep into her sister.

The dock close to the Glass home was a welcome sight, and Conrad waited for them. His face filled with relief and then worry when he saw his daughters.

William jumped out first, and Kai passed Emilia to him, then Vic to her father. He ran with him back to their home. The sun had barely peeked out over the city line as they reached the Glass home. Conrad shoved open the doors, and healers hurried down the hall.

"I need two healers!" Conrad shouted, and they placed the sisters on nearby cots. They must have prepared while they'd been fighting. William stepped back to let the healers work.

He didn't remove his gaze from Vic's pale face. Her lips were cracked from the heat, and dried blood covered her chin and neck. With how hot she felt, he thought she would be redder and less pale. The red in her hair shone as brightly as ever, like a candle flame.

The healer asked William while she checked Vic, "Do you know what happened?"

"She used her magic without a gicgauge."

The healer worked quickly with her partner. "Magic burnout. Take off her boots. Start with her feet. We need to cut off her clothing. Stand-about person, help us."

William jerked to attention when he realized she was talking to him. She shoved a pair of scissors into his hand. He hesitated, then cut off her pants while the healer followed, wrapping her up in blue bandages. Whatever they'd imbued those with, he hoped it would work. He yearned for Vic to open her eyes.

While the healer covered her body, another healer used a different colored bandage on her neck wound. He carefully wiped away the dried blood. "I can't tell where the gicorb is at the moment. After the wound heals, we can check."

The other healer nodded.

At the cot next beside him, they also wrapped up Vic's sister, then piled heated blankets on top of her. Their father smoothed back her hair and whispered to her.

The healers finished with Emilia and stood. "When the blue turns white, flag us down so we can rewrap."

"That's it?" Wasn't there more they could do? Imbued bandages were great for quicker healing, but healers didn't rely on them all the time for more serious injuries.

The healers exchanged glances. "Magic burnout has a low survival rate. She used her body instead of the stone to fuel her relic. It caused massive damage. When the gicgauge breaks, the magic user will usually go through the stone then the body." The healer pointed to the relic. "From my bare knowledge, the stone looks intact." The healers left to go help others. William was thankful for the small explanation, even though he thought they could do more to help her.

"How's her sister?" William asked Conrad.

"Hypothermic but stable." His brow furrowed, and he placed Vic's hands back onto the cot. A tremor entered his voice as he said, "She always did everything the hard way."

William pulled up two chairs. He didn't know where Kai had gone. Probably to look after the reapers. Conrad stayed by Emilia, checking her temperature. Their mother came by often to check their vitals. Apparently, she was a founder from a healer house, and she often got dragged away to direct other healers. William didn't look away from the bandages.

In less than an hour, he had to chase down a healer to put on fresh bandages. In the morning hours, it happened five more times. The latest set seemed to hang on.

Conrad placed a plate of food next to him, and William nodded his thanks. "I'm afraid to ask, but how was the news met this morning?"

"Better than we'd hoped. The lack of comment from GicCorp is worrying, but they've shut themselves in for now." Conrad squeezed his left arm. "We can't predict their next move because we don't know their motivation. If we continue to shoot in the dark, we may all end up dead or a radiant." Conrad left his food untouched. "Sorry for the lack of encouragement." He paused. "I'm guessing your father has mentioned nothing?" He straightened Emilia's blankets.

"He probably would have if I'd stayed to purify people by force. The last time I saw him, he was ranting about his legacy and tried to purify me." William would be happy to never see his father again. He rested his hand on Vic's forehead. She felt cooler, or maybe it was wishful thinking. "I should go have a talk with him."

"Do you need me to come?"

Did he? Then he wouldn't have to deal with it on his own. He ignored the food and rose. Sam came behind him. "He's our problem. I'd like to meet with him first on our own."

Conrad nodded.

William lightly brushed Vic's forehead. "I shouldn't be long."

Conrad raised his eyebrows at William's action but said nothing. "When should we worry?"

"Give us three hours. If I end up purified, I'd appreciate it if you put us to work away from my father." He didn't want to end up dragging people out of their homes in the middle of the night. He doubted his brother would want that either.

"Understood."

William left the father with his daughters, and Sam followed him out of the founder house, walking beside him. The chaos of the house had calmed down while the injured rested. The dead reapers had been left behind at Haven. It would hurt those who'd escaped that they couldn't honor their fallen comrades in the usual way.

The afternoon sun stayed cheerful behind the swirls of blight. William's mood degraded the closer they came to his family home, countering the brightness of the day.

The homes changed the farther they went, from the smoother lines of houses built with magic to those built by hand, with more windows to let in the daylight, but the pathways near the canal were overcome with algae. William paused before his former home. How sure he'd been about the radiant and what they believed in Verrin. That righteous feeling had fled the moment he'd purified his brother. His father, the leader, wasn't out to save people from the blight, but to make them compliant. The truth hurt him and shattered his world.

William tried to pick up the pieces. All those times he'd claimed purification was better, but they were actually making people follow orders instead of living in harmony.

"Higher plane," William muttered. He didn't know what was true anymore. His brother had asked the right questions.

He couldn't stand with GicCorp. For now, that left the

rebellion. Maybe they could find out why the magic had caused the blight.

The thought unsettled him, and he knocked on the door. His mother answered. She frowned at her sons.

"If Father is home, I would like to talk to him out here." William didn't want to go inside the house. He rested his hand close to his wand. He wasn't sure how to use it as a weapon, but it provided him some comfort. If anything, he could poke his father in the eye and run.

She closed the door, leaving them outside.

"Did this ever feel like home to you, Sam?" They'd been raised to be good radiant, not sons.

Sam didn't answer.

After a few moments, his father appeared. The lines of his face were deeper, and his eyes held an unkindness that William had never noticed before.

"What do my traitorous sons want?" His hands stayed at his sides, but William monitored them, staying out of arm's reach.

He didn't know how to start, so he asked, "Why are there radiant in Haven?"

His father sneered. "Do you think I would tell you?"

"No." William felt like he was watching someone else's life unfold as he talked to the man he called Father. "There is still hope in me that my entire life wasn't a lie." He inched his hand closer to his harness. He could grab his wand within seconds.

His father crossed his arms. "The lie is that you're here for the founders and reapers. You couldn't care less about the radiant."

"I care that you're forcing them to change. That isn't the

way you taught me." Why did he bother trying to salvage any part of his childhood?

"We teach you that way to make it easier to accept. The truth has always been that we would rather have radiant than mogs. Now we're being more aggressive about it." His father stepped forward.

William shifted back. "Why? What's going on? Why do you need so many radiant? GicCorp can control the mogs and the radiant. What's GicCorp trying to do?"

"A controlled population is a peaceful population."

"That's it?" He didn't want that to be the truth.

"Either become a pawn or become a king. You made your choice."

"What will happen when GicCorp no longer needs you? Do you think magic users will care about you then?" His father thought he was untouchable. If GicCorp could control the mogs, why did they need the radiant? His father wouldn't tell him, but it had to be important.

"I wouldn't worry about me. Worry about your founder and reaper friends." He focused on Sam. "If you're smart, you'll leave your brother here. He's among the few who don't take purification well. His actions will become volatile if he isn't taken care of."

Sam stared up at the blight, ignoring them. William knew he acted strangely, but no harm had come to him or Vic. "Taken care of? Do you mean killed?"

"Take the meaning however you want, but a radiant who doesn't listen has no moral compass. They will do what they want, and if your brother ends up hurting you, it will be your fault." His father shook his head. "Everyone thinks they can help the radiant rogues until they're killed."

"This has happened before?"

His father didn't reply.

He straightened his imaginary cuffs and dropped his hands to his sides. "This has happened before and you never told me? Does it only happen to those who have been purified by force?" Xiona didn't seem to have a problem.

"I owe you nothing. Get out of here. I don't want to see you again."

The father and sons stood apart across the street. The sound of the canal blared in the silent standoff. William wanted to find the bonds with his father, but he must have never had them in the first place. This man looked at him with no feeling, and emptiness filled William.

He drew his wand and let the magic feel the items in the area. It connected to the stone, the water, and the clothes he wore. His father took a step back, but before he could leave, the wand connected with the relic on his father's hand. Heat flared from trying to contradict the power of the stone. It didn't feel like a normal relic stone. William lacked finesse, but with a pull and a bitter taste of iron in his mouth, he crushed the stone and the metal until it blinked out of existence.

Blood burst from his father's hand as the crushed relic sliced off the finger. The digit dropped to the ground.

His father screamed and cradled his hand to his chest, staining the radiant white bright red.

William's voice remained steady as his father tried to charge at them. "I owe all the lives I purified. I owe Sam and Xiona. If I ever see you again, Father, you better hope it isn't while you're forcing purification on someone. You've bastardized the radiant enough."

With a sick feeling, William turned away from his father. He heard his mother burst out of the house, screaming at him. His ears rang, and he couldn't hear her words. For that he was thankful. Sam followed, ever silent.

"He won't stop hurting the city, will he, Sam?" William's voice shook over what he'd done.

"Do what you must."

What he must? Should he have let his father live? "Why does it seem like I never make the right choice?"

His brother didn't answer as they left the land claimed by the radiant. The sounds of people living their lives surrounded them. They lived while others made choices for them. Maybe a radiant would go into their home tonight and take them away to Haven. Yet the city still teemed with life, as if to say, "I'm still here, living."

"I guess we'll do what we must, Sam." The brothers made their way back to Vic's family home while they forever lost theirs.

Amaya waited to stir until the room had quieted around her. At Haven, she'd soaked in a cold bath for hours and lain still in that empty room forever before they'd found her. She fumed at Tristan. He'd messed with the reaper by saying her sister was dead. Why had she gone through all that to go undercover? Stupid man. He had a cruel streak with others, but she loved the idiot.

She hated acting, but she'd ended up in this body. The others had more faith in her than she had in herself.

Amaya moaned softly and fluttered her eyelids. A man with eyes that matched hers but darker hair leaned over her. She gasped in surprise at how close his face was to hers.

"Sorry. Are you feeling okay?" He sounded worried.

"Y-yes, Father. How did I get here?" Amaya feebly pushed herself to a sitting position. She didn't have to fake it too much since she felt weak. That ice bath had almost killed her.

"Hush, don't get up. Rest. Your sister saved you from Haven. Do you remember anything that happened before?"

He scanned her face, and a furrow deepened in his forehead. His clothing was wrinkled like he'd stayed and watched her all night. He seemed like a decent father. Amaya had lost hers years ago, and she couldn't remember him.

They'd agreed that Amaya needed to keep her story simple. Otherwise, the lies would get to be too much, and it would be hard enough to act like someone she'd never met. Tristan had told her that Emilia was calm and quiet. The idiot man wasn't helpful. From the raging going on inside her, "calm and quiet" didn't fit the description.

She flinched and pressed her hand to her forehead. "They took us past the gate, and then everything went dark. I was in a room for so long that I lost track of the days, and it got so cold. I passed out. How did she get into Haven to find me?" The sewer paths were the only way, but they were cut off from the normal Verrin sewers. And if they wanted to get in through the GicCorp wall, they would have to move the stone with imbs. The stone founder was on their side—mostly. Other imbs could do it, but once you practiced in your specialty, you rarely used anything else.

"Don't worry about it. Just rest."

Like she had a choice. How much would these rebels share with this person?

This man studied her some more. "Your sister is doing better, by the way."

Blight and stone, she'd forgot to worry about her sister. "She was hurt?" Amaya tried to recover quickly and once more pushed herself up. Then she looked at the cot next to hers, at the woman covered in blue bandages and with dark red hair. Her face almost looked transparent.

"Yes. She woke up, so the healers are hopeful she'll recover." He reached out to brush her hair back.

Amaya tried not to flinch away. She didn't like strangers touching her, but to this man, she wasn't a stranger. "What happened?"

"Magic burnout. Apparently, she broke her gicgauge." He sighed. Yes, he was a caring father who often got frustrated with his overzealous daughter.

Amaya supposed that might be why she was the calmer one, while the other charged in. That the woman had broken her gicgauge worried her, but since she'd almost killed herself, there would probably be nothing important to report. Those who broke their gicgauge died shortly after if they tried to use their relics too much. She would somehow need to report to Tristan. The father noticed too much. She couldn't be sure if that was normal or not. She didn't know these people or how they acted.

Get out.

Her jaw twitched. It would be harder to contain her while Amaya was in her environment. Lesson one, never mention the one you tried to eat. They made a difficult meal. Those kinds of things gave the clinging vitals strength. She'd never told Tristan that this one stubbornly clung to her body.

"Can you move me closer to my sister?" That seemed like the right thing to want, didn't it?

The father nodded and pushed the cot closer so Amaya could take the sister's warm and clammy hand. She didn't really want to hold on to it, but it would make sense that she would want to touch the sister. Gross.

Don't touch her! the voice screeched in her head.

Amaya flinched and dropped the hand reflexively.

"Is something hurting?" the father asked.

"Ah, no, just a twinge in my muscles." Amaya neutralized her body. *You can scream all you want. This is all mine now.*

From the depths, a steady scream rose. The voice didn't need to stop for breath in the mind. Amaya closed her eyes and focused on locking it down. She'd made an error in continuing to contact it. If she continued to make rookie mistakes, she would fight for too long over this bag of bones. She tried to shut down the endless droning, her body and mind weak from the ice bath. Amaya would gather her strength and focus on squashing it. Trying to ignore it, she smiled at the father.

"I will sleep for a bit." She thought for a moment and added, "If my sister wakes up again, can you wake me?" That should be right?

"I will."

She went back to fake resting while the voice screamed in the back of her mind. She liked this body, but its soul was obnoxious. They all eventually left or disintegrated. They didn't have time, but Amaya did. Her lips turned up slightly. She would enjoy beating this one.

❦ 21 ❦

VIC

Vic smelled clean linen before she opened her eyes. Her lips curved as she cracked her eyes open. William sat next to her, fast asleep, like she'd somehow known he would be. His head bent forward, and her neck hurt looking at him. Samuel, ever his shadow, slept curled up on a more comfortable chair. In sleep, he could pass as his old self. Her father stood looking at a family picture on the mantel. Relief filled Vic as she noticed Em's steady breathing next to her. As she stirred, William woke.

"How are you feeling?" William asked, his voice rough from sleep.

The bandages, wound tightly around her, made it difficult to breathe. "Kind of like I'm underwater. Can't these be looser?" She struggled to flex her fingers.

"I can cut some of them off, but I shouldn't cut them all. Which ones are the worse?"

Vic tried to take another deep breath. "The one around my ribs. How else do you think I would need to breathe?" Her elbows stayed straight from the tight wrappings.

"Ah, um, let me find someone to help."

"Cut them already. You know how to use a pair of scissors. Or did you miss that class in school?" Vic shifted and took another breath, her ribs straining against the bandages again.

William's face turned bright red, and he grabbed the scissors on the table with other cut-up bandages scattered across it. They must have rewrapped her a few times. He leaned over her and hesitated while holding the bandages around her ribs.

"Come on, glow stick. I want to breathe."

"Ah, yes."

He swiftly cut through the bandages and pulled up her blanket.

Vic took a huge breath of air. "That's so much better. Thanks." She glanced at his red face. "Are you hot or something?"

William set down the scissors and cleared his throat. "It's hot in here. It's been a while since you've called me a name. I think I missed it." He didn't meet her eyes.

Vic grinned. "I guess I need to do better." She touched her sister's hand. "How is she?"

"Your father mentioned she woke up for a bit and talked to him."

At the sound of their voices, her father turned to them and walked over. His eyes contained shadows. Vic assumed he'd been worried about them while they'd slept.

"Her body seems fine." His voice was low to avoid waking Em up.

Vic frowned. "Her body?" Why had he phrased it like that?

After a slight hesitation, he said, "She's fine. Don't worry."

"Now I'm worried," Vic muttered.

He tussled her hair, something he hadn't done in years. "She's fine. Stop overthinking everything."

Vic settled back so she could see them both. "What happened? Did GicCorp do anything while I was out? How long was I out? Did everyone make it out okay?"

Her father held up his hand. "Whoa. The news reported that mogs had infiltrated Haven, so none of the reapers were there illegally. Since then, they've been silent. It's almost night, and from the reaper counts, Boreus lost twenty, Dei lost thirty-one, and Nyx lost twelve. Considering the size of the Orders, Boreus and Dei lost about ten percent." Her father ran his hand through his hair. "Nyx already contained the fewest reapers since they don't recruit as many."

"How did you get them to help?"

Kai had stepped into the room and heard her last comment. "I've been communicating with Becks. She has the fire of their old leader, and she wanted to lessen her involvement with us, but the mention of the mogs in Haven got both Orders into gear."

"So Boreus didn't know what was happening?"

Kai shook his head. "We assumed they were since they're next to us and where the bait was." He sank onto the foot of the bed. "I need to be more careful about who I accuse of being the bad guys."

Vic took his hand. "We all did it. We assumed everyone would take the same deal that Xiona had taken with GicCorp. Or that GicCorp would ask the commanders to change people into mogs."

Kai squeezed her hand. "They weren't even offered the deal. Just Nyx."

Vic's father interjected, "If they got people to turn into radiant instead of mogs, it would be easier to use the radiant to get more people than to use reapers."

"But if they need blight to purify, why radiant?" Vic asked.

They all looked at each other, but they had no answers.

William leaned back in his chair. "That they're compliant helps, but other than that, they aren't the best fighters, unless they already have training. They'll still get a little blight from them when they're purified."

While they weren't looking at her, Vic touched her neck. She'd torn out her orb. She glanced at her family and friends. Vic decided not to tell them for now. When the time came, she would decide, but she had a few days, at most, to think about it. Her mind burned from trying to think of a plan. She for sure didn't want purification, so that meant becoming a mog. Unless ...

"Vic?" William touched her shoulder. "Are you okay?"

She picked at the fraying bandages. "Yeah, just tired."

Kai paused at William's hand on her shoulder, and he let it drop. Kai stood and dropped Vic's hand. "I'm glad I caught you when you were awake. I know we have more to talk about, but you were lucky. Don't charge off on your own again, okay?"

Vic glanced at her sister. "I would have done it for any of you. I can't make promises anymore." It didn't matter, really. She could feel time ticking down.

Kai adjusted the harness straps on his back. He must have been wearing it since last night. "I knew you had a problem with authority from the beginning."

Vic shrugged. "What can I say? I was born to rebel." Much to her family and teachers' annoyance, Vic had always questioned the system of Verrin. Most had assumed it was because she would miss her sister. They had been far from the mark.

Her father snorted, and when Kai left, he followed him out, saying something Vic couldn't hear.

"Is everything okay? Or are they keeping things from me?" Vic asked while watching the retreating forms of her father and Kai.

William's gaze followed them. "They were expecting more from GicCorp. They want to make an evacuation plan."

Her brows shot up. "To where?"

"Your favorite place."

Vic groaned. "If I end up living in the sewers, I'm quitting the rebellion."

William chuckled, and his face lit up. "Yeah, sure you will. You love fighting the man."

"You won't be the one laughing, Mr. Clean, when we're keeping sewage away from our beds." She leaned closer, her face even with his. "Wait until it floods. Feces up to your eyeballs."

William's face turned red again.

Vic placed her palm on his forehead. "You're feeling hot too."

He gently removed her hand. "I'm fine." He continued to stare out the door. Vic thought he wanted to ask her something, but he glanced back at her and said, "I'm glad you're feeling better."

"Okay, then."

Vic wondered why it suddenly felt awkward. William

stared out the window as the afternoon light lit up the room. She felt a bit of relief when she saw Bomrosy.

Bomrosy waited at the door. "Can I talk to you?" She glanced at William. "Alone?"

William got out of his chair, and Samuel woke up to follow him. He took one more look at Vic, then left the room.

Vic shifted on her cot, and Bomrosy sat in William's vacated chair.

Emilia still slept, so Bomrosy spoke softly. "I worried about you when they said you ran off by yourself." She fiddled with a string on her pants.

Vic swallowed. "We didn't leave on very good terms."

"No, we didn't."

"I'm sorry I said it was your fault that the reapers left." Vic tried to sit up straighter. "It wasn't fair of me. I keep thinking I'm the only person who tries to take care of others and saying I understand you and Xiona, but I did a poor job of supporting you."

Bomrosy took a deep breath. "What Xiona did was wrong. If there's ever a trial for a radiant, she should have one." Her eyes grew misty. "I can't forget who she used to be. I owe her my life, Vic. I shouldn't have kept her in the Order, but Kai shouldn't have lied."

Vic tried to hug her friend with her arms stiffly wrapped. It didn't turn out so well, and they laughed. "You're right, and Kai knows it too. I hope our Order can heal before the next thing comes at us."

"Do you think we're that lucky?" Bomrosy asked.

"Not a chance."

"The reapers are settling in. Your mother is a force to be reckoned with. She barks orders better than Landon. She even has him saying, 'Yes, ma'am.'"

It felt good to laugh, especially at Landon's expense. After a while, Bomrosy left, and only Vic and her sister remained.

Feeling creepy, she watched her sister breathe in and out to make sure she really was there.

Em opened one eye. "Are you going to stare at me all night?"

Vic burst forward, and despite her bandages, she squeezed her sister into a tight hug. "I can't believe you're alive."

"Was I supposed to be dead?"

Vic backed away and continued to drink in her sister's presence. "Tristan told me you were dead. I thought ..." Vic drew a shuttering breath. "It doesn't matter. We found you, and you're here, and you won't go back."

Emilia held her hand. "Calm down. I'm not going anywhere."

"Do you want to talk about what happened, or do you need to rest?" Vic took in her sister's pale skin, or was she flushed? Should she call a healer?

"I'm fine. I'm sure I'll rest more, but honestly, I don't remember what happened to me. Maybe that's a good thing."

Em usually kept things to herself, so Vic didn't want to push. "If you need to talk, I'm here. Don't keep it all bottled up."

"Thank you for coming to get me."

Vic didn't want to let go of her hand. "Always." She met her sister's familiar eyes—the same bright green but with shadows that aged them beyond her sister's years.

She would do anything to take those ominous shadows

away. She'd gotten her sister back. Now she could face GicCorp full-on.

The sisters talked into the night, and when Emilia fell asleep again, Vic watched her.

Her father came back and fussed over them. "Your mother won't rest. It looks like you won't either?"

"I'm afraid she'll disappear if I close my eyes." Vic pulled the blanket around herself.

He patted her shoulder, then spoke softly so only Vic would hear. "I've talked to the healers about the stress Emilia may have faced. They think it's best to keep her out of the loop when we deal with GicCorp, for her own mental health."

"Oh? That seems odd. You'd think talking about it would help." Her father's eyebrows creased as he looked at his daughter.

He shook his head and reached into his pocket to fiddle with the bag of sand. "We need to look out for her and help her heal. She won't be part of the fight, but we can keep her safe. Limit any information you tell her, okay?"

Vic didn't completely understand, but she nodded. "If that's what she needs to heal, I'll do it." A feeling grew in her that her father wasn't sharing everything with her. She wanted to trust him. He wouldn't keep any information that might hurt them to himself, would he?

Her father's face softened. "You did so well, my daughter. I'm sorry I let this happen." His voice cracked, and he turned away.

"Everything turned out okay." She tugged at his shirt. "You're overreacting a bit. Em's safe and fine. We'll get through this."

His eyes looked distant. "I wish you didn't have to live in this time. I don't want your spirit to break."

"I'm pretty strong."

Father and daughter sat together in silence. Vic tried to resist drifting off, but she couldn't stay awake anymore. As her vision blurred, she saw her father bury his face in his hands. She stretched her hand out to comfort him, and he gripped it so tightly.

She wanted him to know that she wouldn't go away. "It's okay," Vic mumbled as sleep claimed her.

"I'll fix this."

Not understanding, Vic fell asleep.

In her dreams, shadowy eyes haunted her.

ACKNOWLEDGMENTS

Thank you for joining me again!

This middle book wasn't easy to finish. A particular character decided he didn't like my outlined plan for him and continued to do his own thing. I decided to let him, and we'll see where he ends up in book three.

I'd like to thank Ravenborn Covers for the wonderful work on this series. It was fantastic to work with you, and your beautiful work has inspired me to keep going, even when I felt too tired to finish.

Many, many thanks to the fantastic Elizabeth from arrowheadediting.com. Your attention to detail is amazing. Every time I get a list from you, I vow to make the next book even better! Thank you so much for your time and energy.

And, to Stacy Rourk, The Blurb Doctor for helping me fine tune my blurb.

Also, to my wonderful Alpha readers, thank you. Your comments help me so much, and I appreciate you so much for reading my work! To Angela, Nicollee, Mary, Helen, Bryan, and my mom, thank you for all your help.

Since I live in the middle of nowhere, I'm also thankful for all my virtual writing buddies. The brainstorming and reality checks keep me grounded. I never thought I would look forward to a meeting, but here I am, excited to share in our trials and triumphs. I'm amazed by all your talent, and I can't wait to see what you write next.

Last but not least, dear reader, thank you for picking up my book. All I ever wanted to do was share my stories. I hope you've enjoyed the journey and will finish it with me.

A thousand times over, thank you all.

This is only the beginning.

ABOUT THE AUTHOR

Mari Dietz wrote her first poem about crickets when she didn't even know how to write. Her mom typed it up for her on an old typewriter. From then on, she was a goner to the written word. Over the years, she fell in love with the world of fantasy and thought maybe one day she could write something too.

She took a few side roads and got a major in Theater and English. Then she somehow ended up teaching in South Korea for three years. Now back in the middle of nowhere, she teaches Creative Writing and writes her own books in her "spare time," when not distracted by lesson plans, anime, or K-dramas.

Four rescue dogs give her the privilege of living with them, and they keep her sane-ish.

This is her debut novel and series. If you want to contact Mari, feel free to connect on:

Twitter

Facebook

FacebookGroup

Website

Amazon

Instagram

She can't wait to hear from you!

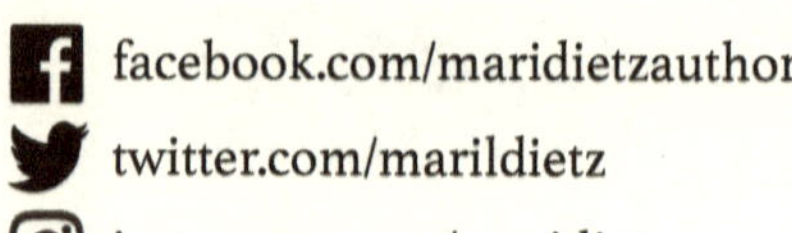